# OPEN

# GRAVE

a BEACON FALLS novel    featuring LUCY GUARDINO

# CJ LYONS

## PRAISE FOR NEW YORK TIMES AND USA TODAY BESTSELLER CJ LYONS:

"Everything a great thriller should be—action packed, authentic, and intense." ~#1 *New York Times* bestselling author Lee Child

"A compelling new voice in thriller writing…I love how the characters come alive on every page." ~*New York Times* bestselling author Jeffery Deaver

"Top Pick! A fascinating and intense thriller." ~ 4 1/2 stars, *RT Book Reviews*

"An intense, emotional thriller…(that) climbs to the edge of intensity." ~*National Examiner*

"A perfect blend of romance and suspense. My kind of read." ~*#1 New York Times* Bestselling author Sandra Brown

"Highly engaging characters, heart-stopping scenes…one great rollercoaster ride that will not be stopping anytime soon." ~Bookreporter.com

"Adrenalin pumping." ~*The Mystery Gazette*

"Riveting." ~*Publishers Weekly Beyond Her Book*

Lyons "is a master within the genre." ~*Pittsburgh Magazine*

"Will leave you breathless and begging for more." ~Romance Novel TV

"A great fast-paced read.…Not to be missed." ~4 ½ Stars, Book Addict

This book is a work of fiction. Any references to historical events, real people, or real locales are used fictitiously. Other names, characters, places, and incidents are the product of the author's imagination, and any resemblance to actual events or locales or persons, living or dead, is entirely coincidental and not intended by the author.

# OPEN
# GRAVE

a BEACON FALLS novel      featuring LUCY GUARDINO

## CJ LYONS

EDGY READS

*"Darkness cannot drive out darkness: only light can do that.*

*Hate cannot drive out hate: only love can do that."*

~ Martin Luther King

# Prologue

*MAY 17, 1954*

DR. SAMUEL MANN steered the Dodge Wayfarer down the corkscrew curves of the Pennsylvania mountain road. The late afternoon sun had been banished by the thick forest, its tall trees leaning together, old women gossiping in the breeze. The drive would have been fun if it weren't for the logging truck in front of them riding its brakes, its load swinging back and forth, making passing impossible.

"Samuel, slow down," Jo said from the passenger side of the bench seat, reaching across sleeping Maybelle to tap his arm.

Four-year-old Maybelle snuggled closer to him; she was of an age where she clung to Daddy. With his irregular, long hours spent at the hospital, she seemed always worried he might vanish from her sight. Josephine pulled Maybelle to her side of the seat, giving Samuel room to focus on the road and the truck swaying past the centerline as it lumbered around each steep curve.

The trees surrendered to the sky and sunshine greeted them as they plunged down one last switchback and reached the valley below. Finally room to pass, which Samuel did gleefully.

Once clear of the truck, he shrugged his shoulders, rolled them forward and back, just like he did in the operating theatre when he'd been on his feet hunched over a patient for too long. He glanced at the clock on the Dodge's dashboard; already four o'clock. "Told you we should have left your aunt's earlier."

Jo inclined her head in a half-nod that acknowledged he was right without coming out and admitting she was wrong. "You were the one who insisted on staying for dessert."

"Polite thing to do. After all, she's your family. They already see me as the usurper, stealing you away." Not to mention he was several shades darker than Jo—something her conservative Cleveland family seemed to think placed him beneath her, despite his education and position. "Plus, it was mighty fine pie."

The magic word woke Maybelle. "Daddy, I'm hungry. Can we stop?"

"I don't know, ask our navigator." The valley was narrow, filled with farmland that followed the curve of the mountain range behind them, stretching out north to south. Another set of mountains, not as high or steep, rolled up before them in the distance. Other than a few scattered barns and farmhouses, there was no sign of civilization.

Samuel was a city boy. He loved DC with its hustle and bustle, constant motion. Even Cleveland was all right—although Jo's family lived in a sedate neighborhood that, during their three days there for her uncle's funeral, had seemed ruled by church ladies who showed up at odd hours, always in twos or threes with their hats and gloves, coming to visit.

While Jo thumbed through the Green Book, he reached forward to spin the dial of the radio. Static, more static, the twang of a country-western guitar, then further down the dial the soft melody of Nat King Cole's "Mona Lisa." He left it there—Jo loved crooners like Cole.

"Nothing until Altoona," Jo announced, closing the book and returning it to the glove box.

"Won't be long," Samuel assured Maybelle before she

could protest. "Besides, I saw you sneak that extra piece of pie—or was it two?"

Maybelle giggled and hid her face, holding up two fingers.

The song finished, the station coming in a bit clearer now, and the afternoon news break began. "Our top story is from Washington, DC," the announcer said. "The Supreme Court returned what is certain to be a historic verdict in the much-debated *Brown versus the Board of Education of Topeka, Kansas* case."

"Turn it up." Jo leaned forward, her right palm planted against the cross that hung between her breasts, clasping it against her heart.

Samuel complied, hoping those nine white men had finally found the courage to do the right thing. Bad enough they'd heard the case twice now; people had been waiting since December for their decision.

"Who's Mr. Brown?" Maybelle asked. "Do we know him?"

"Hush," Jo said. "This is your future." Jo taught elementary school in the District, where segregation was federally mandated; it wasn't only the southern states with a stake in *Brown*.

Samuel steered one-handed, noting signs of civilization

rising up beyond the farmland ahead: an Esso station on the other side of a river. He stretched his other arm behind Maybelle's shoulders, Jo taking his hand in hers as her lips formed soundless prayers. Jo and her family were AME back generations. Samuel considered himself a good Christian, even if he was only a wedding-funeral-Christmas-and-sometimes-Easter churchgoer. But after serving in two wars, he'd come to realize that his God was bigger than any building or date etched onto a calendar. The God he prayed to was always there for Samuel, even if He didn't always answer Samuel's prayers.

He hadn't told Jo—it was one of the few secrets between them—but lately he'd begun stopping in at the Quaker meetinghouse that was on his way home from the hospital. There was no preaching, certainly not the loudmouth, know-it-all type of hellfire and damnation type he'd been raised with in Georgia. No confession, no explaining, no bargaining, no penance. Instead, he'd found a shared silence...and strength.

Jo wouldn't understand or approve—especially since the Quakers he sat with in silence were white. For a teacher intent on bringing change to future generations, who'd spent her school holidays lobbying with the NAACP, and who'd taken vacation days last December to attend the Supreme Court hearings, she could be a bit closed-minded. Jo wanted her schools open, with equal funding and opportunity for all. Didn't mean she ever wanted to actually associate with whites. Maybe because she hadn't seen as much blood as Samuel had. Black or white, brown or yellow, there was no telling from blood.

Samuel had seen more than enough fighting and bloodshed to fill a lifetime. First as a medic in the Second World War, then as an Army surgeon assigned to a battalion aid station in Korea. When he finally came home last year, he'd decided he was done fighting.

Because this new war, this war no one spoke of that coiled and writhed beneath every polite conversation and occasionally reared up to strike with venomous ferocity, this war here at home frightened him...and wearied him. It was all so senseless. As nonsensical as grown men wearing pillowcases for hats, hiding their faces as they terrorized innocent people like his parents and grandparents.

If nine white men in black robes could wave their magic pens and end this war, bring peace to the land, and protect his daughter's future, he was perfectly content to let them.

Jo disagreed. Said it was every parent's responsibility, no matter where they lived, to get involved, take action. She meant every black parent, of course. Which sometimes seemed a bit hypocritical to Samuel, but he knew better than argue. Jo was more than a dreamer, she was a doer. She knew what she wanted for their daughter's future, and she'd never give up fighting. It was why he loved her. She was so much stronger than he'd ever be.

Confused by the sudden tension that gripped her mother, Maybelle turned her questioning expression on her father.

"It means," he told her, "that one day you'll be able to go to any school you want. It means that you can grow up and be anyone you want to be."

She thought about that as the road wound through the fields, the Esso station beckoning up ahead across the river. They were close enough that he could start to make out a few houses, the edge of a town nestled in the forest at the base of the next mountain. He glanced at the map on Jo's lap. Greer. Tiny dot alongside a river. He didn't even remember driving through it on the way out to Cleveland.

"Anyone?" Maybelle asked. "Then I'm gonna be a teacher like Momma and a surgeon like you, and a cowgirl and a singer and a pie baker."

"That all?" Samuel asked with a smile.

"Well, sir, I'm gonna go live in that big white house everyone stares at and crowds around and takes pictures of. Then when I see those pictures, I can tell everyone that's my house and when you live in that house, you're the boss of everyone, so I can tell everyone what to do and when bedtime is." She jerked her chin in a satisfied nod.

Jo rolled her eyes toward Samuel. "In case you ever wondered if she's your daughter."

"Don't blame me. I'd say she takes after her momma, that's for certain." They shared a private smile above Maybelle's head.

"You all making fun?" Maybelle asked, squinting her eyes first at her father then her mother.

"No, baby." Josephine soothed Maybelle's hair, patting down a few kinky strands that had come loose from her braids. "Just that, you know, the president lives in that white house and you can never be president. No Negro can."

Samuel turned his attention back to the road. It was one of the few areas where he and Jo disagreed. They both wanted to raise Maybelle with an honest view of the world, but sometimes Jo was brutal with the truth. After all, his own folks still didn't believe he could be a "real" doctor, saving lives of both coloreds and whites. Last time he'd seen them, his mother had taken him aside and whispered to him, "Be careful about being too uppity around all those white folks. Don't put on airs, let them know you're smarter than they are."

Of course, his grandparents—who'd all died when he was young, their bodies worn out before their time by decades of back-breaking work—never dreamed of his parents owning their own land instead of sharecropping for white men.

"I don't want to be no president," Maybelle said.

They crossed over a ratchedy metal bridge and passed the Esso station. Samuel slowed down as the road led them through a section of tarpaper shacks, white men sitting on porches staring slack-jawed while women hung laundry or worked in gardens. Ahead, he spotted larger houses, once proud Victorians and Queen Annes that had fallen on hard times, paint peeling, shutters hanging crooked.

"You don't want to grow up and be president of these United States?" he asked.

"No, sir. President doesn't know what's right, sending daddies to war and getting them shot at. I want to make pies for the president. I'll live in that white house, make pies as good as Gramama's, and then I can boss him and everyone around just like she does."

Jo arched her eyebrows at that while Samuel stifled his grin. Jo's mother did boss everyone around, and those who tried to resist, she plied with her pies until they fell silent and surrendered to her will.

"And if the president don't listen, then he don't get no pie," Maybelle finished in a shrill voice that sounded exactly like Samuel's mother-in-law. He coughed to hide his chuckle.

"Maybelle Henrietta Mann," Jo rebuked. "You shouldn't— look out!"

Samuel was already pounding the brakes and pulling the wheel. The whirl of pale-colored motion that had darted into the road and fallen in front of the car slowly, painfully coalesced in his mind: a girl. Had he hit her? He hadn't felt a thud or thump, but the Dodge was solidly built and so very much larger than the slight figure that had appeared from nowhere, as if by magic.

Jo crossed her arm in front of Maybelle as the car lurched to a stop. Samuel opened his door and leapt out, scanning the road behind him. The girl was a heap of worn calico and denim, kneeling in the road, dusty pale soles of her feet facing him, head held in her hands, straggling brown hair hiding her features.

A vacant lot littered with the burnt-out ruins of a house

crowded with weeds and saplings lay on one side of the road. The house on the other side hid behind a tall hedge of evergreens, only its roof visible.

No one to be seen, no hands tugging at curtains, no eyes blazing venom at the Negro daring to approach a white girl.

The girl looked up at him, twisting her body like a feral animal preparing to escape.

"Please," she begged through choked tears. "Please. You gotta help. Please. They're gonna kill him."

# Chapter 1

WALTER SHIELDED HIS eyes from the bright July sun and stared up at the stark cliffs of the quarry. The way they loomed above the boat made him feel small, insignificant. He lowered his gaze back to where his brother, Terry, stood at the boat's wheel. Sunlight bounced from the crystalline clear blue water of the quarry and he wished he hadn't forgotten his sunglasses in the truck.

"The judge is gonna kill us, he finds out. Technically, we're trespassing." No technically about it, and they both knew it.

Terry shrugged away Walt's concerns. Like he always did. He was the eldest but far more reckless. "Judge Greer's a good businessman. Knows we can't make a proper bid for the property without fully inspecting it."

"He already told us he wasn't going to sell the quarry." Not over his dead body had been the exact words.

"Just means he wants to make sure we're serious and not wasting his time." Terry turned to face Walt. "We'll need to re-grade the boat access, turn it into a proper landing ramp." He waved to the area on the far side of the water where the truck and boat trailer waited. "That shallow section will be perfect for classes. With a large dive platform maybe twelve-fifteen feet below the surface."

Walt nodded. Terry was the one with the big dreams; Walt's job was to figure out how to make them come true.

"Then," Terry continued, his hands skimming out over the darker waters closer to the sheer cliff walls, "down here on the deep side, we'll lay out dive paths along with decompression platforms. Stock the whole place with paddlefish and interesting objects for folks to get their picture taken with. I was thinking maybe an old weather balloon, if we can figure out how to anchor it and keep it inflated."

"How about a phone booth?"

"E.T. phone home. I like that." He turned back to the

wheel, leaning over their Hummingbird fish finder. "Got something down on the bottom. Around a hundred-twenty feet."

Walt craned to look over Terry's shoulder. "Equipment abandoned when they let the quarry fill?"

Terry's grin turned wicked. "Maybe the stories are true. About the quarry ghosts. Two young lovers leaping from lovers' lane."

Walt's gaze jumped up to the crumpling edge of the cliff overhead. He wished Terry wouldn't joke about things like that. Hard to believe this barren stretch of land had ever been a lovers' lane. Most unromantic spot he could imagine. Goosebumps crawled over his skin as they entered the shadow of the granite wall.

"Looks like a big car," he told Terry, tracing the outline of the object on the screen.

"So they didn't jump. Maybe it wasn't even suicide. Maybe just two drunk, horny kids too busy necking to know they released the emergency brake." He arched his hand up before plunging it in a nosedive. "Only one way to find out."

"What? Today?"

"Sure, why not? We got the gear. If we're going to invest

in this place, open up our own dive school, then we need to check out the conditions, right?" He was already unpacking the tri-mix tanks from their gear bags. Terry lived for technical dives—the deeper and more dangerous, the better. Which left Walt to play mother hen, working the numbers, calculating depth times and decompression stops.

But once they were below the surface, their bubbles sparking through the gleam of their dive lights, all worry fell away. Despite growing up in landlocked rural Pennsylvania, both Walt and Terry had always felt most at home in the water. Terry had even done a stint in the Navy—he'd hoped to be a SEAL but had ended up a mechanic. While Walt—who hadn't passed the physical to join up, something about scoliosis—had worked fishing charters from the Outer Banks down to the Keys during school breaks before he finally dropped out of college and came back home to help his parents with their struggling family farm.

This quarry, surrounded by ancient rock, abandoned as useless once underground springs flooded it, was their family's chance to finally pay off their debt. He and Terry could still work the farm weekdays and open the quarry up on weekends and holidays. Dive enthusiasts were always looking for good spots that didn't entail expensive travel to far off exotic places. Although, as Terry said, finding good, deep water in the middle of the Alleghenies was probably more exotic than heading to the crowded dive spots in the Caribbean.

The crystalline water remained clear even as it darkened at the deeper depths. Little debris, mud, or silt, almost no algae. Some chemical in the rocks maybe kept it at bay while giving the water an unnaturally bright turquoise hue, unlike anything seen around here. The quarry had a surprising number of fish, and they were curious about the two strange new visitors. Both had their video cameras going, and Walt caught a great shot of several fish nuzzling Terry.

Then they arrived at their destination. It was a car. An old one, big and clunky, yet somehow pretty. It glowed an otherworldly shade of blue in the sharp white of the dive lamps.

Terry swam around to the back, his light a tight beam. Walt glided to the front, framing the hood ornament and insignia in his camera shot. The hood was slightly buckled and the front windshield cracked, but other than that, there was no obvious damage; the car looked like new.

Definitely not left behind before the quarry filled with water—no rust. So how had it gotten here? He backed away, counting down the seconds before they'd need to begin their ascent. Terry motioned him in closer, pointing to the passenger side window. Walt tapped his dive watch even though they had a little more time left.

Terry shook his head, pointed to the window, gesturing for Walt to take a look inside the car. Walt really, really did not want to look, but he could never resist Terry. Walt glided into the car, his bubbles bouncing from the glass. At first his dive light was too bright, reflecting from the glass, and he couldn't see inside. He reached to adjust it, accidentally knocking it too far, plunging him into darkness.

He fumbled the light. Its beam shuddered in his hand, bouncing in time to his pulse. His ears roared—he was hyperventilating. As he fought to slow his breathing, his temples throbbing and eyes burning with pressure, his hand finally steadied the light.

The black void pierced by the beam broke into a star-shaped shadow. No. Not a shadow. A hand—or what was left of it. Pressed against the car window.

Beyond the hand the light hit a skull. Snaggled hair and greasy fat clung to it, its lower jaw hanging open on one side in a gaping, ghoulish grin.

# Chapter 2

SHE'D TAKE OUT the leader first, TK O'Connor decided. Hard jab to the throat, leg sweep. The combo would send him to the pavement. Question was: would the three—no, four, she'd missed the skinny kid by the mouth of the alley—others attack or give her time to escape?

She blamed her predicament on the heat and sloppy city planning. One side of the street was lined by a row of burnt-out houses, their roofs bowed in surrender behind a hastily constructed eight-foot tall chain-link fence.

Opposite, stood a ragged yellow brick four-story apartment building. Both the fence and the building were plastered with election signs. TAKE GREER TO CONGRESS! they read, the words circling around a photo of JR Greer, the mayor of Greer, smiling like a used car salesman. Seemed like a long shot for a small-town mayor, but since JR was the one who'd hired the Beacon Group to assist with a cold case, she wasn't about to argue the point.

But she did blame the mayor for her current predicament. The street she'd intended to cut down to get to the police station from her hotel was closed. Not for construction, for demolition.

From what she'd seen so far of Greer, there was a whole lot of the town ripe for demolition. Starting with this group of corner boys who'd decided a pretty young blonde walking alone made for an easy target. No matter it was broad daylight and ninety-some degrees. They were bored and aimless—two things that made any pack of men dangerous.

Her messenger bag was slung across her chest and she wore cargo pants, her Merrill combat boots, and a loose-fitting sleeveless blouse. Along with two knives, one in her boot, the other in her front pocket, and a Beretta nine millimeter at the small of her back. Definitely overdressed for the occasion.

The uniform of the day if you were a Greer street thug consisted of baggy shorts, a variety of colorful short-sleeved shirts, hanging unbuttoned and untucked over wife-beaters, ball caps optional. Plus tatts. Even on the skinny kid near the alley who surely couldn't be more than thirteen. Skin inked like a billboard.

Except for a smattering of freckles on her shoulders, TK's arms were bare, mainly because she'd never gotten drunk enough to join her squad and have the insignias she was entitled to emblazoned on her flesh.

"Lady, are you seriously ignoring us?" The leader, not taller or bigger than the others, but the one with the deadest eyes who did all the talking that mattered. "We pay you compliments and you don't even thank us?"

She met his gaze. Oh yeah, he was definitely going down. It was the two linebackers flanking him that she was worried about. One at a time, she could take them, but not with the others blocking her escape route. No. Only way out was through Mr. Dead Eyes.

"C'mon," one of the others sang out. "At least give us a smile." He favored her with one of his own, sunlight sparking off gleaming gold inlays shaped like pistols.

The others joined in, crowding her, herding her, closing ranks around their prey. They didn't seem to realize that she was actually steering them toward the spot she'd chosen to make her stand. The entrance to an alley between two apartment complexes. Narrow enough to take the linebackers out of the equation for the few seconds she'd need, leaving her with only the skinny kid after she dropped Dead Eyes and the guy behind him. Poor Skinny Kid. Should have stayed home, watched cartoons.

Other than a quick glance at a map before leaving her hotel, she didn't know the town of Greer, but she knew alleys. Here, Fallujah, back home in Pittsburgh running a parkour course, alleys were all the same. Narrow and crowded with opportunities. Beyond the kid, she spotted the rungs of a fire escape dangling eight feet off the ground. Drop Dead Eyes, plow through Skinny Kid, vault onto the top ledge of the dumpster, short leap to the fire escape, up the building, and gone...

TK flexed her fingers, bounced on her heels, eager to flee. She *could* do it...but...*should* she do it? Physically assaulting at least two people, maybe three? For what? A barrage of innuendoes and trash talk?

Yet, her only crime was being a woman walking alone down the wrong street at the wrong time. Why should she have to deal with their BS?

No good answer. She flicked her gaze from the alley,

shifting her attention from her mental choreography of parkour moves and close quarter combat strikes back to Dead Eyes. Who actually, despite his bravado, was just another teenaged kid, pretending to be a man. Smart enough to keep his boys in check—no one had laid hands on her; she almost wished they would, it would make her decision so much easier—but not smart enough to find gainful employment or a better use of his summer vacation than slouching against a crooked lamppost on a street corner, marking his territory.

As TK continued her halting forward progress, the pack of youths surging with her, she wished she was better at clever comebacks. Seemed like it was always the next day when she figured out the perfect response to situations like this—so much easier to resort to primal fight or flight. Easier, but not better.

"Leave her alone!" a man shouted from behind her.

TK glanced over her shoulder and saw a white guy, college-aged, which made him a few years younger than her own twenty-six, dressed in slacks and a white shirt buttoned all the way to the top despite the heat. His hair was nicely trimmed, and he could have been a youth minister or a librarian or maybe an office worker out for a morning coffee run, caught like her in the maze of blocked streets.

Either way, he was a civilian and a complication to the carefully balanced social algebra she and the corner boys had silently negotiated. Dead Eyes leered at the approaching man, the two boys behind TK turning to face this new target. Leaving TK squarely in the middle.

"I'm fine," she called to the man, hoping he'd get the message and make his escape before things escalated. She'd had this under control. Until he came along.

"I said," his voice low and yet carrying effortlessly to them, his pace slow and certain as he continued his approach, "leave her alone."

A lone woman, she didn't pose enough of a threat to instigate any violence from the group of boys, but a man might. Especially this guy with his bland looks and confrontational attitude—the perfect contradiction of easy target and ego-threatening challenge that would make it difficult for the corner boys to back down peacefully.

"You telling us what to do?" Skinny Kid shouted, his sudden assertiveness surprising TK and from the look on his face, himself as well. "We got every right to be here. Free country."

Dead Eyes stepped up beside Skinny Kid, the others

squaring off beside him, forming a solid wall of muscle and flesh between TK and the white guy. She moved into the street where she had them all in view and room to maneuver. She could have simply taken off, made her own escape, but she felt responsible for the civilian now caught squarely in the corner boys' sights.

The white guy didn't back down or show any fear; instead he stood his ground, his bland expression taunting the boys. TK couldn't see a weapon on the man, but she sensed that he had one—the source of his confidence.

The corner boys tensed as the white guy reached into his back pocket—but they didn't draw any weapons of their own, proving TK right when she'd decided that they were unarmed. The white guy didn't pull a weapon, at least not anything with lethal force; instead, he drew out his cell phone and aimed the camera at Dead Eye's crew.

"I asked you to leave this woman alone," he narrated. "This is a live stream of your response. Want to see how quickly you end up in jail if you choose wrong?"

His calm tone irritated even TK. He was much too confident for someone so young, outnumbered five to one—not including her, of course, but it was obvious that to the white guy she was a damsel in distress, not someone to count on if things turned violent.

The idea of needing to be rescued—or even being perceived to be helpless, powerless—rankled. She'd had things under control. Hadn't needed or asked for his help. And now she was caught, unable to protest or say anything until the standoff was decided. She was tempted to leave, let the testosterone storm dissipate on its own.

A short squawk from a police siren interrupted the standoff. Dead Eyes shifted his attention to the street where a patrol car pulled to the curb, its front bumper sagging to scrape the uneven pavement, hurling random sparks.

"My man, Karlan," Dead Eyes called to the officer behind the wheel. "Verdict in?"

The officer rolled down his window. "Not yet." He jerked his chin at the white guy who joined TK at the police car. "Everything all right here, Grayson?"

"Nothing I can't handle, Detective Karlan," the white guy, Grayson, said. Somehow he made it sound as if he was the cavalry riding in to save the day.

The police officer, a black man in his fifties, turned his attention to TK "You TK O'Connor?"

"Jamel Karlan?"

He nodded. "Hop in."

Grayson opened the passenger door before TK could reach it, holding it for her, his back to the corner boys.

Dead Eyes didn't seem to notice his prey escaping. "You know," he said to Karlan in a conversational tone, "they let that cop get away with murder, we gonna have us a Fourth of July party no one's gonna ever forget. Starting with some home cooked barbequed pig."

As TK settled into her seat, shifting so her knee wouldn't knock against the shotgun secured below the dash and edging away from the computer canted on the center console, she watched for Karlan's response to Dead Eye's threat.

Karlan didn't take Dead Eye's bait, instead calmly said, "How about we wait for the grand jury to decide if it was even murder or not?"

Dead Eyes rolled back on his heels and spit on the sidewalk. "I should believe a bunch of folks too stupid to get out of jury duty? No way. Round here justice ain't just blind, it's deaf and dumb."

Grayson, still on the sidewalk with the others, shook his head. "Already making excuses so you all can have a riot no matter what the verdict is."

"Don't need no excuse when there's never any justice," Dead Eyes shot back. "Not that you'd ever know what that's like."

Karlan's lips tightened at that, but otherwise his expression remained neutral. "No need to take an attitude, Franklin. How about if you all just head on back home? And you, Grayson, can I offer you a lift?"

"No thank you, Detective. I'm fine walking. Nice meeting you, Miss O'Connor." TK was impressed he'd remembered her name—Karlan had only used it once.

Grayson nodded to her and continued to stroll down the street. Franklin, aka Dead Eyes, frowned after him, then caught Karlan's raised eyebrow and sauntered in the opposite direction, his crew following.

Peace established, Karlan rolled up the window and pulled away from the curb, the corner boys in their rearview mirror before he released a sigh. "Gotta say, finding that damn car couldn't have come at a worse time."

"Thought we were meeting at the police station?" Karlan was the detective assigned to the cold case that had brought TK here from Beacon Falls.

"Chief wants everyone in uniform, visible presence, until

the grand jury comes in on Jefferson. Had to go to the maintenance garage to pick up this junker, so when I saw you and the mayor's son conversing with some of the city's fine upstanding lowlife—"

TK bristled a bit at the thought of his thinking that she needed rescuing. If she'd followed her first impulses, it would have been several of the corner boys who needed saving, not her. She found herself perversely defending the kids. "They didn't do anything wrong."

"No, not most of them. Except Franklin. Been to juvie twice. Just turned seventeen, so next time he'll be doing real time as an adult." He gave a shake of his head. "Boy's a lit fuse, and those others, they're moths dancing around his flame, seeing how close they can fly without getting burnt."

A cop and a poet. She bet Karlan never had trouble thinking of a comeback. "Grayson is the mayor's son?"

"Yep. The Greers go back to the town's founding father. Back before the Revolution, even, when this land was a trading post on a river landing."

Guess that explained Grayson's confidence. And a guy like Franklin was too smart to antagonize the mayor's son. "This Jefferson case, I take it a cop's involved?"

"Officer-involved shooting. Happened last month. You haven't seen it in the news?"

"I don't watch the news." TK would never admit it to anyone, especially not David Ruiz, her investigative-reporter boyfriend, but she despised the news. Not because she didn't want to know what was happening in the world but because she hated feeling manipulated into how to think and feel about what was happening. She preferred collecting her own information and deciding for herself, thank you very much.

"Jefferson was totally justified, no way the grand jury will indict, but—"

"That will just make things worse with the public."

"Exactly. Only reason the DA took it to the grand jury was because she's up for re-election, doesn't want to look like she's coddling police officers who are simply doing their jobs. Nothing to do with the facts. Now we've got protesters coming in from all over; TV and news broadcasting every time a cop's hand goes anywhere near his weapon; Staties, DOJ, and FBI talking about monitoring the department…"

Which explained why the Greer police department didn't run to the State Police or FBI for help with their new cold case. Although a blue-collar, down-on-its-luck city like Greer didn't have the resources to take it on themselves. Not that TK minded—first time Lucy had sent her to lead a case. Plus, how often did you get handed an unknown case from sixty years ago and have the chance to be there during the actual initial investigation? "Sounds like a hell of a time for an unidentified body to be found, especially one that might date back to the last century."

"Recovery divers said the vehicle is a '49 Dodge Wayfarer." He shrugged. "Maybe it's a classic car lover, got lost, drove into the quarry by accident."

"Someone with a distinctive classic car like that and no one reported him missing?" Good luck with that.

"Yeah, it'd be too much to ask for. If it really is an unidentified body from sixty-some years ago, then we're up against some impossible odds. We're a small force, understaffed, underfunded—only have twenty-three sworn officers for a town of nineteen thousand...twenty-two, with Jefferson out on administrative leave."

"Don't worry, that's what you have us for. The Beacon Group specializes in solving the unsolvable." As soon as she said it, TK regretted the words. Cheap and cocky. Lucy would have never said anything like that. Neither would Valencia Frazier, the Beacon Group's founder. Less than fifteen minutes into her first case as lead, and she was already screwing things up.

TK gritted her teeth. It wasn't cheap or cocky if you made good on your promise. Which was exactly what she planned to do. Impossible case or not.

# CHAPTER 3

KARLAN DROVE TK past a block of brick row houses dating back to the Second World War, more than a few with eviction or foreclosure notices, all covered by graffiti. At least three generations of adults sat on porch stoops or old-fashioned lawn chairs, the kind with the wide webbing that sagged if you sat too long. It reminded TK of the neighborhood where she grew up back in Weirton, West Virginia. Same blank expressions, same worn-out, faded gazes as they watched the younger generation play in the street.

The kids, despite the heat, exuded energy. Older boys congregated at the mouths of alleys and around street corners, glaring across the pavement at each other, a silently fierce battle over contested territory. Dead Eyes' competition, TK guessed.

Most didn't deign to raise their faces to acknowledge the patrol cruiser; the few who did spat wads of phlegm that pinged off the side of the car or raised their middle fingers. As if a single cop car was beneath their notice. They had better things to do.

Then they spotted TK, and their expressions changed. Eyes tightened, gazes lasering in on her. She suppressed a flinch as she glanced back in the side view mirror. Despite the fact that she was in a vehicle, with a police officer, she felt more threatened than she had during her encounter with Franklin and his friends. Why was that?

Her stomach knotted as she realized that perhaps she had totally misjudged the situation with the corner boys. She'd felt so excited about taking lead on this case, so confident in her abilities—so safe facing a few kids on a sunny street on a summer's day.

She started to slide her phone from her pocket then stopped herself. Now was not the time to separate herself from the world with earbuds and her language lessons—her usual recipe when anxiety closed in on her. No. She was here as lead field investigator from the Beacon Group.

An investigation that she'd have no new details to work with until the divers raised the car. She cast around for a topic of conversation and landed back in her well of fears. "What's the first thing you notice when you meet someone?"

"Someone? As in one person? Because the first thing I notice is how many potential threats I'm facing."

Good point. "One person."

"Their hands. Then if they're a man—sorry, I know it's not politically correct, but odds are a man is going to be a person of interest a lot more often than a girl."

Woman, she corrected silently. "And then?"

"I don't know. I guess race. I mean, I know that shouldn't matter, but it's how I'm wired, probably how everyone is wired, right?" He shrugged. "Maybe age. Although we have plenty of eighty-year-old grannies around here I wouldn't turn my back on."

She smiled at his joke but said nothing, busy mentally dissecting her encounter with Franklin and his crew. She hadn't seen them as men, hadn't seen a real threat, only a potential one...more of a puzzle to be solved, an obstacle course to navigate. Had her instincts been wrong? If she couldn't trust her gut, after all her training and everything she'd been through here and overseas, what could she trust?

Karlan kept the car moving slowly—not only to avoid

accidentally hitting one of the wayward kids, but also so he could take his time, making eye contact with each of them. Not a glare or contemptuous stare, but a neutral smile and nod. An expression that said, "I'm not going anywhere. I'll be here when you need me."

The younger kids, they weren't as restrained as their older counterparts. Gaggles of boys would turn, make faces, call out taunts and jeers, while the occasional bold ones would race up and slap the car, young warriors counting coup.

"You serve?" Karlan asked abruptly as he steered with one hand draped over the wheel. "Look like you served."

"Marines."

He made a noise of acknowledgment. "Same as our mayor. Talk is, he's headed to Congress."

"From mayor to congressman? That's quite a leap."

"Don't I know it." He didn't sound impressed by Mayor Greer's political success. More like suspicious. "You deployed? Iraq or Afghanistan?"

"Both." She didn't elaborate. Easier to let Karlan do the talking.

"Never understood that winning hearts and minds BS. I mean, I agree with the concept—should be the foundation of any police or military strategy. But how to do it? I've lived here all my life, been a cop going on three decades now, and these people need us."

He raised his hand to gesture at a two-story frame house, its porch roof sagging in defeat. A woman rocked in a chair near the front door while a teenaged boy wearing a pair of Beats headphones sprawled on the steps, palms drumming in time to music.

"Saved her when the boyfriend beat her so hard she was in a coma two days. Stopped their son from going after the bum and ending up in jail himself."

A jerk of his chin directed her attention to the brick ranch style house across the street. "Got that old man to the hospital after he was carjacked. Caught the gangbangers who did it, but case got thrown out when he wouldn't testify. This neighborhood, they *need* us. But they don't *want* us."

TK was beginning to like the detective. She'd bet if it wasn't for the old patrol car with its constant shimmy and recalcitrant steering requiring a firm grip on the wheel, Karlan would be talking with both hands slicing the air, to hell with the driving.

He continued in a doleful tone, "If we can't win hearts and

minds here at home, how the hell are we ever going to do it in a place where we don't speak the language or understand the religion or jack shit about anything?"

TK wished she had an answer.

# CHAPTER 4

*MAY 17, 1954*

GOD HELP HIM, but despite the little girl—she was a spindly thing, no more than eleven or twelve—and her plea for help, Samuel's first instinct was to stop and look around for an ambush. His father had told him tales of men caught in similar circumstances. All ending with a rope, a tree, and a noose.

And with the Brown decision being announced today...the newsmen had said there were already riots and protests in the South. He strained to remember if Pennsylvania was one of the states impacted by the Supreme Court's decision.

He glanced up and down the road. No one in sight. Ahead, the road took a sharp turn, vanished as it meandered through the streets of Greer before heading back up into the mountains.

Then he saw the little girl's arms. Covered with bruises—all ages, but the fresh ones were the most vicious, fingerprints red with fury against her pale skin. Her bare calves showed below her denim skirt. More bruises plus welts that could only have come from a belt buckle.

Mind made up, he looked back to the Dodge where Jo huddled with Maybelle in the front seat.

"Wait here," he called.

Jo shook her head no, her lips pursed against the idea of him getting tangled up in white folks' business.

Samuel helped the girl to her feet; she leaned against him as they walked back to the car.

"I'll be right back," he told Jo through the open driver side door. "Just want to see her home safe."

"Sure her folks are going to see it like that?"

"Can't leave her alone in the street, can I?" He edged his gaze down to Maybelle, and Jo relented. "Lock the doors. If I'm not back in a few minutes—" He hesitated, no idea where to send his wife and daughter that they'd be safe. The girl tugged at him, already pulling him away from the Dodge.

"Hurry. They're gonna kill him."

He let her pull him through the vacant lot, her urgency forcing him into a jog despite his much longer legs. "What happened? Who hurt you?"

"It's all my fault."

Scraggly weeds tore at the cuffs of his slacks—one of his two pairs of Sunday slacks, worn especially for Jo's family—as they cut across the vacant lot. It ran through to the next street over.

As he stumbled over the crumbled curb, he saw that the main road intersected this street as well, two blocks farther up.

Then he heard the shouts and looked the other way down the street, past a cluster of frame houses crowded shoulder to shoulder with no space to breathe between them. In the middle of the street, five white boys, all teenagers, were kicking and stomping someone at the center of their circle of flailing limbs.

"Help him!" the girl cried, shoving Samuel at the white boys.

He glanced at the houses, hoping to find another adult who could relieve him of duty. Preferably a white adult who knew these boys and their families. No one. Not even a flutter of a curtain in a window.

Working class neighborhood like this, maybe even the

mothers had jobs out of the house, no one home when the kids got off school? Pretty obvious the boys weren't expecting any adult intervention as they continued to pummel their victim.

Samuel stood tall and strode forward, using his best "I'm the surgeon, and no one's going to die on my watch," tone, and said, "Leave him alone."

He didn't shout, barely raised his voice. But they heard him. All the boys froze in place except one, the leader, he suspected, who heaved all his weight behind one last vicious kick. "Now, what's going on here?"

The boys didn't look up, seemed fascinated by their feet. Except the leader, a sandy-haired kid a little bigger and a little older than the rest, who slowly turned to face Samuel.

"None of your business. You'd best move on now." His words were a threat, his posture knife-sharp when he spied the little girl cowering behind Samuel. "Winnie, you get away from that Negro. Now, you hear me?"

The girl shuffled out away from Samuel a step, then two, but didn't move forward. "Is he dead? Did you kill him? He didn't do nothing wrong."

"Shut the hell up!" The boy lashed out at the girl, bringing fresh tears as if he'd struck her. "You're coming with me." He lunged in her direction but Samuel sidestepped to block his path.

The boy reared up, fists raised, ready to hit Samuel. And there wasn't a damn thing he could do to stop him—not a white boy, not without knowing what was going on here.

The boy's friends, emboldened now, moved as well, edging into a circle to block Samuel's escape. He glanced past them to their prior victim—a colored boy, young, barely a teenager himself, lying face down on the cracked pavement, not moving.

Samuel ignored their threat. They were just boys and there was nothing he could do here except his job. "Let me through. I'm a doctor and that man needs medical attention."

The leader blinked at that. "I'm a doctor?" he scoffed, mimicking Samuel's tone of command. "If this monkey's a doctor, then I'm President of these here United States!"

His laughter was cut short by the shriek of a siren. Only a two-second blast as a police car turned down the road, but it was enough to spook the girl, who took off faster than a deer, vanishing between the houses. The boys separated themselves from Samuel, acting innocent. Their leader strode right up to the police car as the door opened and an officer emerged.

"That's him," he pointed down the road at the

unconscious boy. "He's the one who tried to rape Winnie Greer. We got him all ready for you, Archie. Unless you want us to finish the job? My dad'll be home soon; he'd love to take care of business."

The boy's words were fed by anger and adrenaline—but also some strange shade of pride that Samuel hadn't encountered since he'd left the battlefields behind. Same pride he'd heard in soldiers who'd fired on defenseless villagers, killing dozens in the hopes of killing one of the enemy. In their eyes, they were all the enemy, there were no innocent victims of war.

He'd never understood that, not even after surviving two wars on three continents. Jo said that was a good thing. But it left him feeling sad and vulnerable, not being able to dissect what made men—of all colors and races and creeds—so damn blind, deaf, and dumb to human suffering.

Samuel turned to tend to the injured boy. He was still alive, breathing a bit irregular, no surprise given half his ribs were caved in on one side. Pulse rapid but strong. Airway clear. No obvious spinal fractures.

"Hey, what're you doing?"

Samuel looked up to regard the police officer. Archibald Thomson, his nameplate read in well-polished silver letters above the badge pinned to his chest. Beside him, the white kid stood, bouncing on his heels, thumbs hooked in the pockets of his dungarees, beaming at his handiwork.

"I'm a doctor, a surgeon. This boy needs medical attention."

"Your boy needs to learn his lesson—"

"Shut up, Philip," Thomson, the police officer, snapped at the boy. "You run home. I'll come talk to you later."

"No. I want to—"

"Are you deaf? Do as I say. Now!"

Philip hesitated a rebellious beat before turning and stalking away. "I'll go home," he said over his shoulder. "Just long enough to tell my father. He'll want to talk to you about this, Archie Thomson." He hurled the last as a threat.

Thomson ignored the kid and knelt beside Samuel. "What can I do to help?"

"Head trauma, possible skull fracture and lung contusion, multiple facial lacerations…this boy requires a hospital."

Thomson shook his head. "Closest one that will accept Negroes is Altoona, and I don't have the manpower to transport him and guard him long enough to get him there alive. Not with what the Greer boy is accusing him of." He looked up at Samuel.

"If we take him to the station, can you help him? I can protect him there."

Samuel wasn't naive enough to ask who the injured boy needed protection from. He sighed. Jo was going to kill him, getting involved.

"This boy didn't hurt that girl. You know that, right?" Why was he sitting here arguing with a white policeman? Trying to save a stranger he knew nothing about from a town he knew nothing about. It was insane. But somehow Samuel felt like Thomson understood, knew how wrong this was.

"No. It was her pa. It's always her pa. But Winnie will never say nothing. She always runs to the Rawling home when things get too bad. Usually it's the women who shelter her until it's safe for her to go home, but looks like today she ran into Henry, more's the pity." He glanced over his shoulder. "Help me get him into my vehicle?"

The boy, Henry, regained consciousness as they moved him into the car. He seemed disoriented and in pain, but his breathing stabilized once he was sitting up in the backseat of the police car.

"I need to return to my family," Samuel said, closing the door on Henry. He was uncertain about leaving the defenseless teenager in the care of the law, but Thomson seemed a better option than the hooligans out in the street. White boys allowed to act like that meant white men who'd taught them.

"Hold on, now." Thomson's voice carried the authority of his office. "Thought you said he needed doctoring."

"He's stable until you—"

"Look around you. This look like a town that can support a doctor? Closest we got is Bruce Macauley at the mill, and that's only because he was a corpsman in the Army. It's you or no one. At least not until Henry's folks get off shift tonight and can drive him over the mountain to Altoona. If those boys don't bring their fathers back and take him first."

Samuel drew up short. This was the twentieth century, this was Pennsylvania. Not the deep South where Jim Crow reigned. "You'd let them do that? You're an officer of the law. You'd let them take him?"

The look on Thomson's face said it all. Same look Samuel had seen on Korean prisoners of war right before the anesthesia took them under: utter defeat. They were certain the white devils—or in Samuel's case, even worse, a black devil—were about to butcher and torture them, yet they'd lost the will to fight and surrendered to their fate.

"Not sure I'll be given much choice in the matter. Philip Greer's dad pretty much owns this county. The chief is best friends with him. I'm just one man. We got two more part-time officers I can call in, but they aren't about to risk their paychecks, much less their lives, not for a colored boy."

"And neither are you." Samuel glanced around at the rundown houses, the lack of any adults, the general feeling of a town ground to dust. His own hospital was in one of the poorest sections of DC, but even it didn't seem as hopeless as this place.

"Doing the best I can. You can leave, or you can stay and help. But we need to move now." His voice snapped through the air like Samuel's old drill sergeant. Samuel was immune, but before he could answer, a small figure crept from the shadows of the house across from them. The girl. Winnie, Thomson had called her.

She darted closer, stopped at the edge of the street, her body wavering as if the slightest breeze could blow her back into the shadows. "You gonna help him?"

Her words barely carried to him. With them came the fear and courage it had taken for her to step forward.

Samuel drew in a breath. "Let me get my family. We'll follow you to the police station, stabilize him, and then I'll drive him to the hospital in Altoona myself." Jo was not going to like it, but it was the boy's best chance for proper health care—and to avoid another beating. Or worse.

Thomson nodded. "Station's two blocks over. Brick building beside the courthouse."

Winnie said nothing, merely tightened her lips in determination, and marched over to the police car, climbing into the back seat beside Henry.

Lord help him. What had Samuel gotten himself into?

# CHAPTER 5

TK REMAINED SILENT, waiting for Karlan to continue. They crossed through an intersection and continued into another residential area, this one a step up, not by much but a little, from the last neighborhood.

The people here weren't as angry or indifferent to the sight of the police car; many waggled their hands in acknowledgement or nodded their heads. Except the kids—they were just like the ones in the other side of the square, laughing and yelling and playing. No counting coup here; only a few middle fingers raised as Karlan leaned on his horn to break up a football game so he had room to roll past.

"Most of the segregation around here isn't racial." Karlan steered them past post-war colonials, mid-seventies ranch houses, and Craftsman bungalows. "It's economic."

TK nodded, although she noticed there definitely seemed to be more whites on this side of Main Street, but also African-Americans, a few Hispanics. There was no new construction but plenty of obvious repairs and fresh paint.

Karlan continued, "Last century we had the railroad, the quarry, paper mill, even an electronics assembly plant once upon a time...all that's gone. Now our biggest employer is the college. Most folks who work there, the professors and the like, they don't live in town. They live up the mountain, where you have a view of the river or in one of the fancy gated communities built on what used to be old family farmsteads. But those of us in town, we're victims of geography. Hemmed in by mountains, the river and the college. Leaves people feeling trapped. Powerless."

She was silent for a moment. Had a feeling he was talking about a lot more than geography or economics. "The officer-involved shooting you mentioned, I'm guessing the victim—"

"Was black. And the cop was white." He gripped the wheel as he plowed over a pothole rather than steer around it. The struts squeaked, the car groaning at the impact.

"I was Jefferson's T.O." A training officer was any police

officer's first real mentor after the academy. "Kid's a damn fine cop." His sigh rolled through the car like a tsunami. "*Was* a damn fine cop. Even if he's in the clear with the grand jury, no way he'll come back from this. Not in this town. Maybe not anywhere, way the news and everyone keeps putting his face and name all over the internet."

His lips tightened, and it was a moment before he continued. "This town, this department has a target on it right now. I need you to understand why it's important to keep our calling you in for assistance on this case as quiet as possible. We don't need any rumors that we're incompetent, can't do our jobs."

"You need? Or your chief?"

"Actually, it was Mayor Greer."

"No problem. We prefer to stay out of the limelight."

"That's what the Justice Department said. Right before their press conference where they about crucified Jefferson."

"It's not your fault," she tried but immediately regretted it as the wrong thing to say.

"Of course not. Not anyone's fault except the actor's." Police slang for a person taking action to commit a crime. "He put himself there in that alley that night. Jefferson did nothing except do his job."

"What happened?"

He was silent as they came to an intersection with a four-lane highway. On the other side, nestled in the curve of the mountains behind it, was Greer College.

She could see what Karlan had meant about the geography working against the town's working-class population. The streets surrounding the college had mature shade trees, and the homes were larger, a few new, mostly well-maintained classics: Tudors that resembled fairy tale gingerbread houses, Craftsman-style bungalows, large Colonials with lawns mowed in meticulous diagonal patterns visible even from the street.

Karlan followed her gaze. "College already expanded up the mountain as far as it could—razed an old mobile home park and took over some State Game Lands in a deal with the government. Now there's nowhere left to go but headed into town." He gestured at the pristine houses they were passing. "Because no way are the professors and folks over here going to give up their pretty homes." His tone turned bitter.

TK waited, understanding that Karlan would tell the story at his own pace.

"Call came in as a routine domestic. Which are never routine. But Jefferson knew the address, knew that usually by the time the cops arrived, the fight would already have burned itself out and the guy would be sitting on the porch nursing a forty, waiting for the missus to let him back inside, and she'd be on the phone complaining to her friends about her low-life, low-rent guy who maybe really wasn't so bad and what the hell were the cops doing banging on her door disturbing her peace. Seen it so many times, Jefferson could practically run the script word for word in his head as he cleared the job he was on—a vehicular collision over on Broad—and started to the domestic."

"No back-up?" TK hated domestic disputes—when she was stateside, between deployments, she'd occasionally pulled that duty as an MP. Never knew the right thing to say or do to help the victims, especially the ones who didn't act like victims, who just wanted to be left alone.

"None available." He waved a hand. "We're stretched pretty thin, usually do okay, but sometimes a busy Friday or Saturday night can overwhelm the system. Not much you can do except keep clearing calls and moving on."

"So, Jefferson responded to the domestic."

"Yeah. Thinking about what he was going to say—you

know the drill. You assess the situation, and if it's nothing actionable, you have your words of wisdom, trying against all odds to prevent being called back again later that night. You talk to the man, telling him to stop stealing his woman's money, spending it all on booze or drugs, to appreciate his hard-working beautiful lady the way she deserves to be appreciated. You chat with the woman, invite her to leave with you if she feels unsafe, let her know there are people ready to help if she feels trapped or things get violent—that usually is the last thing you say because she'll kick you out of the house then, yelling at you that she's no victim, the cops are useless, and why the hell did she call you to begin with. But you do it anyway because sometimes they take the card you give them and make the call and rarely they'll leave with you. All part of the job."

"But not that night."

"Not that night. Jefferson arrives just in time to see Eggers run out the front door, gun in his hand, blood on his shirt, neighbors screaming, shouting. Jefferson runs inside, finds the wife, beaten but alive, holes shot up in all the walls, place trashed. Calls for EMS and back-up, puts out an alert on Eggers, starts his pursuit, first in his vehicle, then when he spies Eggers hopping a fence, crossing through yards, waving his pistol at anyone who pokes their head out, he follows on foot."

They continued down the highway, passing a few shopping centers and a large commercial office park. Within less than a mile of leaving the college, they were surrounded by cornfields on one side and trees on the other.

"You ever been in a foot chase after an armed felon?"

TK shook her head. When she'd been deployed with the Female Engagement Team, she'd been in active combat situations—most still classified, couldn't talk about them even if she wanted to—but never had to chase someone through the night, jumping obstacles, trying to keep from tripping in the dark, little cover, unable to see much of anything, never knowing when the guy you're chasing is going to take a breath and turn to shoot at you. "I would imagine that it's a lot like being in a close-quarters firefight."

"Damned right. Pulse racing, chest heaving, hauling your butt over fences, stumbling through yards and alleys and trash heaps, trying to keep up on the radio so you don't get mistakenly shot by one of your own guys, hoping the guy you're chasing doesn't decide to make a stand and start shooting civilians or you or your backup. Most foot pursuits don't last more than a minute or two—this one lasted about three. But then Eggers runs down the wrong alley, one the city had barricaded for demolition."

"The one near where you found me this morning?" TK remembered her path being blocked by the future demolition project.

"Exactly. Jefferson catches up to his subject. Finds enough breath to yell at him to put the gun down and raise his hands over his head."

"But the guy didn't?"

Karlan paused as he slowed and turned onto a narrow two-lane road marked only by a sign that read: GREER QUARRY AND STONE WORKS. HAZARDOUS CONDITIONS AHEAD. DANGER: NO TRESPASSING

"Eggers still had the gun in his hand when he turned to face Jefferson."

"So, pretty clear-cut. A clear and present threat, right? Bodycam video would show that."

He grunted. "We can't afford decent squad cars; think we can afford bodycams?"

"So it's Jefferson's word only? Were there any witnesses?" She guessed not.

Karlan shook his head. "Jefferson ordered him to not

move, to freeze and not turn around. Three times told him to slowly lower the gun to the ground in front of him—away from Jefferson. Instead, Eggers turned around."

They stopped at a chain link gate at the entrance to the quarry where a uniformed officer waited with a clipboard in hand. The police wanted to minimize traffic to the crime scene— evidence recovery scene, really—which was the whole reason why TK was riding with Karlan, but she cursed the timing. One thing for sure, Karlan was a damn good storyteller.

"Good timing," the officer told Karlan as he made a note of their particulars for the evidence log. "Divers just got the float bags under and are bringing her up now." He waved his pen to a spot on the other side of the gate. "We're asking everyone to park on the far side, away from the action. The forensic folks and coroner are already at their tent, ready to process the vehicle and whatever's inside it." His grin turned ghoulish. "My money's on a mob hit."

Karlan shook his head, rolled his window back up, and waited for the officer to open the gate for them. "Mob hit, my ass."

"You were telling me about Jefferson."

He eased the car through the gate. "Oh, right. Eggers

turned all right. With his hand coming down with the gun. Monday morning quarterbacks like the DA say he was he trying to lower the gun to surrender. Or maybe he was just too damn tired and disgusted and knew he was caught and was trying to end it all by forcing Jefferson to defend himself."

"And Jefferson shot him."

"Yes, ma'am. Jefferson shot him. By the time it was all said and done, turned out Eggers's gun was empty—no way Jefferson could have known that. No idea if Eggers even realized it. But technically, that made him an unarmed man. Then the woman came forward, said the domestic disturbance call was a mistake. That it wasn't Eggers who'd beaten her and shot up their place, it was an unknown intruder."

"She defended him? After all that?"

"Love. Or greed. Maybe she sees a chance at a new life after she sues the city. Who knows with domestics? But her story now is that Eggers wasn't threatening her or Jefferson, he was chasing this unknown, apparently invisible intruder that no one else saw and that was never caught on any traffic cams or surveillance of the chase. Not that anyone cares about evidence when you've got a juicy story to tweet about, right? Blue on black murder victim was the hash tag."

He hauled in a breath, his chest expanding, shoulders lifting. The kind of deep breath you take before battle. Then he released it, the weight of it so heavy it collapsed in on itself without even a hint of a sigh. "Jefferson got to stay alive, go home to his wife and kids, and live another day. But if the grand jury indicts, he may end up losing everything. Hell, even if they don't, he's already lost."

With that sorrowful sentiment echoing through the air, he parked the patrol car between a van from Greer College's forensic anthropology department and an ambulance emblazoned with the county coroner's shield.

TK climbed out of the patrol car and blinked into the bright morning sun reflected from the walls of the quarry. The granite acted as a natural reflector, sparking the light in a myriad of directions before it was swallowed by the shadows deeper down the steep walls. They'd parked to one side of the inclined area of hard-packed stone that had once allowed excavation equipment to enter the quarry's lower levels. A police tow truck idled there, waiting for the divers to finish their work in the deep sapphire water beyond.

Along the edge of the cliff, a group of eight college students crowded, watching the events unfolding out in the water—they weren't that much younger than TK, but somehow seeing their enthusiasm made her feel old.

When TK had learned the county coroner was a college professor and that she and her students would be responsible for the crime scene, she'd had her doubts. Bringing up an antique car without unduly disturbing its occupant from a hundred and twenty feet below the surface? And do it all while preserving any evidence? She couldn't even begin to imagine the logistics—and all only two days after the body was discovered.

"Dr. Madsen really knows her stuff," Karlan said, following her gaze. "We're lucky she took on the job of coroner," he continued. "Before then, it was always one of the mortuaries—more than a few times, I had the feeling they were more interested in saving money than getting to the truth. Guess they did the best they could with a limited budget."

"It'd be nice if Pennsylvania had a real medical examiner system like other states." The gravel crunched beneath their feet as they crossed the empty expanse to the idling tow truck.

"Hell, most of our county sheriffs still only serve papers, leave the real police work to the locals and the Staties." Karlan nodded a greeting to the tow truck operator, also a police officer, thus able to maintain the chain of custody once the vehicle was excavated, preserving any criminal evidence.

*If* there even was a crime, TK reminded herself. Her first case as lead investigator could be over before it began, depending on what they found inside the car.

# CHAPTER 6

LUCY GUARDINO STEERED her Subaru onto the exit ramp leading to Altoona. The city sat on a shallow plain in the heart of the Alleghenies, surrounded by mountains and newly completed highways. A city constrained by geography even as its citizens built new ways to escape it.

Or maybe that was her gray mood talking. She'd love to escape this particular task. Despite the bright sunshine and brilliant blue sky—or maybe because of it—she felt nothing but sorrow.

"Thanks for coming with me," she told her boss, Valencia Frazier, owner of the Beacon Group. "We're never really trained for this kind of thing at the FBI. Local law enforcement or medical examiner offices usually handle next of kin notification."

She wished she'd gone to Greer with TK—a cold case

from sixty-odd years ago was eminently more appealing than what she faced now. But this was important, and she needed to get the job done right.

Valencia's smile was comforting despite its lack of mirth. "You never really get used to it, I'm afraid. But at least when we arrive, families know it's with answers instead of more uncertainty. Even if those answers are years or decades in the making."

Fourteen years since eleven-year-old Benji Randall stepped off his school bus but never made it home. Fourteen years Lucy had been working his case. First, using it for her thesis on interagency cooperation in law enforcement. Revisiting it when she was working on the FBI's geographic profiling system, as well as using it as a teaching case when she was stationed at Quantico as an instructor. Then, assigning it during slow times to her team after she was promoted to Supervisory Special Agent in Pittsburgh. And finally, now, bringing it to completion.

Ironically, it had taken Valencia and her coalition of civilian resources, including NamUs and the Doe Network, to help her discover Benji's fate. And his body.

Fourteen years the Randall family had waited, never

leaving their home on the outskirts of Altoona. As the mother had once told Lucy, how could they? They had no choice but to stay, just in case Benji found his way home.

"What do I say to them?" Lucy asked, surprised by how nervous she felt. It was a breathtaking responsibility, handling a moment that would forever change a family.

Valencia was silent for a long moment. Lucy edged a glance in her direction. When Nick had first met Valencia, he'd described her as all the best of Michelle Obama and Audrey Hepburn combined. She boasted impeccable taste, had an aura of refined elegance and intellect, but most of all, she genuinely cared about the people who came into her life, especially the families of the victims she'd created the Beacon Group to serve.

"You've never met them before?" she asked Lucy.

"No. Early on, the case was an exercise, a research project. I was mainly drawn to it because it happened so close to where I grew up. Thinking back to when I was a kid, both parents working and then after my dad died, I pretty much ran wild. There was never anyone at home, we didn't have cell phones, we'd ride our bikes over the mountain to the dam, go swimming even though there was no lifeguard, stay out all hours when school was out over the summer.

"At least that's how it started. I wasn't even focused on the victim, more the patchwork system of coroners, small town police departments, larger regional coalitions, the lack of uniformity in county sheriff agencies that actually do more than serve papers and perform actual investigations. I couldn't believe how haphazard it all was. There are literally areas of the state where you can get away with murder, falling between boundaries of law enforcement agencies so that if the State Police aren't called in, no investigation would occur. County coroners elected with no medical backgrounds and what little forensic backup they might have—usually hiring an outside private pathologist—limited by their budget. Anyway, that's how I first started, using Benji's case as an example of the limitations and need for better interdepartmental cooperation along with some state-wide authority providing oversight." She paused. "But while I was working on my thesis, I got pregnant with Megan."

"And after that, Benji was no longer an anonymous case or file."

"Exactly. Still wasn't my case or my place to interfere with Smitty—Matt Smith, the detective who caught the case, worked it until he retired, even after, basically until he died. That was two years ago now. Once he was gone, I did speak with the mother a few times, just to let her know that even without Smitty around, someone still remembered Benji, was still working it. Wanted to give her someone she could call, just in case."

"Do they know why we're coming?"

"No. They've had their hopes raised and dashed so many times, I couldn't bear it. And it didn't seem right, not over the phone. But..."

"How to tell them their son is dead? They know. But you still need to say it. And even when you do, they won't believe you."

"Surely after fourteen years—" Lucy stopped herself. "I'd never give up, not if it was Megan. Of course they still have hope. It's going to break their hearts."

"And it's your job to make sure they understand the truth. You won't be doing them any kindness by lying or hedging, not even if you think it will ease their pain. You can't leave any room for doubt, nothing that will gnaw at them from the inside out. This is their chance to finally get the answers they've been waiting for, even if it's not the answer they were praying for."

"What if they ask if he suffered?" It was the question she'd been dreading.

The corpse buried beneath the tool shed had been reduced to a skeleton—but the pathologist had found multiple broken bones in varying stages of healing, along with evidence of severe malnutrition and prolonged confinement. Benji hadn't died quickly, had probably been alive for months before the skull fracture that killed him. He most definitely had suffered.

"They deserve the truth," Valencia said. "Don't interpret the facts, just deliver them in plain language. Answer everything the best you can. It's the only way."

The nav system signaled the final turn. They arrived at their destination, a modest two-story colonial nestled into the forest above the reservoir.

The driveway was filled with vehicles so Lucy pulled up to the curb. "Maybe I should check in with TK first."

"She would have called if she needed anything." Valencia knew Lucy was stalling, of course.

Lucy appreciated the older woman's patience. She got out and joined Valencia at the far end of the walk. They stood together in silence.

Lucy twisted her wedding ring. In her old life as a FBI agent, it was always her touchstone before she began any dangerous operation. Nick often accused her of magical thinking with her need to always try to fix everything, save every victim, solve every case. As if by restoring balance to the world at large, she could somehow protect *her* world: Nick and Megan.

"There are some things in this world that you can never make right," Valencia said in a low tone, startling Lucy because it was exactly what Nick would have told her if he'd been here. No big surprise. Nick and Valencia were two of the smartest and wisest people she'd ever met.

Despite everything she'd seen and done, Lucy stubbornly refused to give up on the idea that anything was possible if she just threw enough of herself at the problem. It was as if some part of her psyche was stuck in mid-adolescence and she would never fully mature into a pragmatic adult like the rest of the world. Times like this, she wished she could allow herself to accept that evil sometimes won—oftentimes won—and that there was nothing she could do about it.

They walked up to the front door together. Valencia stepped aside to let Lucy ring the bell. The door opened.

"Mrs. Randall? I'm Lucy Guardino. We spoke on the phone." Lucy's mouth suddenly went dry. "It's about your son. Benjamin."

# CHAPTER 7

TK AND KARLAN walked down the incline behind the tow truck to where the water lapped the edge of the stone. The bottom dropped off precipitously, making her wonder if there had once been a collapse, cutting off access to the lower levels of the quarry.

A woman wearing polarized sunglasses and holding a pair of binoculars stood observing the boat on the far side of the quarry. Karlan tapped her elbow. "Dr. Marcia Madsen, this is TK O'Connor, the investigator from Beacon Falls. Here to help us figure out who's in that car and how they got here."

Like Karlan, Marcia Madsen was older than TK, in her mid-fifties, with close-cropped gray hair and the athletic build of someone more accustomed to fieldwork than life behind a classroom podium. She took TK's hand with a firm grip. "Nice to have you on board."

"Ever do anything like this before?" Last night, after Lucy had told her about the case, TK had read Madsen's online bio and knew she was an accredited forensic anthropologist who'd worked in war zones including Bosnia and Argentina as well as mass casualty events like the Indian Ocean tsunami and 9/11.

"Body recovery from submerged vehicles, yes. Part of being a coroner in a county with so many rivers and lakes. But they were all fairly fresh. Never had the good fortune to work one submerged at such a depth in a relatively anaerobic environment like this one and definitely never one this old."

Clearly the professor had a warped idea of "good fortune." They peered out at the boat in the distance. It and the divers had arrived last night, on loan from the Pittsburgh River Rescue team.

"What's the plan?" TK shielded her eyes and focused on the boat bobbing in the gentle swell created by the wind circling the quarry walls.

Madsen's team would be doing all the heavy lifting as far as retrieval—then it was TK's job to cobble together tidbits from the examination of the body and other evidence so that Wash, their technical analyst back at Beacon Falls, could use it to scour his databases and hopefully track down an identity. Once they knew who they were dealing with, TK would be the boots on the ground trying to re-create his or her final journey while Wash searched for any living relatives.

"The dive team is filming everything—both for educational and evidentiary purposes. Once they've documented as much as they can without disturbing the car, they'll set float bags beneath it and fill them with air."

"That's it? It just floats up?" Seemed a bit anticlimactic.

"That's it. Then the boat will pull it to the ramp where we'll attach a winch and tow it onto dry ground."

A diver popped up to the surface, water glistening as it rolled off his wetsuit, and shouted something to his comrades in the boat. The diver swam away from the boat and the expanse of water between them became agitated. TK couldn't help but think of a horror movie where a monster slowly emerged from the deep, ready to devour the unwary and unsuspecting.

The water churned for a moment, air bubbles rupturing against the surface, and suddenly a light blue car popped up as if by magic. Around them the grad students clapped and cheered.

Madsen nodded, and her students turned and got to work

unrolling a large tarp between the tow truck and the water's edge. "Once the car's on land, we'll collect anything that drains free as the water runs out, then move the car onto the flatbed and under the canopy for further examination."

"Why not just haul it back to the police's evidence garage?"

"I'm worried about losing potential evidence. As soon as the car hits the air, everything associated with it will begin to suffer oxidative damage. We'll document as much as we can *in situ* here, collect the remains, transport them to my lab, while the police will remove the vehicle for more complete analysis."

Out on the water, the divers finished their task of attaching the tow lines to the boat, and the boat began to slowly return to shore, the car floating alongside it.

"What are you expecting to find?" TK asked. "After so long underwater?"

Madsen smiled as if she'd been waiting all morning for that question. "Anyone?" she addressed her students. "Sixty plus years submerged, what do we expect to find?"

Her tone turned professorial. TK felt herself blushing for having asked the question, hoping it didn't make her sound like an amateur. But Madsen herself had said that she'd never worked a case like this, so there couldn't be much precedent—certainly none that TK and Wash had found when they got the call last night and had done a quick search for similar cases.

"Temperatures would have held steady, just above freezing at that depth," one of the students—in TK's mind she thought of him as a kid, although he might have actually been older than her own twenty-six years. But his face was uncreased, his eyes clear; obviously he wasn't older as far as experience, even if he had more formal knowledge than she had.

"Near anaerobic conditions and the contained environment would have prevented much predation," another student, this time a girl, chimed in.

"Not all of it," someone else corrected. "Small fish would have gotten in. Plus, we don't know the pH of the water at that depth. Excessive acidity or an alkaline environment could lead to enhanced degradation of any organic material."

TK glanced at the assortment of future forensic scientists, all eager to prove themselves to their professor. To spend your life listening and learning, soaking up knowledge—it seemed like paradise to someone like her who'd joined the Marines straight out of high school. She'd thought about trying to go to college—Valencia and Lucy said she could take the time off, and the

Beacon Group would help pay the costs—but whenever she saw students like this, she realized she would never fit in. They may be studying crime, but they had no real knowledge of it.

"The body will be mostly skeletonized with some adipocere clinging to the bones," another student voiced his opinion, beaming when Madsen nodded her agreement.

"The clothing will probably be dissolved, unless the car went in during the winter and the occupant wore several layers." This from the first student, the man with a wispy beard that TK wasn't sure was even actually meant to be a beard or more of a statement that he was too preoccupied with more important things than personal grooming. He frowned. "Not sure what kind of synthetics they wore back then. And leather...that might be preserved."

They continued their debate as the boat reached the landing and the divers, Karlan, and the tow truck driver worked to attach the truck's winch to the car.

TK marveled at the discussion. No, she'd never fit into the academic world. None of these kids had ever witnessed bloodshed, she was certain. None of them had ever looked into the face of a man they would kill or feared for their own life.

Just like she'd never fit into normal civilian life. Only

people she'd ever fit in with were others who were just as broken and battered—like her former squad or her new team at Beacon Falls.

"Any evidence may be hopelessly degraded," again from Mr. Wispy Beard, this time with a tone of authority that rankled with TK.

"You keep saying evidence—we don't know that a crime has occurred." TK's attention was on the car now being winched free from the water, carefully positioned over the tarp. She had to admit, the old car was a beauty—a shade of robin's egg blue you'd never see nowadays and a sturdy yet elegant design.

Madsen answered. "We don't know that any hasn't. Best to take the time to preserve things now instead of regretting it later."

She and TK moved to join Karlan on the far side of the tarp as the students positioned themselves around it. Madsen signaled the tow truck driver and the winch began to slowly turn, raising the car. "Besides, I want my students to see things done correctly, learn how to take their time despite any pressures placed on them."

"Pressures?" From the laughter coming from her students as water sluiced from the car, splashing them, they didn't seem to be under any undue pressure.

She shrugged. "Law enforcement wanting answers, politicians wanting everything to go away, reporters looking for a story, your grant running out, forcing the dig to shut down, security telling you rebel forces aren't happy with you unearthing their war crimes. You know, the usual."

"Right. The usual." TK smiled. She was starting to like the professor's pragmatic view of the world at large.

Karlan stood between the tow truck's cab and the lift mechanism, giving the driver directions. He had the operator stop when the car's rear end was raised to about twenty degrees, water and debris draining into the waiting tarp. The students surged forward to examine their treasure trove.

"Want him to keep going, doc?" he called.

Madsen waved her hand. "Yes, please." The car raised a few more degrees, releasing another wave of water that quickly subsided. "Okay, that's good, you can position it on the flatbed and move it beneath the canopy."

TK joined the students, being careful to stay out of their way. The tarp had been staked so that nothing could slide back into the quarry. The students were happily straining the water, collecting their finds in plastic buckets. So far it didn't look like much except normal debris: clumps of algae, a few rocks, bits of unidentifiable metal.

When the water had finished draining, she, Karlan, and Madsen paced the truck as it slowly hauled its cargo beneath the canopy on the other side of the landing where the pavement was flat.

"No one in here without protective gear," Madsen told them, pointing to the cardboard boxes at the entrance to the canopy. They all pulled on Tyvek suits and booties designed to avoid contaminating any evidence. It was like zipping her body into a portable sauna, TK thought as she tightened the hood around her hair.

Beneath the canopy, several students were already at work. One filming with a video camera, the other snapping still photos, as a third laid out measuring tapes around the car. There wasn't room on the truck's flatbed for more than one person at a time to walk around the car, so they took turns, careful not to actually touch the Dodge.

Then the photographer hopped down and plugged her camera into a laptop Madsen had set up on a folding table. TK had her own laptop in her messenger bag, but no sense in adding to the crowded conditions—everything was being stored in the cloud where she and Wash, back at Beacon Falls, could access it remotely. She did grab her phone to make sure Wash was on line, watching the uploads, but before she could dial him, he called her.

"Are you seeing this?" he asked in a breathless tone. She could hear his keyboard clicking furiously in the background. "This is incredible."

She squinted at the images on the screen before her then turned back to the vehicle. Madsen had set up a ring of halogen work lights around the edge of the flatbed, but the images were still dark, their secrets waiting to be uncovered as they were processed and enhanced.

"I'm not seeing much of anything." Except the backs of the students gingerly climbing around the car's exterior.

TK itched with curiosity, wanting to jump up and just open the damn car doors, see what was inside, but she understood the need to move slowly and methodically. Didn't mean she liked it. Without the water to buoy it up, the skeleton inside the car had slid down out of sight. Not that you could see much beyond the silt-streaked windows.

"Take a look at this one that I just enhanced," Wash said.

TK opened her own laptop and turned it on. A few

moments later her screen filled with a photo that now revealed actual detail. It had been shot through the driver's side window, aiming across the front seat.

She made out a steering wheel—big, old-fashioned, it looked like something to wrestle. On the far side of it the light reflected from a glistening mound of greasy yellowish material covering what could only be a rib cage and skull.

"Is that what I think it is?" Wash asked. "On the far side, near the door handle."

TK zoomed in on the area. "You might want to see this," she called to Madsen who was busy directing the students and waved her hand in a "be right there" gesture. TK turned to look for Karlan; he'd definitely need to see. The detective caught her eye and sauntered over. "Look there."

He lowered his head until his nose almost touched the screen then leaned back again. TK couldn't restrain herself any longer. She grabbed a pair of the nitrile gloves and hopped up onto the platform. The student nearest her looked up as if TK had just trespassed on sacred ground. "Dr. Madsen?"

Madsen and Karlan crossed over from the table. "It's okay." She nodded to TK. "Go ahead. Open it. Slowly. Peter, keep filming this."

TK pulled at the passenger door. She was expecting resistance, imagined that an almost seventy-year-old car dragged up from the bottom of a quarry would be rusted shut. But the door practically fell open at her touch. As if it had been waiting for this exact moment, as if it wanted to unveil its secrets.

She allowed it to open only an inch or two, just far enough to confirm what the camera had seen.

"Looks like just the one occupant," Karlan narrated from behind her. The videographer gestured for him to get out of the way and he moved aside.

"We definitely have a crime scene here," TK finished for him.

She stepped back so Madsen could see for herself what Wash had glimpsed in the photo. The camera flashed, and there was no mistaking the hard glint as the light sparked from the steel handcuff fastened around what remained of the victim's arm, a few frayed dark threads all that remained of the skeleton's clothing. The other end of the handcuff was locked to the door handle.

"Our corpse wasn't the driver," TK continued. "He was a prisoner. With no hope of escape."

# CHAPTER 8

THE POLICE CAR stank of piss and throw-up and blood. Winnie ignored all that as she crouched on the floor, her body pinned between the back of the driver's seat and the seat Henry lay on. His breathing wasn't right, and his face was smushed in. At least what she could see of his face through the blood.

All because of her. "I told you not to."

His eyes fluttered open and his lips tried to make words. She leaned closer.

"You...right?"

"I'm fine. Philip Greer and his bullies weren't whaling on me."

"No. Your...pa...hurt you?" His question lingered in the

air as Officer Thomson climbed into the car and began to drive.

Winnie leaned down until her lips were at Henry's ear. "Pa never can hurt me. Not for real."

Her words surprised her. It was as if she'd just now figured out something she should have known all along, something she should have learned on her own. But it'd taken seeing a colored boy willing to stand up for her; someone not even her blood who thought she was worth something in this world.

And that was everything.

"You two all right back there?" Officer Thomson called over his shoulder as the car lurched over the railroad tracks and headed away from the river toward the town center.

"Henry's bleeding real bad," Winnie answered, not sure what to do about the split above Henry's one eye that kept spurting blood.

Her father said Negro blood was different, tainted, but it looked and smelled just like her own whenever he slapped her hard enough to make her nose gush. Smelled better than his when he got drunk and threw up blood mixed with whiskey, missing the toilet so she had to clean it up by hand.

"That colored man was a doctor. He's going to patch

Henry up, take him to Altoona to the hospital."

"Before Philip Greer and those boys come back with their fathers?"

"That's the plan."

"He didn't touch me. Henry was trying to protect me."

Officer Thomson made a noise that sounded like he already knew that. "Your father? Again?"

"Wasn't fast enough," she admitted. "Should have seen it coming."

"I need to know, Winnie. What exactly happened?"

She turned her head far enough to stare at him in the rearview mirror. "Why? No one ever does anything about it. Except Henry and his mom and aunt."

"I meant, what did Henry do."

She grit her teeth in anger. So typical. The only people she could count on when things got bad and now this hopeless, helpless policeman wanted her to get them in trouble. Then where would she run? "I told you. Nothing. Not that anyone cares. Just because Henry's colored doesn't make him bad. And just because others are white doesn't make them good. Why can't anyone see that?"

Officer Thomson looked away, his eyes pinched tight like

she'd said something that smelled like road kill.

He turned down the alley between the police department and the Woolworth's, slowed the car and pulled up to the metal door with the heavy hinges and massive lock—the one they used for prisoners since the town's only jail cell was back there. It was the door other kids' mothers used to scare them, hauling them down by their ears, telling them to take a good look at their future.

Winnie's mother had long ago run off to find her own future so it was usually her meeting her pa here out in the alley, bringing him a coat with his bottle in one pocket and his cigarettes in the other, once he sobered up enough for the police to let him go.

Most times she'd wait, ignoring the police officers' stares—always filled with pity but never actually doing anything to fix her father or stop him. Except Officer Thomson. More than once she'd seen him through the bars on the window arguing with her father; a few times he'd even come outside to check on her, ask her if she was all right.

Today was the first time she'd ever had the courage to look him in the eye and answer. Funny, she thought finally telling the truth would change things. But it didn't; people didn't change because of mere words. Heck, if seeing her own blood on his hands didn't change her dad, nothing would.

Officer Thomson opened the rear door of the police car. Henry's hand had gone limp and his breathing was raspier.

"Maybe we shouldn't move him?" she said as she scrambled out to give him room. "Not until the doctor's here?"

Hard to believe that Negro was a doctor but she'd heard of things like that in the cities. Nowhere around here. Big places like Pittsburgh or Philadelphia. Still, a Negro doctor was better than no doctor at all.

Unless her dad or any of the men he drank and played cards with found out. Even worse—if Philip Greer made good on his threat and got his father. More than the mayor, Mr. Greer owned everything and everyone in town. If he got involved, there'd be hell to pay—for Henry and the colored doctor.

She didn't understand why most of the men around here, the white ones at any rate, seemed so angry all the time. Lashing out at the colored, the Italians and Hungarians, anyone who wasn't just like them. As if being different meant coming to steal what little anyone else had in this world.

Winnie couldn't imagine anyone wanting to come steal

anything her dad had. Empty bottles of whiskey and beer, a house about ready to fall apart with roofing shingles patching holes in the siding, a daughter he barely seemed to know was alive except when he was looking for someone to scream at or something to hit.

Henry's parents were Negroes, but they never shouted or hit or stole or got drunk, not that she could see. They'd been their next-door neighbors since before her mom ran off, and if it weren't for Henry's mom and aunt, there were winters when Winnie might have frozen to death or gone hungry while her dad was off on one of his trips to find better work. Somehow, he never made it farther than Altoona and always came home drunk, broke, and smelling of cheap perfume.

The Rawlings were good people, always there for her when Winnie needed shelter. And yet white boys like Philip Greer and his no-account friends jumped all over Henry for being colored and helping her get away from her dad.

No one jumped all over her dad for being white and hurting his daughter. His friends laughed and pounded him on the shoulder like they were proud every time they came over and saw her with a black eye or new bruise. "Gotta keep 'em in line. Can't let her grow up wild like her momma," they'd say.

Winnie wished she'd just for once find a way to hit back. Lately, when her dad got that deep drunk, sleeping like the dead, she'd stand over him, watch him breathe. She would go to hell, she knew she would, but she couldn't help sometimes praying to Jesus to make him just not take another breath. Just to never wake up. But he always did.

Officer Thomson reached inside the car, trying to rouse Henry, when another car pulled into the alley. A pretty robin's egg blue sedan. Nicer than any car around here—except the fancy black ones the Greers had, but they always had someone else drive them while they sat in the back seat.

The colored man from before drove the blue car. A lady wearing the nicest go-to-church suit Winnie had ever seen and it wasn't even Sunday sat in the passenger seat. Between them was a little girl in braids and a gingham dress. The man and woman were obviously in the middle of a serious discussion, their heads bobbing back and forth as their mouths moved, but just then Henry's breathing turned into a shrill gasp, and she knew he couldn't wait any longer.

She ran to the sedan and pounded on the driver's door, then leaned her weight back, yanking it open. "He can't breathe! You need to come now. Help him. Please."

The man climbed out of the car, striding past her to where Officer Thomson had pulled Henry from the back of the squad car and stood cradling him in his arms. The colored man didn't need more than a blink to see what was going on.

"Get him inside, onto a flat surface. A table or the like," he ordered Officer Thomson. He turned to the woman. She was already out of their car and at the trunk. "Bring my bag. Quickly."

Within moments, they'd all rushed inside the police station. Officer Thomson bundled Henry into his chest, Henry's long arms and legs hanging limp. He hesitated when they passed the jail cell but kept on going down the narrow hallway into a room that had a big table in the middle, a kitchen sink, hot plate, and set of cabinets. There, he gently lowered Henry onto the table.

The woman ran to the doctor, handing him his bag. He was already shrugging free of his suit jacket then reaching into the black bag for a stethoscope. Henry wasn't making any noise, none at all.

"Is he dead?" the little girl whispered to Winnie as she crept into the doorway, following her parents at a distance.

"No," Winnie said in an authoritarian voice even though

she had no idea of the truth. Henry sure looked dead. She took the little girl's hand in hers and squeezed it. "He's gonna be okay."

The little girl beamed up at her and patted her arm. "Of course he is. My daddy's the best doctor in all of Washington. Maybe the whole country. He can fix anything."

A heavyset woman appeared in the hall, coming from the front of the police station. Mabel Parker, the town's phone operator and police dispatcher. Nosyparker was what the kids called her behind her back.

"What's going on here?" she yelled. "Little girl, you can't be in here. Winnie, what on earth are you doing bringing a colored girl here?"

Then she drew close enough to see Henry sprawled out on the table. The doctor held a shiny scalpel, about to slice into Henry's chest. "Stop it! Archie Thomson, what in darnation are you doing? Get that colored boy off our break room table!"

"He's hurt, Mabel." Officer Thomson was busy holding the boy still as the doctor got into position.

"I don't care. We eat off that table."

"He has a tension pneumothorax," the doctor explained as his wife poured alcohol over Henry's bare chest. "A collapsed lung. He'll die if I don't release the pressure."

Before Mabel had a chance to respond, the doctor sliced into Henry's chest with one hand, the other sliding a metal tube though the slit he cut. A whoosh sounded through the room and Henry gasped, his chest heaving up and down. Breathing. That was good.

"I'm calling the chief," Mabel said, strutting back toward the front where her desk at the switchboard was. "We'll just see about this."

The doctor ignored her, instead held a hand, palm up, out to his wife. "4-0 silk."

The wife rummaged in his bag and had what he needed in his hand before he finished speaking.

"See?" The little girl squeezed Winnie's hand. "I told you my daddy could help him."

"Is your mom a nurse?" Winnie wanted to be a nurse when she grew up. Wanted to help people like Henry's mom and aunt had helped her time and again.

"No. But she learned. There's always hurt people coming to our house middle of the night." The little girl let go of Winnie's hand and turned to face her. "Almost forgot my manners. I'm Maybelle Mann."

Winnie nodded, her gaze still hooked by the misery that was Henry's battered body. All her fault. "Winifred Neal."

"Most pleased to meet you, Winifred." The little girl actually curtsied.

Winnie clamped both hands over her mouth, strangling her laughter. Henry's blood dribbled over the edge of the table and dripped onto the white linoleum.

"He gonna be all right?" Officer Thomson asked, relaxing his grip on Henry's shoulders as the boy stopped struggling and began to breathe easier.

"Once we get him to a hospital." The doctor tied a complicated knot around the metal tube, fastening it to Henry's chest wall.

Officer Thomson jumped up as Mabel shouted something from the front of the building. He ran past Winnie and the girl and out to the front of the building.

"Where is he, Archie?" came a man's voice.

Its whiskey-fueled rage about curdled Winnie's blood. Her father.

"Where's that Negro who attacked my baby girl? I'm gonna kill that bastard."

# CHAPTER 9

DESPITE THE DRAMA of their initial find, Madsen kept her students in check. TK watched as she reminded them of the need for confidentiality, including any social media, and the solemn responsibility they owed the victim and their family. "No matter how long he or she has been dead, it is our duty to help them reclaim their lives and achieve justice. Remember that."

The students nodded and continued their work, more subdued than before. As they explored the passenger compartment of the car, carefully lifting anything they could find onto sterile sheets to be sifted and sorted and documented, Madsen herself took over removal of the human remains. TK and Karlan watched, Karlan acting as videographer, while TK assisted the coroner.

"Here, see here?" Madsen lowered TK's hand to cradle three pieces of bone wrapped inside the waxy gray-beige decomposed tissue Madsen called adipocere.

TK was glad she was breathing through a mask although it felt as if the sickly-sweet smell might be absorbed into her own flesh. Two of the bone fragments had sharp edges, and she realized, once she oriented the anatomy, that she was looking at a broken forearm bone running alongside an intact one.

"He fractured his wrist trying to get free?" TK asked the anthropologist. "This is about where someone trapped by a pair of handcuffs would try to yank the door handle off if they were panicked." She demonstrated the motion with her free hand.

"No." Madsen shook her head sternly. "We can only observe and document. We can't draw conclusions—it's too easy to misinterpret. Tell me what you see, not what you think happened." Madsen rolled the two sharp edges of the broken bone so they fit together in her gloved palm.

"They're sharp, the cut or break is clean," TK tried again.

"Not cut. No kerf marks from a tool. Definite break. How close to death did it occur?"

"Very close. No signs of healing, right?" TK wished Tommy Worth were here. The former pediatric ER doctor would be much more in his element—she was barely treading water.

But Madsen nodded. "I'll know more back in the lab once I get it under the microscope. It's almost impossible to pinpoint completely without any of the surrounding soft tissues intact enough to examine, but I agree, it's a peri-mortem injury."

"So it could have happened right before he died or right after—maybe from the impact of the car?"

"Maybe. Maybe a lot of things. Like I said, all we can do is document our findings. What makes you think it's a he?"

TK turned her attention to the grisly skull that lay at a strange angle on the collapsed set of ribs, remnants of leather—a belt, maybe?—and vertebrae. With the flesh gone, the only tissue holding the bones together was the greasy adipocere. She'd heard it called corpse wax and now she knew why. It was weird how it clung to the facial bones, creating a wrinkled mask that looked like a kid's Halloween mask with its stringy dark hair and collapsed eye sockets. Less than human.

Except this was a human. Someone who all evidence pointed to having died a terrible death.

"Not sure. Just looks like a man—jaw's wide, forehead is kind of thick, the way his eyes are set."

Madsen nodded her approval. "I agree. Also the shape of the pelvis and a few other skeletal features. Again, once we have him back in the lab, cleaned up, I can give you more specifics. I can tell you that he was shot—years before he died." She gestured to the large thighbone where there was a dimple with a bit of dull metal at the bottom. "Notice the callous formation of bone over the old wound."

"But no medical hardware to tell us who he is."

"Wouldn't help if there was—they didn't start keeping registries of that information until fairly recently. Same with DNA databases. But his petrous bones appear intact as do several molars. I might be able to extract DNA to perform familial matching. If we find any family."

TK didn't know how to read bones, but the man's belt and the handcuffs intrigued her. As Madsen carefully lifted the body, piece by piece, into a waiting body bag, a tinny ping rang through the car.

Karlan aimed the camera's light to follow the noise. "What was that?" he asked. "Another coin?"

The students had been collecting as many coins as possible to help narrow their timeline. So far the most recent one they'd found was a dime dating back to 1953. That combined with the 1953 license plate that expired in June of 1954, meant that whatever happened had happened in 1953 or 1954.

Madsen hopped down from the flatbed and carried her now-contained body over to a waiting exam table for more photographs before she took it back to the lab. That gave TK room to get down, almost eye level with the floorboards.

"Not a coin," she said, reaching for the camera to document her find before she moved it. "A bullet. And there are two more down here." She held it up for him. "Unfired, casings intact."

"Handcuffs, bullets..." His voice trailed off as he glanced at her in dismay. "What's left of that belt, pretty heavy leather, don't you think? Designed to do more than just hold up a pair of pants."

"A duty belt. Except, I don't see a holster or signs of a weapon."

The leather seat was slimed with adipocere where the body had sat, and was partially decomposed around those areas, with tangles of springs and horsehair exposed. Karlan aimed the camera with its bright light over the seat as TK slowly, carefully probed each crevice. Her fingers stretched, feeling something shift, it had hard edges and felt metallic.

"Something's down here." She gently spread open the slit in the upholstery and finally fished out the object that had fallen between the springs.

A badge. The insignia was obscured by decomposed material, but when she ran her gloved finger over it, she could feel some of the etchings. They'd be able to clean it up and find out where it was from. Except…

"What's a cop doing handcuffed alone in a car at the bottom of the quarry?" Karlan asked the question foremost in her mind.

"And why the hell did no one ever report him missing?" she added.

"Maybe it was suicide and he used the handcuff so he wouldn't chicken out?" He backed out of the car and turned off the camera.

"Then wouldn't he be in the driver's side?" Her neck and back creaked from being twisted in such an unnatural position for so long; she gladly took his hand as he helped her down from the truck bed.

He stretched his left leg as if measuring the distance across to the wheel and the accelerator. "I guess he could have put the car in gear, then moved across the seat, secured himself, and reached over with his left leg to hit the gas pedal."

"You're that desperate to kill yourself, wouldn't you just put a bullet in your head?"

He frowned. "Maybe he was a prisoner? This definitely isn't a cop car. Maybe some kind of jail break, he was taken hostage and the actor bailed out at the last minute?"

"Without anyone knowing about it? No one ever reporting it? A cop going missing or being taken hostage would make the headlines." Knowing the car was built in 1949, they'd both already scoured what news archives there were from the time period. Not that there were a lot of digital records from back then, but Wash hadn't found any trace of a missing person associated with a car like the Dodge—and if he couldn't find it, with his Internet magic, it wasn't there to be found.

"We need to find out who owned this car," Karlan said.

"Exactly why you have me. My tech guy got nowhere with the plate number. Other than it was registered in DC in 1953. Unfortunately, there was no mandated national vehicle identification number system in place back then, but he's already amassing a database of all the original serial numbers and factory-issued VINs for 1949 Dodge Wayfarers. He says if we can get him the numbers from this vehicle, he can probably find the original dealer. Hopefully that will lead us in the right direction."

She turned to Madsen, who was measuring areas on the skull. "Professor, okay if we pop the hood and trunk here so we can try to get some identification numbers? It would save us time instead of waiting until we take it to the police garage."

"No problem. Go ahead." Her tone was absent—now that she had some bones to play with, it was as if the car that had been their casket for so long was no longer important.

Karlan grabbed a student to take over filming while he and TK worked to get the hood open. The latch mechanism was wedged shut from the dent in the hood, but the tow truck operator had tools to pry it free. While the men worked on the front part of the car, TK took the keys—still dangling from the ignition, appearing in almost pristine condition when she slid them free—and opened the trunk.

Several inches of water sloshed around the bottom of the cavernous area. But that wasn't what made TK freeze, one hand still on the trunk lid, the other going involuntarily to her throat.

"Dr. Madsen." Her voice was a mere croak. No one could hear her over the multiple conversations and the tow truck's engine. "Dr. Madsen! I think we have a problem here."

"What is it?" Madsen sounded annoyed, not turning away from her examination of the skull.

But Karlan recognized the tone of alert in TK's voice and joined her. She gestured to the contents of the trunk. He called to Madsen, "You're going to want to see this, doc."

Madsen left her worktable and came over. "What?"

"I'm counting three?" TK meant it as a question because she really hoped she was wrong about what she was seeing.

"Dear lord," Madsen breathed. Then she turned to the student with the camera. "Peter, get over here. We need to document this completely before we touch anything."

The student crowded onto the narrow platform with them, the camera light playing across the dark space, casting shadows across the collection of bones and their three skulls, their eye sockets all riveted on TK as if pleading for her help.

# CHAPTER 10

BENJI'S MOTHER KEPT her hand on the door, opening it only far enough to scrutinize Lucy and Valencia, her expression at once both hopeful and guarded. Her posture was strong, ready to ward off any threat to her remaining family. A family who now milled behind her, all silently watching.

There were two older men and a woman: the surviving grandparents. A man just a few years older than Jennifer Randall's forty-five but appearing much more worn and haggard: the father. It was a small miracle they'd stayed together through all these years. The odds were against them, Lucy knew from the research. Tragedies like theirs tended to splinter relationships. Beside him was the younger daughter, now in her twenties, standing close to a man, one arm cradling her obviously pregnant belly. All here to learn a little boy's fate.

"You found him," Jennifer Randall breathed the words, her lips barely moving.

Lucy kept her focus on the mother—she couldn't help but think how she'd feel if she was in her place. The thought brought with it the image of Nick and her daughter, Megan, when she'd left them this morning, happy, healthy, whole. As much as she ached for this mother, nothing could prevent a twinge of relief that her own family was safe—followed immediately by a dose of guilt for feeling that way and tempting fate.

"Yes, ma'am," Lucy answered. Jennifer swayed and Lucy continued, "Maybe we should all sit down?" She took Jennifer's arm and guided her inside as if it was Jennifer's idea. Valencia followed, closing the door on the too-bright July sun and the world outside.

Lucy reflexively made note of the room's obstacles—a sectional sofa and two recliners facing a large screen TV above a fireplace, a glass-topped coffee table in the space between—and the exits—a staircase, French doors off the dining room at the rear of the house, a kitchen beside it, no doubt with a door to the garage. Most of her attention was on the people, watching for their reactions, observing their posture, where their feet were pointed, what their hands were doing. Always the hands.

Unlike Lucy, Valencia didn't hesitate, sweeping into the room like a maternal force of nature, settling the sister in one of the recliners, Jennifer in the other, letting the others fend for themselves as she made the rounds introducing herself and Lucy, shaking hands and collecting names, making eye contact with each of them. While Lucy's training kept her at arm's length—a defensive posture, ready for anything—Valencia breached everyone's defenses, getting up close and personal.

It was the better way, Lucy saw as she watched from where she stood beside Jennifer's chair. At least for this particular task. Valencia's calming etiquette allowed a transition for Benji's family from frightening unknown to familiar social reflexes.

Lucy tried to see how Valencia worked her magic, but it was lost on her. She made a mental note to ask Nick. He was a psychologist who specialized in trauma; maybe he could break it down into a skill she could learn.

Then, suddenly, everyone's attention was on Lucy. Valencia moved to the far wall, near the kitchen, allowing her to take the lead. Lucy didn't want to force Jennifer to look up at her, so she sat down on the coffee table, facing the mother, even though it went against every reflex, putting her back to the others. Benji's father moved to stand beside his wife, their hands interlinked.

"I'm sorry," Lucy began. "We found Benji's body. He's dead. Has been for a long, long time."

She paused, feeling as if her words were blunt weapons bludgeoning the mother. Jennifer's eyes glistened with tears that she blinked back, but she nodded.

"Are you sure?" one of the grandfathers asked from behind Lucy. "We've been here before you know."

One of Smitty's regrets—almost a decade ago when the case was still relatively fresh, they'd found a boy's body up in the state game lands. He'd been certain when preliminary dental comparisons were a match that it was Benji, had come to tell the family, prepare them for the final identification. Only to discover a few weeks later when the DNA came in that it wasn't Benji but another family's lost son.

"We're sure. The forensic pathologist confirmed both his DNA and dental records." Usually it would be the local coroner who examined the body along with the detective working the case who made the next of kin notification, but this case was anything but usual, having out-lived the lead investigator.

"When can he come home?" Jennifer asked. Her husband leaned forward, his face creased with concern, whispering something in her ear. She jerked away. "I understand that. I know he's dead. I've known it for a long, long time. Here." She pounded her free fist against her breastbone. "But I still want him home. He deserves that at least. And so do we."

"Yes, you do," Lucy answered. "The pathologist is finishing up their examination. If you let us know the name of the funeral home you prefer, we can arrange for him to be transported back." She glanced at Valencia, who'd spoken with the morgue administrator about the logistics. "They said they'd release him tomorrow, right?"

"Yes."

"We don't have to see him?" the father asked, his voice trembling. "To make any identification?"

"No, sir. It's all taken care of."

He blew his breath out. "McKinley Brothers. That's who we want to take care of him."

"I can call them, if you like. Start the arrangements," Valencia offered.

The father shook his head, seemed relieved to have something to do. "No. I know Ted McKinley. Went to school with him. I'll call." He separated himself from his wife and headed toward the kitchen.

"Tell me everything," Jennifer Randall said.

Her husband missed a step, stumbling and catching himself against the fireplace before fleeing out of sight. Valencia left her position to go after him, leaving Lucy to answer Jennifer's questions.

Questions there were no adequate answers to. Questions no mother should ever have to ask about her child.

Lucy leaned forward toward Benji's mother. "Ask me anything. I'll tell you what I know."

There was much of the story she didn't know for certain, only had theories. Those she wouldn't share. Only what she was absolutely certain of.

"Where he was he? Not near here, not for all these years?" Jennifer's voice was tainted with anguish at the thought that her son had been near and somehow she hadn't found him in time. Lucy was grateful it was a question she could answer and provide some slight comfort to the woman.

"No. The man who took him, his name was Darren Wilson, he took him into the mountains near Cumberland, Maryland."

"He took him, who?" She looked around at her family. "I've never heard of any Darren Wilson." They all shook their heads. "Why did he do this? Why my son?"

This Lucy was less certain of, although Wilson's suicide note and other evidence they'd found at his cabin filled in some of the blanks. Nothing specific to Benji's case, but it was clear Wilson had had a type. "Benji wasn't the only boy he tried to take. Wilson attempted to abduct two others, both of whom looked just like Benji and his own son."

A look of horror filled Jennifer's face. Beside her, the pregnant woman, Benji's sister, made a gagging noise. Her husband helped her to her feet and led her out to the kitchen, her sobs trailing in the air behind her.

"Did he kill them, too?" This came from one of the grandfathers behind her.

Lucy turned to meet his gaze. He was in his late sixties, maybe even early seventies, but his expression was one of lethal intensity. "We found two other bodies near Benji's. One a boy about his age, Wilson's son. The other a woman, his mother. We've identified her as Wilson's wife. According to the tests, they both had been dead years longer than Benji."

"Did he suffer?" Jennifer asked the question Lucy had

been dreading. "Did my boy suffer?"

Jennifer grasped both of Lucy's hands in hers as if fearing Lucy would try to escape. She hauled in a breath and answered. "Yes. I'm afraid he did."

"How long? How long was he still alive, how long was he hurting? What did that monster do to him?" Her voice trembled and dipped low as if she didn't want anyone else to hear either the questions or the answers. Her grip on Lucy's hands tightened, her knuckles pale, unyielding pebbles.

"I'm afraid we don't have all the answers. It's been too long, and Wilson didn't leave anything to help us." Unlike many pedophiles, Wilson hadn't been interested in recording his activities to relive and re-experience. "I can tell you that Darren Wilson is dead. Killed himself."

"All this time, and the only way you found him was because he killed himself?" The grandmother's voice was chiseled with hatred.

"He killed himself because we'd found him. We found him through the work Detective Smith did before he died and the work of the National Center of Missing and Exploited Children, as well as the Beacon Group."

Lucy didn't bother to mention her own work on the case

even before she'd joined the Beacon Group. It was her painstakingly built geographic profile, teasing information from every report of a child abduction or assault that remotely fit the signature of Benji's abduction, following up on every lead, no matter how unlikely, that had finally led them to Wilson. He'd chosen to take the easy way out with his shotgun rather than facing justice.

"Why did it take so long?" the grandmother asked. "Was it because we're black? I see you all finding lost white girls all the time—sometimes even still alive, even after years."

"Was this Darren fellow black?" one of the grandfathers, the one who'd been silent until now, broke in.

"No. He was white. His wife was African-American."

"But he was white. Of course he was. Maybe that's why it took you so long to find him." He made a disgusted noise behind her and stomped off.

Lucy felt their anger heating up behind her, but she kept her focus on the mother. She didn't take it personally—it was an unbearable situation, leaving them powerless. Of course they were angry, lashing out at anyone they could.

Jennifer closed her eyes, her grip slipping away from Lucy's hands, her chin sinking low onto her chest, her new reality too heavy to bear.

"I'll stay as long as you like, answer any questions I can," Lucy told her. Jennifer nodded, her eyes still shut. "Once they've finished processing all the evidence, getting a better picture of things, the state police and pathologist will also be happy to help. Whatever you need."

The mother's eyes snapped open, and Lucy wished she hadn't added that last. Because no one on the face of the earth could give Jennifer Randall what she truly needed.

"What I need is my son. Home safe and sound," she said. "Living the life he was meant to live. What I'll settle for is finally seeing him buried, back home where he belongs. With us."

# CHAPTER 11

TK DEBATED CALLING Lucy for help but decided not to. Just because her single cold case had now turned into four extremely cold probable-homicides, there was no reason she couldn't handle things.

Instead, she asked Wash, their tech analyst back in their offices at Beacon Falls, to make sure Tommy, their medical expert, freed up time tomorrow to go over all the medical findings with Madsen. By then, she hoped the forensic anthropologist would be able to give them a better idea of what they were dealing with. If she knew how their four victims had died, not to mention basic info like sex, estimated age, and ethnicity, it would help her find out who they were.

"Three people dead in a trunk and another handcuffed up

front?" Wash asked breathlessly.

TK secretly suspected Wash of using their cases as fodder for retro-noir pulp graphic novels or maybe as the storyline of a video game. He got so excited and caught up in each one, despite the fact that he had the most boring job imaginable: cranking info through the computer. He never went into the field. Although she'd heard Valencia and Lucy both offer to accommodate his wheelchair, he always declined. TK wasn't sure she'd ever understand him; she'd die if she were trapped behind a computer day in and out, but she couldn't do her job without him.

"Is this another serial killer, you think?"

"I don't think anything yet," she said, mimicking Lucy's prim and proper tone. After fifteen years with the FBI, Lucy was a stickler for procedure—at least in her underlings. TK noticed that Lucy somehow seemed to ignore all the rules whenever she liked.

"I'm running with everything I have. Detective Karlan sent me all the identification numbers he could find on the car, and I've been going through all the uploaded photos and videos, looking for anything to ID our victims."

"There was a badge in the front seat."

"Like a police badge?"

"Maybe. Who knows, could be a food inspector found too many rats. Or it could be fake. As soon as we get it cleaned up, I'll send you pictures."

"Yeah, but, if it was someone official and they went missing, then there has to be a trail I can find. That kind of story is going to make it to newspapers, police bulletins, church newsletters, police fundraisers for family left behind... It's the kind of thing an entire community would get involved with. Even after so many years, there's bound to be some kind of digital footprint left behind." His keys chattered happily, excited by a new direction to pursue. "I'll call if I find anything." He hung up.

Wash was on the case. Which meant there was nothing more for her to do until Madsen was done and TK could start to examine what little evidence the car had given them. Corroded bits and pieces of the lives that had been lost. That was all she had to forge a trail into the past and discover what had happened sixty-three years ago.

She pulled her phone free. No, she was not going to admit defeat and call Lucy just because her case had grown tangled and complicated. But there was someone else used to putting together timeworn puzzles who might help. She dialed David Ruiz.

"Hey, Ms. Lead Investigator," he answered. His voice was a tinny monotone, the cell phone stripping it of what little affect it strived for. From the way the sound echoed, she thought he was probably in his car, heading out to a new story for the national crime blog he worked for now that his career as a TV investigative reporter had ended. "Tell me about this big case that cut our weekend short."

"I left early to give you time to recuperate. Figured you'd need it after Friday and Saturday night."

"Not to mention Sunday morning." A traumatic brain injury while embedded with troops in Afghanistan had left David without the ability to express or understand verbal emotions, but despite the fact that his voice never changed inflection, she knew he was grinning.

"Actually, it worked out okay," he continued. "I'm on my way to Pennsylvania to cover another officer-involved shooting protest. This time the Klan, neo-Nazis, and Tea-Partyers are organizing a counter-protest to the Black Lives Matter folks. Poor little town, middle of nowhere. It's never gonna know what hit it."

She frowned. "You're coming to Greer?"

"Yeah. How'd you know? The story just hit our radar after the FBI announced it was performing its own independent investigation no matter what the local grand jury's verdict is. And my sources say there might be public corruption involved. Maybe the DA, maybe the cops, I'm not sure." His words practically boomeranged against each other in his excitement.

"Greer is where my case is. But," she warned him, "you can't report on it or tell anyone I'm here." Damn, she really wanted to ask him for advice, but how could she do that without breaking confidentiality?

"Tiffany, don't be a tease." David was the only person other than Valencia Frazier, owner of the Beacon Group, who ever called her by her given name. And he only got away with it when it was over the phone and she wasn't close enough to punch him in the arm. "What's the story—I mean case? You said it was really old, a body that was unidentified. Who'd you find?"

"I never should have said anything. Sorry."

"Is it a criminal case?" he persisted. "Not just some old family bones folks forgot where they were buried? Was it murder? If so, I could help—write a story, get the word out, maybe help you get an ID. Who knows, maybe there's

something to this corruption charge and our stories are linked."
David didn't believe in coincidences—neither did she, usually.
But how the hell could a car filled with bodies from the 1950s be
linked to a grand jury hearing now?

"I doubt that. My case is from sixty-some years ago.
Besides, we're not that far along yet. I've only been here a few
hours."

"More than enough time. I've seen what you can do in a
few hours. Didn't take you much longer than that to find the
evidence we needed to free my father from prison."

She had to smile at his faith in her crime-solving abilities.
"Not this time. In fact, that's why I called. Off the record," she
stressed, "how would you go about identifying someone from
sixty-three years ago?"

"Sixty-three years? Like," he paused to calculate, "1954?"

"We think. Maybe late 1953. I don't have anything paper,
so no ID or business cards. What I do have is a car. Registered in
Washington DC in 1953. Wash is running a search on the serial
numbers and license plate, looking for an owner."

"DC? And the car was found in Greer? It's pretty much
the middle of nowhere now, couldn't have been a popular
destination back then. Maybe they got lost?"

Wouldn't explain the handcuffs or three bodies in the trunk, but she couldn't tell him that—it would be like offering a tiger catnip. She'd seen David on the prowl for a story; he could follow the slightest scent to uncover all sorts of treasure caches of buried truths. If it wasn't for the need to keep the investigation quiet, his help could be invaluable. Maybe if she hit a dead end, she could convince the mayor that a little publicity, done with discretion by the right reporter, could be helpful.

"You're not going to find any computer DMV records from that long ago," he continued. "But maybe Wash can work with classic car collectors? They have all sorts of online communities that might help him trace the car's origins. Narrow your geographic search?"

"He's already on it. What we have so far doesn't match any missing persons cases in our database, any ideas on where to find paper records?" That had been one of Valencia's greatest accomplishments at Beacon Falls: consolidating the myriad of government and NGO data collections into an easily searchable information clearinghouse.

"Sure. Old newspaper archives. Look for stories of missing persons and don't forget to check the personal ads— loved ones would often place ads hoping to get information.

What else…if they were local I'd suggest old police blotter files. Some departments keep them for historical value. You might get lucky with DC; if the person was ever reported missing there, they might still have records archived, but with a tiny town like Greer, I doubt it. Especially if the missing person was from out of town; none of the locals might even have known them at all."

"Which means if they were reported missing in DC, that fact might have never made it to Pennsylvania, much less a tiny police department like Greer. So, if they weren't local, just passing through, no one local would have known to look." TK thought about that. Still didn't explain their police officer victim—no way would a DC cop drive to a place like Greer in his private vehicle while still in uniform.

"Was it a homicide? Maybe Greer was just a convenient, quiet dumping ground."

TK thought about that. Maybe the police officer—or whatever kind of law enforcement officer he ended up being— was local, maybe the car belonged to one of the victims in the trunk, and the cop was just in the wrong place, wrong time, saw something he shouldn't have? But then why wasn't he reported missing?

"That's your Venn diagram," he said. "Greer crossed with

DC. Find who fits that intersection and you can narrow your search."

"Thanks, David."

She started to hang up, but he said, "Hey, if we're both in the same town, what about getting together later? I promise I won't ask about your top secret case—at least not on the record."

"Call me." She hung up, slid her phone into her pocket and began the laborious process of struggling back into her sweat-soaked protective clothing. She glanced toward the tent where she'd left the badge with one of Madsen's students. Madsen had warned her it was a slow process, removing the decayed debris without destroying the brittle metal underlying it, but surely they had to have something she could use to track down her handcuffed front seat passenger.

Her cop turned prisoner. He was the key, she was certain.

# CHAPTER 12

"I CHANGED MY MIND," Karlan told TK as she returned to the heat and humidity trapped beneath the canopy. "I'm going back to my original theory of suicide. Three bodies in the trunk makes the sonofabitch a serial killer. I think he was only impersonating a cop, using a fake badge to lure his victims, but after he killed them, he felt enough remorse to kill himself."

"Maybe they were all victims; our actor just ran out of room in the trunk."

"Then why the handcuffs?"

"Maybe they weren't dead before the car went into the quarry," TK suggested. Hard to tell in the glare of the work lights and with his dark skin, but she swore his lips went pale at the suggestion.

"Can you imagine? Watching, seeing the water rush up at you, not able to do a damn thing about it? Or worse, being trapped in a trunk, no light, no one to hear your screams..." He shook his head, a muffled curse escaping. "I want to get this SOB. I don't care if he's been dead fifty years, I still want to nail his ass, let people know what he did."

"What who did?" a voice came from behind them. TK turned, surprised to see Grayson Greer standing there, his white shirt still buttoned up to the top button, not a trace of sweat blemishing its pristine cloth. Unlike her own most decidedly wrinkled and sweaty appearance. "What did you find?"

"What are you doing here, Grayson?" Karlan said. TK detected a hint of disdain in his tone for the mayor's son. "This is a crime scene."

He used the bulk of his body to back the younger man up beyond the canopy. TK followed them outside, grateful for the chance to unzip her Tyvek suit and shuck the constraining hood.

Grayson didn't seem to take offense at Karlan's tone. "Dad sent me to get you. Didn't want to say anything over the radio or phone, but the grand jury is coming back with their verdict on Jefferson. He's thinking of announcing it this afternoon. He wants every available officer there."

"I can't leave. This is an active investigation."

"It's a sixty-year-old cold case. Dad said your boss said you and the patrol officer need to get back now. The officer driving the tow truck can maintain the chain of custody for the car, and Dr. Madsen will take care of the rest of the evidence. Dad said it's just a matter of paperwork anyway."

"Paperwork that can get a case thrown out before you even go to court," TK protested.

"Dad doubts a case this old will ever make it to court."

TK wondered if Grayson had a thought in his head that wasn't put there by his father. Seemed like the mayor didn't trust her to do her job without someone holding her leash. The thought rankled, but she kept her expression bland. Leashes could pull in both directions—and they were apt to tangle and trip the ones who thought they were in control.

"Anyway," Grayson continued in an officious tone, "I'm here now to escort Miss O'Connor."

Karlan frowned. "Go," TK told him. "I'll let you know when we find anything."

"I'll catch you up later." With a curt nod to Grayson, he stripped free of his Tyvek and trudged back to his squad car.

"So, what did you find?" Grayson asked eagerly. "The

Lindbergh baby? Jimmy Hoffa?"

"Worse. A possible serial killer." Let him run to daddy with that little tidbit of a shocker. Only thing worse for a town's image than a collection of unidentified bodies was a serial killer stalking the town, getting away with murder.

"A serial killer? Here? No way." He shook his head in disbelief. "Nothing that exciting ever happens in Greer. What makes you think we had a serial killer?"

"We found four bodies in that car."

"Really? Can I see?"

"Can't risk contaminating the evidence." She looked past him as Madsen emerged from the canopy, sipping at a bottle of water. "How's it going?"

"Definitely four sets of remains. We've gathered all of the major bones—in cases like this, there are often smaller bones missing. Sometimes dissolved by the elements, or just lost in the debris. But I think we've gotten all we can."

TK nodded—she'd seen how painstakingly careful Madsen's students had been as they sieved the water and combed through the car. "You okay to release the car, then?"

"Yes. I'll transport the human remains and the other evidence back to my lab. Should have some preliminary results later today or tonight—at the very least, sex, size, ethnicity, maybe even approximate age."

"It'll be a start." TK's job had just gotten that much more difficult, now with four victims to identify rather than one. But having four times the data might help as well. "What about the badge I found?"

"We cleaned it as best we could. Looks like it's from Greer." Madsen handed TK a clear plastic evidence bag. Grayson peered over TK's shoulder, staring at the decades-old badge.

"No name or number on it," TK said. Of course not. That'd be too much to ask for. But, knowing the police officer was local at least gave her a starting place.

"That's not how our badges look," Grayson protested. "Maybe it's a fake."

"It's from the 1950s," Madsen told him, annoyance in her voice. TK had a feeling that the coroner had been forced to tolerate Grayson's babysitting before and liked it even less than she did. "Good chance the city has changed its design at least once since then."

TK handed the evidence bag back to Madsen then peeled the rest of her Tyvek overalls off, rolling the sticky, sweaty mess into a ball. "Let me grab my gear, and I'll head out with the tow truck."

"I can drive you," Grayson volunteered. "Sounds like you'll need another pair of hands anyway. My summer internship is with my dad's office, and he assigned me to liaison between his office and the police. Another reason why my dad sent me to help out."

That and to make sure TK kept quiet about the case, she thought. She wasn't sure how much longer it would be before someone leaked info, despite the mayor's wishes. A vehicle with an occupant who'd driven into the quarry sixty years ago was one thing…four victims of what had to be foul play was entirely another.

In the meantime, she was stuck with Grayson. It was damned irritating that he always seemed to be rescuing her—in his mind, at least. She hadn't asked for his help, yet they were now somehow partners in all this.

"Let's go," TK said to Grayson.

Madsen finished her water. "We're heading back to the lab. Hopefully more will come to light once we've finished drying the organic material." The stuff that used to be cloth, paper, and cardboard, TK translated. "Our best bet will be the bones, but tell the mayor, it will take time."

One of the students called to Madsen from where they were packing up the van. She nodded to TK, then left.

The tow truck drove out, stopping in front of TK and Grayson. The car had been secured beneath a tarp, protecting it from the elements as much as possible during the trip to the police garage.

"You riding with me?" the driver asked. The coroner's ambulance pulled up behind him, leaving only the students in charge of removing the canopy and TK and Grayson left to leave.

"No, I'm taking her," Grayson answered for TK. "We'll meet you there."

The truck and ambulance drove off, a cloud of dust billowing behind them. TK gathered her belongings and Grayson led her to his car, an anonymous silver Ford Taurus. Inside, the center console was crowded with a police scanner and radio. Grayson took his duties as an intern seriously.

"Why aren't you helping out at the protests?" she asked as they drove down the narrow road leading back to the highway. "Karlan said there'd be trouble either way the grand jury ruled."

"My dad thought it might look bad if I helped with crowd control. At least with that particular crowd. Not politically expedient is how he put it."

"What do you mean 'that crowd'?"

In answer, he unbuttoned the collar of his shirt and pulled it back. At the base of his neck was a tattooed eagle, its wings spread wide, stretching up onto his collarbones. Clutched in its talons was a globe. Covering the globe was a blood red swastika.

# CHAPTER 13

SAMUEL FOCUSED ON the boy with the same intensity he'd give any patient in his brightly lit hospital operating theatre. Breathing stabilized, airway clear, pulse fast but steady. As long as his makeshift chest tube didn't clog and none of those broken ribs moved to lacerate the lung, the kid had a chance.

As he took all this in, he finally realized that the shouting beyond the break room had grown louder. He glanced up, startled for a moment to find Jo there, staring at him, waiting for him to tell her what he needed. Then he looked past her and saw Maybelle standing in the doorway, clutching the white girl's hand.

This wasn't his hospital. This war zone might be more

dangerous than any he'd seen in Italy, North Africa, or Korea. Fear clenched his bowels—fear he'd never dreamed he'd feel here, back on home soil. "Jo, take Maybelle and bring the car to the back door."

Jo snapped his bag shut, nodded—the tight-lipped chin jerk that meant no more than yes—and turned. The boy, Henry, the policeman had called him, grabbed at Samuel's shirt.

"He'll kill her. Leave me. You gotta get Winnie outta here." Each word drew a grimace of pain but the boy never let go.

"Don't worry, son. No one's getting killed. Not here, not today."

Even as Samuel said the words in his most reassuring tone, Jo turned to frown at him. She had Maybelle by the hand, the white girl shuffling away to give them room to leave.

He raised an eyebrow at her and she reluctantly nodded to the white girl, a tacit invitation to join them. The girl's eyes widened in surprise but she quickly recovered, taking Maybelle's other hand.

Once they were gone, Samuel bent over to help Henry sit up. The boy's eyes welled with tears, but he only made a soft groan, even as he trembled with pain.

"Our car's out back. Think you can walk that far if I help?"

Henry nodded. He braced both hands against the edge of the table. Samuel held him under his armpits, gingerly placing him on his feet. Before he could take even a half step, he cried out in pain and collapsed back against the table.

"Let me pass," an angry man's voice thundered from the front of the building. "Goddamn it, she's my daughter! I've got rights!"

"Come on, now," Samuel urged. The boy was too big for him to carry alone, not without risking the chest tube—move it the wrong way, and it could puncture the lung or worse, the heart. "We don't have much time."

To his credit, the boy—Samuel adjusted his estimate of his age down, the kid was maybe only twelve or thirteen at most—tried, lurching forward, most of his weight on Samuel. But even that was too much. He had to stop to catch his breath before trying another step. At this rate, they'd make it to the car by Christmas.

"Leave me," Henry gasped. "Take Winnie and your family. I'll be fine."

"Stop wasting breath on talking," Samuel snapped.

The sudden sound of a shotgun being chambered stopped

them both.

Henry looked at Samuel, fear widening his eyes until every red capillary shone bright. Samuel leaned Henry's good side against the wall. The boy promptly slumped down to the floor, groaning with pain.

Samuel crept out into the hallway. Before he got far enough to see the front room, the sounds of scuffling, fists pounding, and a man swearing came.

He took another step. A woman screamed—not Jo, maybe that white woman? Glass broke. Something thudded to the ground. Then a door slammed shut, followed by the clang of a heavy lock being bolted. Samuel froze, preparing himself for battle.

# CHAPTER 14

"LOOKS LIKE THIRSTY WORK." Grayson reached behind TK to pull a bottle of water from the rear seat. As she drank, he drove them down the rutted two-lane road leading away from the quarry, staying far enough back that the dust from the ambulance had time to settle.

"You're a Nazi?" No wonder Karlan had been so anxious to separate Grayson from Franklin and his crew this morning.

"I'm a patriot." He glanced at her, his smile never diminishing. "I stand for the Constitution and the freedom of the American people. Just like my father did when he served. Just like you do, Marine."

"Nothing like what I did as a Marine," she snapped.

He shrugged. "The way Franklin and his thugs threatened

you this morning, you don't think that had anything to do with the color of your skin?"

"I think it had to do with the fact that I'm a woman. And they weren't threatening anyone, they're just kids being kids."

"Boys too ignorant to know any better. How to treat a woman right. Act with civility."

"That's not what I said."

"It's what you meant." They came to a red light. He held his hands up in surrender. "I know, you think I'm awful, but I'm not. I'm just honest. Most people are hypocrites, denying how they feel about people of color. They're the real racists, the dangerous ones. Me, I let everyone know the truth about how I feel. Besides, I'm not a racist. I don't hate the blacks. Our problems aren't going to be solved by hate. In fact, I want the very same thing the Black Lives Matter organizers want."

"How so?"

"Like I said, I'm not a racist. I'm a separatist. Which is exactly what they want as well. They want their communities to be policed by their own people and not white outsiders. I agree. In fact, I say let them have it all."

"I don't understand."

He made the turn. They had been driving past the college,

but with that turn, they were back in the neighborhood Karlan had driven her through this morning. The one where resignation filled the air thicker and more stifling than the July humidity.

"Look around. What I'm talking about is what is already happening in every city on the planet. You were a Marine. You've traveled. Have you ever lived anywhere where people didn't self-segregate? Think about it. It's not socio-economic status that determines neighborhood boundaries—in fact, many well-to-do blacks choose to live in lower socio-economic communities to be with their own kind." He shrugged. "Guess they like being a big fish in a small pond. Or they feel more comfortable there. With other people who identify more as Africans than Americans."

"Yeah, you're definitely not racist," she scoffed. She hated to admit it, but he sounded exactly like her father and grandfather back in West Virginia.

"Realist," he corrected. "When you ask *African*-Americans what they want, they say the same thing: police who understand them more than white police can, schools where their children fit in, self-government, a say in decisions about their communities."

He swept one hand out wide, gesturing to the stoop-sitters who followed them with their glares. Even the kids playing in the streets edged away, recognizing Grayson's vehicle as off-limits. "I say, give it to them. They're already isolating themselves, why not draw the boundaries, make it official? Let them run the show, divide their resources like any other city."

"Your people already tried that with the Jews. This is America; you can't round people up in train cars and herd them behind barbed wire."

"No barbed wire. No rounding up. If you build it, they will come. Believe me, everyone will be happier."

She shook her head at his delusion. How had this country come to this? Where a self-proclaimed Nazi acted as if he was the voice of reason? "You're crazy."

"Really? I just graduated from Princeton with my degree in public policy. That was my honors thesis. The university is going to publish it in the fall."

It was difficult to resist slapping the smug smirk from his face. His gaze swept across the street and the people they drove past as if he owned the whole damn world. A world gone mad if they listened to people like Grayson.

"So," she challenged him, "after you put the blacks in their place, in their ghettos—"

"Communities," he corrected. "Asians and Hispanics as well."

"Whatever. Then you have a problem. Because now just about everyone's who's left is white. So who do you target next? Homosexuals? Jews? The Irish or Italian or the handicapped or...who? Where does this self-segregation end? And who decides where the lines get drawn?"

"It's Darwin at his finest. Well, Social Darwinism. The beauty of it is that no one has to decide anything. People sort themselves out. Always have, always will. It's basic psychology: joining a tribe that shares your values and protects each other."

"Fine. So no laws, you just give each of these communities the right to self-govern? Like the Amish do here in Pennsylvania."

"Good example, the Amish. Although if you want to meet real racists, talk to a few of them some time."

"My point is, we are a democracy."

"None of that would change. Unless politicians decide to redraw voting districts, which they no doubt will. But if they didn't, if they let things be, it would make for more challenging political races and force politicians to answer to a more diverse electorate, maybe even keep them honest and intent on actual governing for the people rather than grandstanding for themselves and their party. How is that a bad thing?"

She wished David were here. He could find the right questions to ask, arguments to make that would shoot down Grayson's crazy ideas.

Crazy because they represented everything she despised— the idea that judging a person based on their appearance was okay.

She wasn't stupid; she knew it happened all the time, every day...she was as guilty of it as anyone. She thought of her encounters with Iraqi and Afghan civilians while she was deployed. Decisions made in the heat of fear and battle fury, some of which she regretted. These were the moments she couldn't let go of, especially deep in the night when sleep was a distant memory.

Somehow Grayson made those snap judgments sound so damned reasonable. Was that because she really was racist? Maybe his words felt tempting because part of her agreed with him, Eve tasting the apple and finding it so very sweet and irresistible. That's how her granddad would have put it.

He would have had no problem with any of Grayson's

ideas. It pained her to admit it, but neither would her father. Could Grayson somehow know the truth of who she really was, a truth she was too afraid to admit? Not even to herself?

No. She wasn't racist. She was an objective observer. Collecting facts, analyzing them. Whatever the situation. Like this morning with Franklin and his friends. Or working alongside a neo-Nazi.

Actions, not words. That was where the truth lay.

"Anyway," Grayson continued. "Tell me about the police officer killed. Whose body you found."

"Why?"

"Because if he was really a Greer police officer, then I might know how to find out who he was."

# CHAPTER 15

*MAY 17, 1954*

JO STEPPED OUT onto the steps leading down from the back exit of the jailhouse. Her shoe skimmed against a splatter of the boy's blood, still wet on the concrete. What was Samuel thinking, dragging them into this? It was no business of theirs who that boy was or why he'd ended up in trouble. From the looks of the white girl, it had to do with her. Figured. Boys always chasing after the ones they couldn't have, even when they should know better.

"Wait here," she told Maybelle and the girl. "I'll be right back."

Maybelle nodded, clutching the white girl's hand. Another problem they were suddenly saddled with, thanks to

Samuel's Good Samaritan complex.

Jo started down the concrete steps, avoiding touching the soot-stained brick baluster. Dirty town. She glanced at the Woolworth's across the street. Its Colored entrance stood alongside the trash bins. Faster they were out of here the better.

Her heels clacked against the broken pavement as she skirted the police car parked haphazardly at the bottom of the steps. Surgery in a jailhouse. On the table the white folks ate off. The last made her smile, but it was quickly dimmed by the hollow echo of her footsteps against the alley walls. Place was too quiet. And yet, she couldn't shake the feeling that someone was watching her.

She glanced back at Maybelle, but her head was invisible below the brick balustrade, all Jo could see was the white girl, her face twisted with fear. What did white girls know about fear anyway? She nodded to the girl and turned back to continue to their car at the mouth of the alley. She couldn't keep Samuel waiting.

That man. He'd be the death of her for sure. When was he going to learn that he had nothing left to prove to anyone? But she knew why he'd done it, helped that white girl with her pathetic sobs and dirty clothes, helped that boy they didn't even know. It wasn't pride. It was something far more dangerous: hope.

Despite everything he'd seen in the wars, Samuel still dared to hope that this world and the people in it were good. He'd done what he'd done not for Jo, but for Maybelle. To show her what a good man was, how a good person lived his life.

Jo believed in a better future but she knew it would come at a cost. A cost their daughter would pay. She knew better than to fill Maybelle's head with fantasies about what her life could be. Not Samuel. He was a dreamer.

Her own fault. That was what had attracted her to the handsome but too-quiet, too-serious medical student he'd been when they met. Not his talent or intellect. His ability to still dream, despite everything.

She'd just never imagined it might end with them stranded in a dirty little town with dirty white men screaming and threatening to kill them.

Her steps quickened down the alley. The bright blue car filled her vision. The car. An impossible dream on its own.

Maybelle hadn't even been crawling yet when the Army drafted Samuel back into service with plans to send him halfway around the world. They'd bought their house because it was close to his hospital; she was meant to quit teaching, at least for a while, stay home and watch over Maybelle. But then the Army sent that letter and all their plans went to ash. If they wanted to keep their home, she'd have to go back to work teaching. Which meant getting up before the crack of dawn and taking three buses across the city.

She'd argued for leaving their home, renting it, taking Maybelle with her back to Cleveland where she could live with her family. Samuel had seen that as a defeat.

The day before he left for the Army, he'd come home with the car. A gift from a rich patient he'd saved when the man's gall bladder ruptured. It was against the rules to take gifts—definitely against Samuel's pride, as well. But he'd sacrificed his pride, working out a deal to pay off the car once he returned from the war. A promise that he would return, safe and sound.

He might be the death of her, with his silly dreams of a world where color made no difference and their little girl could grow up to be President, but he was the best man she'd ever met. Not even war could take that away from him.

A stray piece of pavement almost tripped her as she rummaged in her bag for her car keys. She grabbed them and looked up, only a few feet away from the car and their escape out of this hellhole of a town.

That's when she saw the man. A white man. Leaning against her car as if he owned it. As if he owned the world.

Jo stopped, her stomach clenching tight. Where had he come from? He wore a business suit. And a smile that chilled with its row of icicle teeth gleaming in the afternoon sun.

She glanced over her shoulder. The girls were out of sight, probably hiding below the bricks that lined the police station's steps. She prayed that that white girl had the good sense to keep quiet, to keep Maybelle safe.

"Excuse me," she said. It never boded well, speaking first to a white man, but he hadn't said anything, and she needed to keep his focus on her, away from the girls. "That's my car."

His gaze slid over her like a drunk's greasy palms. "Is it, now?"

From the corner of her eye, she saw two more men, also in suits, but not ones as nice as their leader's, approach her from the far side of the alley. She wanted to run, was desperate to scream, but she knew that would only whet their appetite for blood.

Instead, she stood tall, dared to meet his gaze. She was no

kitchen Negro; she knew her rights. Most importantly, she had a family to protect. Best way to do that was to deal with whatever this white man wanted or at the very least draw him and his friends away from the police station, give Samuel time. "Yes, sir. That's my car. Now, if you could please move away? I'm afraid I'm running late."

"And I'm afraid, this is now my car. You see, it's been abandoned. Illegally. I'm mayor of this town. We'll be impounding this vehicle. Immediately."

The two men sidled up to stand on either side of her. Not touching her, but their intent was clear.

Jo swallowed hard. Men like Samuel got to play hero for their daughters. But it was the women who couldn't afford heroics. Not with men like this. Men like this, they wouldn't give up, not until their pride was assuaged, paid for with Jo's dignity. She lowered her gaze, fear trumping her rage.

"I'm sorry," she said, despite the fact that she had nothing to apologize for. "If there's a fine, I'll pay it."

"Oh, you'll pay all right." He jerked his head and another man appeared, along with a young boy. "Was she with him, Philip? The Negro who laid hands on you?"

The boy shuffled forward, eyed Jo with an expression of

disdain. His eyes were lit with primal cunning instinct, and she knew he was debating which answer would help his own cause the most, no matter the cost to her.

"I think so." He straightened, nodded. "Yeah. She was with him."

"I've never seen you before, young man," Jo protested.

"You calling my son a liar?" The man's hand swept through the air so fast Jo didn't see the blow coming until it was too late. His slap sent her sprawling to the ground. Before she could crawl back to her feet, the other men grabbed her arms and hauled her up.

"Go home, Philip," the man told the boy. "You've done enough. Go home."

The boy started to protest but then sped off, running down the alley without looking back.

The man regarded Jo, his gaze empty of anything except cold calculation. "Anderson, get the men. Tell them we've caught a couple of Commies trying to indoctrinate our Negroes. They attacked a white girl and now the whole lot of them are going to pay. Tell them to bring their bats and pistols. You know the drill. Make sure they're wanting blood."

"What do we do with her?" one of the men holding Jo

asked.

"Do what you want, but keep her close. We'll feed her to the crowd, once they're riled up and ready to go." The man nodded as if he'd just completed a particularly satisfying business transaction. "Won't be any more union talk around these parts. Not after tonight."

The two men began to drag Jo away. "You can't do this," she protested. "Stop. I've got rights!"

Her only answer was a blow to the face. She felt her nose crack, the pain so sharp that tears gushed from her eyes. A second blow followed immediately, this one snapping her jaw out of socket and rocking her head back so hard and fast she felt as if she was falling, tumbling down a black well of pain.

She tried to scream a warning to Samuel and Maybelle, but her words were choked by blood gushing down her throat.

Then darkness swallowed her whole and she wondered if she'd ever see the light again.

# CHAPTER 16

THEY TURNED ONTO the street where TK had met Franklin and his friends earlier today. Now she understood their reluctance to engage with Grayson—not only was he the mayor's son but also a neo-Nazi. Although, to his credit, he'd yet to show any violent tendencies. In fact, he'd disarmed Franklin and his bunch with only his cell phone. Did neo-Nazis espouse Gandhi-style protests? Was that even possible?

She didn't see any sign of Franklin or his cohorts. Instead, the street was crowded with TV news vans and a small group of curious onlookers.

"Still waiting for the verdict," Grayson said as he steered them down a side street. "Dad said he'd ordered the block around the town square cordoned off for the protesters. It's okay, though, they'll let us through."

"Where is the police garage?" TK had envisioned a large lot with impounded cars.

"All the town offices including the coroner's are in the government center, an old Woolworth's building behind the police station. The police garage is in a warehouse beside it. Makes everything convenient."

"Your city hall is an old Woolworth's building?"

"No. Well, kind of. The mayor has his offices in the courthouse along with the judges and county offices. Seems only fitting since it was a Greer who founded both the town and the county, and we built the courthouse along with everything else around here." Pride laced his voice as he waved his hand to include everything in sight—a boarded-up hardware store, a dingy newsstand-slash-sandwich shop, and a barber shop.

Grayson didn't seem to notice, just as he didn't seem to realize he was using the royal "we" to talk about events that had taken place over two hundred years ago. Modern-day Greer hadn't quite held up to the promise of its legacy, TK thought.

She glanced at the buildings across the town square. There was the courthouse, regal with its dome gleaming in the afternoon sun. Beside it was a red brick, squat building with bars on its windows: the police station.

Right now, the swath of green space that was the town square was a swirling mass of humanity separated mainly by skin color and the signs they held overhead.

White people and swastikas on the left, black and brown-skinned people with signs reading "We can't breathe!" and "Hands up, don't shoot," on the right. Both sides had a scattering of American flags; each co-opting the symbol of democracy and free speech for their own cause.

They turned down a narrow street—an alley, really—behind the courthouse. Here the buildings crowded together with no breathing room between them. The rear entrances to the courthouse and police station were on one side of the alley while on the opposite stood the employee entrance to the government center—a faded Woolworth's sign visible on the bricks above the first floor's row of windows—and the secured entrance to the police warehouse.

Grayson pulled into a parking spot marked "Reserved for G. Greer" behind the town's government center. Like the police department and courthouse across the alley, the old Woolworth's building and the warehouse beside it butted up against each other, their outer walls touching.

TK had seen similar construction back home in West Virginia, usually in cities that had begun life as company towns, where every square inch was designed with profit in mind. She'd never liked it. It made the buildings, no matter how lovely their architecture, feel as if they were looming, shouldering in on each other, fighting for the light. And, other than the courthouse, Greer was distinctly lacking in any lovely architecture, so these buildings in particular suffered from the antiquated urban design.

Grayson led her through the open garage doors of the warehouse. The tow truck with the Wayfarer had already arrived; it now held the place of honor in a fenced-off service bay. Even covered by its protective tarp, you could tell it was a unique car with distinctive lines.

She smiled at it as if it was an old friend. TK wasn't usually a car person—she'd never owned one, used an old Harley she'd bought off a Vietnam vet for transportation, mainly because it was cheap to maintain and she could do most of the work on it herself—but she liked the Wayfarer. Despite its gruesome cargo.

There weren't any other cars in the warehouse, but she saw the familiar cages of an evidence storage area behind a counter at the rear, and there was a flatbed truck laden with several pallets of wooden crates parked against the wall.

"Oh good, they finally made it," Grayson said, strolling over to examine the truck's cargo. The crates were all stenciled with a Chinese dragon cradling two large firecrackers in its talons, ready to hurl them to earth. "The fireworks for the Fourth. We launch them from the river." He turned to smile at her. "Hopefully you'll still be here to see it. We may not be a large city like Pittsburgh, but it's going to be amazing."

"Let me guess. Your dad let you plan it?"

He nodded. "Don't tell anyone, but I even used my own money to throw in an extra special surprise at the end. A five-hundred-gram finale called the Black Dahlia."

Behind the truck, she spotted the coroner's ambulance and realized why the two buildings had been designed the way they had: the warehouse must have serviced the store. A large set of double doors, big enough for a small truck to drive through, connected the warehouse with the old Woolworth's. Right now, the ambulance was backed up into the doorway, but there was room for her and Grayson to pass through.

They emerged into a large storage area that had several dumbwaiters and a set of old-fashioned wooden conveyer belts, one leading up to the floor above and one leading down to the basement. All appeared as if they hadn't been used in decades. The doors immediately across from them were open and led into a tiled area. Grayson led her through them, and she realized they were in an industrial-sized kitchen.

"You turned the kitchen into the morgue?"

"Not just the kitchen," Marcia Madsen said, turning to greet them from where she and two students were cleaning bones at the old dishwashing station. She gestured past the stainless steel exam tables to the old pass-through windows. Through it, TK glimpsed the other students seated and hunched over microscopes and laptops. "The entire lunch counter. Genius, isn't it? I can use the old walk-in refrigerator and freezer, I even have a separate decomp room. When I took over as coroner, I moved some of my equipment here and used grant money to help with the upgrades. Considering what most county coroners have to deal with in terms of budget, I think we've done quite well for ourselves. I get more privacy and room than my lab on campus, the students get a better real-world experience, everyone wins."

"Except the corpses," Grayson chimed in with a chuckle that fell flat as everyone turned to stare at him.

"Especially the people we serve," Madsen corrected. "We're able to do a proper examination and give their loved ones the answers they need. Most of the time, at least."

"Speaking of answers, got any for me?" TK asked as she watched the students form an assembly line, one person pulling bones out of a warm solution that had a faint chemical solvent smell, the next gently wiping the greasy adipocere from the bones with a paper towel, and the third taking them to a steel prep table and placing them in their anatomically correct position.

Madsen stripped free of her gloves and protective gear and led them through the swinging doors to the lunch counter. Here the students were examining bones already cleaned as well as the other artifacts found in the car.

"Answers? A few. First, the badge you found. Once we got it under the microscope, we realized that on the back," a student handed TK an evidence bag with the badge, now clean of debris, its brass shining, "there were some faint scratches. Initials. A. T. Might help with identification."

TK peered at the back of the badge, could just barely make out the markings. "It's a start. Anything else?"

Madsen frowned. "Not sure. I want to verify my

findings—they're preliminary speculation at most."

"Now you're sounding like a professor, professor. If you have anything that can start me in the right direction—"

Madsen led them over to a far corner where they couldn't be overheard. Grayson leaned in toward her while TK merely waited. "I've been doing this for some time, so I think I'm right. But..."

Before she could say anything, Karlan barreled through the outer door, his arms filled with food containers.

"Thought you guys might need some provisions," he called out jovially. "Where do you want them, doc?"

The students all looked up eagerly—and hungrily, TK noted. She'd only had a protein bar for lunch, and it was now almost three in the afternoon, but food was the last thing on her mind, especially with the stench of decomposition that had permeated every breath ever since she'd opened the car door back at the quarry.

"No eating in the lab," Madsen said. The students fled out to the warehouse, grabbing the food from Karlan's arms like locusts stripping a field bare.

He laughed and turned to Madsen, hands empty. "Guess I'll have to escort you to lunch personally. Can't let our county coroner go hungry." He smiled and nodded to TK.

"Aren't you on duty?" Grayson asked, his tone officious.

Karlan rocked back on his heels, ignoring Grayson. "What do you say, doc?"

"What about the verdict?" TK asked.

Karlan's smile widened. "Grayson didn't tell you? The grand jury found no grounds for an indictment. Jefferson's in the clear. For now, at least."

"The crowd seemed pretty quiet when we got back. Why aren't they protesting?" Madsen asked.

"DA and mayor decided to wait and make the official announcement tomorrow morning. They're bringing in reinforcements from the State Police tonight for crowd control." He grew serious. "Not a moment too soon. Our guys have been pulling overtime since this damn thing started. Unfortunately, that also gives the protesters—on both sides—time to bring in more bodies as well."

"We made some progress as well," TK told him. "Looks like our front seat passenger was a Greer City police officer, initials of A. T."

"We're headed over to the station to check their records," Grayson said.

"Doubt you'll find much from that far back. Whole place flooded back in '72 with Hurricane Agnes. Flooded again a few years ago with the winter melt." Karlan thought for a moment. "You might try the library; they have archives of the old *Greer Gazette.* Or the courthouse."

"The courthouse?"

Grayson snapped his fingers. "Of course. If there's one thing people never destroy, it's tax records." He turned to the door. "C'mon, TK. They close at four; after that we'll have the place to ourselves."

"Let me just get freshened up first." TK made it sound like some mysterious female undertaking, but really, she wanted to hear what Madsen had started to tell them before Karlan arrived. The anthropologist had clearly been uncomfortable talking around Grayson.

"Okay. I'll be right outside. I want to check the fireworks inventory."

Once he'd left, TK turned back to Madsen and Karlan. The two were discussing possible dinner plans. They made a cute couple with their matching gray hair and intense personalities. "Dr. Madsen, what were you going to tell me earlier? About your preliminary findings?"

Madsen's smile faded. "Not for public consumption, just between us..."

"Want me to leave?" Karlan asked, surprising TK with his sensitivity.

"No. Just don't mention it to the mayor or his son. Or anyone. Not until I finish my calculations."

"Calculations? You mean to tell if the victims were male or female?" Madsen had mentioned a variety of measurements she'd need to perform to verify the sex of each set of remains.

"That and..." Madsen blew her breath out, lowered her voice even more. "Look. Here's what I think. We have one Caucasian adult male in the front seat."

"Our presumed police officer."

"Right. And in the trunk..." She paused again. So unlike the forceful certainty she'd exhibited at the crime scene. "In the trunk, we have one set of adult female remains, one adult male, and one juvenile male. All African-American."

TK blinked. But it was Karlan who spoke first. "A black man, woman, and kid? All together? From the 1950s? Doc, do you realize what you're saying?"

Madsen nodded. "It gets worse. In the victims from the trunk I found evidence of a severe pre-mortem injuries consistent with beatings. And all three had traumatic fractures at C-2. What laymen call hangmen fractures."

Everyone was silent.

"No," Karlan protested. "No way. Not here. I don't believe it. It must have been some weird serial killer fetish. Like a, what do the feds call it in their profiling classes? A family annihilator. That's it. Because nothing like that ever happened here."

He couldn't even use the word they were all thinking, TK noted.

Madsen's lips thinned. "I won't be sure, not until I finish my examination. But I thought you should know. Be looking for three missing African-Americans along with your police officer."

Karlan shook his head and started for the exit.

"What about lunch?" Madsen called after him, a wistful tone coloring her voice.

"Sorry, doc. Lost my appetite. Rain check." He turned back. "I promise. Figure my time's better spent helping these two figure out who our victims are so we can figure out what really happened." He nodded to TK. "I'll get a start on the old tax records, you and the kid can start with the police archives. Meet you over there."

# CHAPTER 17

LUCY'S THROAT WAS tight and raw from answering the Randalls' questions, but she refused to leave until she was certain she'd given them everything she could. Her discomfort felt like small penance for not bringing their child home alive.

Finally, as the afternoon sun began to peek through the tops of the drapes, silence fell upon the gathering. Lucy waited, now focused not just on Jennifer Randall but the entire family. The daughter had retired to a bedroom, her husband leaning against the banister at the base of the staircase, head tilted as he listened for her. The father paced between the kitchen and the fireplace. Lucy couldn't help but notice the way his gaze stretched toward the back door when he reached the far end of his loop and then the front door when he reached the living room, searching for an escape.

The grandparents had collapsed on the sofa and chairs while Jennifer had left her seat to bustle around the room, offering drinks and snacks that no one took, her nervous energy buzzing through the air in her wake. Valencia stood silent at the far wall, watching, waiting for any chance to help.

The noise of Lucy's phone vibrating startled them all. Jennifer froze and released a gasp of fright, drawing her husband to her. Lucy jumped—she was already on the edge of her seat—and slid the phone free from her pocket. She was about to ignore it when she saw it was David Ruiz calling.

"I'm sorry, I'll just be a moment." She walked into the kitchen, their stares following her. It was a relief to leave their sight—the first time since she'd arrived. Her shoulders ached with anxious tension as she leaned against the window facing the patio and the rusted, lonely swing set standing at an awkward angle in the backyard. "Guardino here."

"Lucy, did you send TK to Greer? Alone? Do you know what's going on here?"

"I can't talk about—"

"Not your case. The protests. I was sent here to cover them."

"What protests?"

"Don't any of you read the news? The grand jury is coming back on an officer-involved shooting case today. Blue on black. We've got everyone here from the BLM to the KKK."

"Violence?"

"None so far. The police have things fairly well contained so far, but—"

"But TK can take care of herself. You know that."

"Yeah, but—"

Lucy smiled. She liked David—he was such a stabilizing force for TK. She really hoped they stayed together. But last thing she was going to do was meddle in TK's love life or let David interfere with TK's career.

She and Nick had had to figure out their own give and takes, balancing her career with the FBI and the needs of their relationship and family. It had taken work and heartache and a fair amount of tears and shouting before they found their path. No way in hell was she about to tell anyone else how to live their lives.

"David," she cut in before he could say something he'd regret. "Are you asking me to pull TK off a case and send someone else to do the job because you're worried?"

There was a long pause before he answered. "No. Of course not." Even with his traumatic brain injury and inability to express emotion with his voice—tonal agnosia, Nick had said it was called—she felt his misery. "I'd never ask you to do that."

She glanced back to the living room. The family was now huddled together. Maybe it was time to leave them to their private grieving.

"Tell you what. How about if I join TK in Greer tomorrow? Not to take over her case, just to check in."

"Thanks, Lucy. I knew I could count on you. Oh," he hesitated, "do me a favor."

"Don't worry. I won't tell TK you called. See you soon."

A few minutes later she and Valencia had made their farewells and were back in the Subaru heading toward Beacon Falls. It'd felt that the family was as glad to get rid of them as Lucy was glad to be leaving.

"Maybe it would have been better coming from you," she told Valencia as they left the interstate and turned onto Route 22.

"Why, because I'm black?"

"Because you're older, more comforting." Lucy paused, felt her pulse finally begin to settle back into its familiar rhythm.

She hadn't realized how tense she'd been throughout the day—her body felt as if it had survived an attack. "Okay. To be honest, yes, also because you're black. They just seemed so angry. I get that. If anything ever happened to Megan—"

Anything *had* almost happened to her Megan. Twice now. Lucy had pretty much gone berserker on the men who had threatened her family. Her rage had also spilled over onto the well-intentioned but too slow, too objective, too rational, including her own FBI team, who'd stood in her way.

"Anger is an important part of the grieving process," Valencia reminded her, once again sounding just like Nick. "People need to vent their fury. Far worse if they try to keep it inside."

"So I gave them an easy target to lash out at." She could accept that. When her mother had died earlier that year, Lucy's own grief hadn't just gnawed at her. It had grown fangs and claws and threatened to shred her apart. "That doesn't bother me. I understand it. But there was more. What she said, about Benji's case taking so long to solve because he was black... You don't believe that, do you?"

She hated the doubt that crept into her tone. Lucy knew the work she'd put in on Benji's case—even when it wasn't officially her case—and never once had she made him a lower priority because he was black. At least, that's what she wanted to believe. "I mean…fourteen years. It's a long time to wait with no answers."

Valencia shifted in her seat, her fingers fluttering to smooth imaginary wrinkles from her already flawless silk dress. "Do I think if Benji had been a white girl, all pigtails and smiles, he might have gotten justice sooner, then yes. I do."

Lucy was surprised. She'd been expecting Valencia to assuage her guilt. Hell, she wasn't even sure why she felt guilty in the first place. "Really?"

"Really." She shrugged. "I've been doing this longer than you. Missing persons. Families with no place else to turn to for answers. And if you run the numbers, look at the case files and how zealously they were pursued, glance at the amount of media attention, the odds are against a family like Benji's. Not just because he was black. Also because he was a boy, he lived in a rural area with limited resources—"

"Smitty did the best he could. He never gave up." Lucy felt obligated to defend the deceased detective.

"Obviously his best wasn't good enough. Not for the Randalls. Not for those other boys who came after Benji."

"Those other boys, they're what led me to Wilson. Smitty didn't have access to that information."

"You mean he didn't look beyond his own patch. You were the one who looked wider, who realized that Wilson might go after the same type of boy but was smart enough not to keep looking so close to home." Or in Benji's case, work—Wilson had been a traveling school photographer.

"Basic geographic profiling," Lucy muttered. "Just because Smitty didn't have training in it doesn't make him incompetent or racially biased."

"Of course not. It makes him human. As humans, we're prone to take the easy way out. Especially if we're overworked, underpaid detectives with a desk full of families like the Randalls hounding us for answers."

"Benji's case haunted Smitty until the day he died." As it would probably still haunt her. The look in Jennifer Randall's eyes—stricken was the only word Lucy could think to describe it. No. *Shattered.* Her world hopelessly broken by two strangers ringing her doorbell on a sunny summer day.

# CHAPTER 18

*MAY 17, 1954*

OFFICER THOMSON REAPPEARED, his uniform shirt torn, nameplate and a few buttons ripped away. In his hand was a shotgun. "Bought us some time. Won't have to worry until Mabel gets to the chief, and he brings his keys. Henry doing okay?"

"Good as can be expected," Samuel answered. "Help me move him to the car, and we'll be out of here." Not a moment too soon.

The door at the far end of the hall opened with a clatter. Samuel glanced up, expecting to see Jo waving at him to hurry. Instead it was the white girl, tugging Maybelle inside, hugging the wall as if afraid of being seen.

"Philip's father," Winnie said, her voice strangled with fear. "He and his friends. A whole bunch of them."

"They hit Mommy!" Maybelle cried, racing down the hall to Samuel. "Called her bad names. Those men, they're mean. Why did they hurt Mommy?"

Samuel's first instinct was to run down the hall and out the door, do whatever it took to get to Jo. But Maybelle clung to his legs, a weight he couldn't deny.

He pulled her up into his arms, one hand wiping her tears, while his mind fought to make sense of the insanity that had engulfed them. All he could keep thinking was that this was Pennsylvania, not Georgia. Things like this weren't supposed to happen here.

Fool, he cursed himself. Men were men. And they were always going to hate, never going to change. No one cared what the Supreme Court said—it was all just lies and empty promises. There was no equality. Not in this country. Not for men like Samuel or boys like Henry or a girl like Maybelle.

"You can't let them take her," he told Thomson, surprising himself with the menace chained within his voice. "We have to stop them."

Instead of answering, Thomson rushed past him to the

end of the hall, securing the door and snapping down blinds over the windows. He turned to face Samuel. "There's at least a dozen out there, and they're armed. Winnie. Tell me the truth. What did Henry do to you?"

She backed away, eyes on the floor, shoulders hunched like a beaten animal. "Nothing. He didn't do nothing."

"Then why does your father and Philip Greer think he did?"

"Henry didn't do nothing." She jerked her chin up, defiance snapping her posture straight. "I did. This time Daddy had a knife. I was scared, so scared. I thought he would kill me for sure. But Henry heard me screaming and came—even though Daddy could kill him easy, he's so much bigger. He distracted Daddy, gave me time to run, then he ran, too. Daddy couldn't keep up, he just stumbled and fell, right there in the dirt. And Henry and me, we, we were laughing so hard, it felt so good, and I—I kissed him."

"You let a colored boy kiss you in front of your father? And Philip Greer saw as well?"

"No. He didn't kiss me. I kissed him. It wasn't Henry's fault. He got scared, grabbed my hand, and we kept running. But then Philip and his friends caught up."

Silence thudded through the narrow space as Samuel met Thomson's gaze. Winnie and Henry were just kids. Of course, they should have known better, but...

"They're gonna kill him," Thomson said.

"No," Winnie cried. "They can't. You have to stop them. He didn't do anything wrong. It was me, my fault."

Thomson's lips thinned as his eyes moved from Winnie to Maybelle and then, finally, to Samuel. They were under siege. It was clear Thomson had already sacrificed his job, would maybe even go to prison for his actions if Winnie's father decided to press charges. Henry might still die if Samuel didn't get him to a hospital for proper care. How much was Samuel willing to lose?

"They have my wife," Samuel said. "She's no part of this. She can't be a part of this. Neither can my daughter."

That was his price. He could give up about anything. Including his freedom. As long as Jo and Maybelle lived.

# CHAPTER 19

AFTER ASKING MADSEN to keep her updated, TK joined Grayson out in the garage where he was prattling about dahlias, peonies, glittering silver fish, and crackling chrysanthemums.

"This is going to be spectacular," he told her, proudly patting the stacked crates of fireworks. "Wait and see."

"How about if we focus on finding out who our Officer A. T. is?"

"Sure, sure. C'mon, follow me." He waved to the police officers, none of whom looked up or acknowledged his presence, then led her back outside.

They crossed the street to the police department's rear entrance. Grayson fished a badge from his pocket and swiped it into the security lock, then pulled the door open for TK.

There were two sidelights on either side of the door, both crossed with bars, creating a strange spider-web effect where the afternoon sun cast its shadow on the linoleum floors. The hall was narrow with a old-fashioned holding cell on one side, empty despite the protests out front. TK wondered if that spoke to the restraint of the Greer police department or simply a lack of manpower.

"This way," Grayson said, leading her past a small break room to an unmarked door. He opened it and a wave of musty, damp air assailed them. "It's not so bad, you get used to it."

He switched on a light, and they carefully made their way down rickety wooden steps. The basement was much larger than the narrow police station and TK realized that the storage space extended beneath the courthouse as well. "The oldest records are back here."

She followed him to the farthest corner, dodging sagging bookshelves stacked with bound volumes stained with mouse droppings. "How can you find anything in this maze?"

"Used to play down here all the time when I was a kid and Dad brought me with him to work," Grayson said in a cheerful tone. "Mom died of cancer when I was little, so it was always just me and him. And the judge, of course. My grandfather."

Right. Because a rat-infested, toxic mold-infected basement was the perfect place for a child to play. TK shook her head. No wonder Grayson had turned out the way he had.

"Okay. I think these will probably be our best bet." He stopped at a worktable beside a wide file cabinet with thin drawers, the kind libraries use to store maps or documents that had to remain flat.

"What's in here?"

"Photographs." He opened one of the drawers, releasing a tangled nest of yellowed black and white photos and film negatives. "If we can't find him here or with the tax records, we'll check the library. But any photos they have would be copies from here; these are the main archives, so I figure this is our starting point."

She glanced at the file cabinet. There had to be over two dozen drawers—and another cabinet just like it on the other side of the table. "Are they in any order?"

"Kinda." He didn't sound very certain.

TK closed the drawer he'd chosen from the middle of the cabinet and instead opened the top one. She scooped out its contents onto the table and turned on the gooseneck lamp. Thankfully the bulb was good and strong.

"Anything from 1940 to 1960 that has names that might fit keep, the rest goes back into the drawer. Anything you're not sure of, give it to me."

He nodded and they waded in. As they worked, TK called Wash and updated him.

"Police officer, initials A. T. Got it." As always, the sound of computer keys clicking served as background noise.

"Any luck with the car?" she asked.

"Those pictures you sent are a huge help—I edited out any of the gory details and uploaded them to a bunch of classic car fan sites. There's one called the Horseless Carriage Foundation that looks particularly helpful. Oh, and Mopar, the car parts dealer; they have scanned all of their catalogues, so I'm running a search for the serial numbers."

She made a grunting noise of acknowledgement, knowing that Wash wouldn't need more encouragement. She and Grayson quickly plowed through the first drawer—it was all from the 1990s and early 2000s, probably the end of the department using real film for its archives—and moved on to the next.

"Did you get a good look at the hood ornament?" Wash continued. "From a distance it looks like an angel with its wings folded back, but up close it's a ram with elongated horns curling around. Anyway, I'm working on some leads to narrow in on a possible dealership. No luck with the DC registration records; those are long gone, but maybe I can find out where it was bought. It'll be a start."

"And we're now looking for missing persons reports of three African-Americans. Adult male, adult female, and a teenaged or pre-teen boy."

"As in, you think there's a whole family gone? No, can't be. I would have seen a report like that. Even though the paper police records are pretty much gone, there'd have been something in the newspapers, right?"

Grayson glanced up from his work, and she remembered he hadn't heard about the victims in the trunk. Now that he knew, his dad would soon as well. Nothing the mayor could do about it—and Madsen worked for the county, not Mayor Greer, so even if Greer could silence TK, he couldn't silence the coroner.

"David said to try personal ads," TK told Wash. "Said back then people used them when they were looking for family members they lost touch with."

"Good idea. I already have access to all the scanned

newspapers, I can focus on the African-American ones. Which, by the way, have a much more robust database and search engine than the police archives. Just saying..."

His disapproval at the slipshod police record-keeping wasn't new. Almost every cold case they had, they had to overcome the simple fact that not everyone hoarded data the way Wash wished they would.

Suddenly Grayson jerked around, thrusting an eight-by-ten in front of TK. "Look. 1953 Greer Police softball team." He flipped it over. "Second baseman, Officer Archibald Thomson. That's him. Has to be."

She flipped it back, squinted at the man in the center of his teammates. Not a whole lot to distinguish him as far as looks, but what they really needed was demographic information. "Find me more."

Grayson plunged back into the pile of photos.

"Wash, we think we've just ID'd one of our victims. Officer Archibald Thomson. Can you see what you can find on him? Date of birth, when he was last seen, any mentions."

"Sure, but you know I won't be much help on the real question, right?"

"Yeah. How the hell did he end up in a car belonging to

someone from DC at the bottom of a quarry?"

"And why didn't anyone in his own department report him as missing?"

# CHAPTER 20

TK CALLED KARLAN with what they'd found. A few minutes later he called back from the courthouse. "Got him. Last paycheck issued May, 1954. Nothing in the records at all after that—no sick leave, no vacation, no paychecks, just a note that he never picked up his final check. As far as the paper trail, it's like he jumped off the face of the earth."

"Or the side of a quarry," she added in a grim tone.

"If you don't need anything else, I'm headed back to my office—still have work to do on my current cases before I can head home."

"Thanks, Karlan. I'll catch up with you tomorrow." She hung up and turned back to Grayson, who'd managed to unearth a few more photos of Thomson, including one that showed a good, full-face image. She scanned them with her phone and sent them to Wash and Madsen.

"Don't suppose there's any way to access Thomson's case files?" she asked, turning to look around the shadowy basement.

Somewhere in this detritus of a police department's bygone years, there would be citation books, arrest reports, duty logs—evidence of what Thomson had been working on before he ended up in the quarry.

Grayson shook his head mournfully. "Not that I know of. I've been through a lot of this stuff, trying to catalogue and organize it for my dad, but I don't remember seeing anything from 1954."

"It was a long shot. Not that a patrol officer would have kept much in the way of files. Besides, he may never have had a chance to put anything in writing."

Still, it would have been nice to flesh out Thomson's character. Was he a good cop? Back in the fifties organized crime still ran gambling and protection rackets, not to mention union-busting and moonshining. Any of which could have gotten Thomson killed, good cop or not.

"Is this what it's always like? Mucking about with dusty old photos and documents, searching for that nugget of gold?"

Grayson seemed both disappointed by the mundane investigatory procedure and excited that he'd been the one who'd found their "nugget of gold."

"Afraid so. Most times it's even more boring—and you go it alone. Then we feed all the data we find back to Wash, and he works his magic with the databases. Once we have a few solid leads and as much data as we can mine, we'll hit the ground, start knocking on doors."

"Why not start there?"

"Because we're dealing with cold cases, and people's memories can be faulty, so we try to arm ourselves with as many facts as we can first. Helps to weed out the red herrings, like when people combine events thinking it all happened at the same time or when they get the date or location wrong." As she spoke, TK yanked open a few random cartons but quickly realized the futility—especially after the last one yielded a dead rat's carcass.

"Are they lying to you or is that just normal human behavior?"

"Both. Often they don't even realize they're lying—to them it's just shading their memories in their favor. Or to tell a better story. People like stories and they want them to be logical, for there to be a good reason why things happen. Real life isn't like that."

He considered that as he led TK up a second set of steps out of the musty basement and into the brightly lit courthouse that stood next to the humble police station.

"This building is the family jewel," he told her, nodding to the high ceilings with their hand-carved cornices and the large leaded-glass windows designed to pull light in from both sides of the building. The way he talked, his voice hushed so as to not echo from the marble floor and walls, he could have been inside a church. For a Greer, the courthouse probably was the equivalent of a house of worship, she thought. "When it was first built, it was the largest building in the county. Its dome stood higher than any church steeple."

She nodded absently. Time for the grand tour later. "Where's your father's office? I should update him."

"This way." He led her up to the second floor, above the courtrooms and county offices, to a lavish set of intricately carved dark oak doors with a deceptively simple gold embossed title: Mayor's Office.

"Has Greer ever had a mayor who wasn't from your family?" she asked as he opened the door and waved her in with a proud flourish.

"Not sure. I don't think so. But not all Greers were mayors. My grandfather. He was the black sheep—became a judge instead. But his father was mayor for over forty years, most terms running unopposed, until he handed the baton over to my dad."

"And now your dad is running for Congress. A big step from small town mayor to the nation's capital."

"Not for Dad. If he wins, there will be a special election for mayor." He blushed and glanced away, reminding her how young he was. "He wants me to run. That's why I'm working for him. Learning the ropes."

No trace of embarrassment over the obvious nepotism. Guess it was just the way the world worked if you were a Greer. No wonder the kid believed in social Darwinism and all that Nazi crap.

The mayor's reception area was designed for intimidation. Dark oak paneling, lush carpets, antique furniture that would be impossible to get comfortable in, even the receptionist's desk was on a dais, allowing the mayor's assistant to look down upon the humble masses come to petition him. On the walls hung somber portraits of the Greers who'd held the position: all men, all with the same glint of destiny filling their gaze. As if they ruled a nation rather than a bankrupt town in a forgotten corner of Pennsylvania.

Grayson ignored the furnishings to glance at the grandfather clock in the corner. Almost five-thirty. "I didn't realize how late it is. Everyone's left for the day."

He moved behind the receptionist's desk to the door to the inner sanctum and knocked gently before opening it.

"It's me," Grayson interrupted. "We found something. Thought you should hear."

"Well then, come in. Don't stand there dawdling in the doorway."

The door was yanked open wide, revealing two men. One tall with broad shoulders and hazel eyes the same shade as Grayson's but more piercing as they raked past him to examine TK

"You must be O'Connor. I'm JR Greer, the mayor." He waved her and Grayson into the office. The second man was older, in his seventies, with white hair and soft, blue eyes. "This is my father, Judge Greer."

"Call me, Philip, please," the older man said as he stepped forward to extend a hand to TK. "I've been retired for over a decade now."

"Nice to meet you both," TK said, shaking the judge's hand and then his son's. The three generations of Greer men stood side by side, and she couldn't help but compare them. The judge with his warm smile, the mayor, whose smile was wider but less genuine, and Grayson, whose attention was solely focused on his father, lips parted in an unconscious imitation of an eager baby bird, searching for the faintest hint of sustenance.

"We know who was in the car at the quarry," Grayson gushed, his body buzzing with excitement.

"You've already identified the bodies?" the judge asked. He stepped back—or was it his son the mayor who stepped forward, taking charge?

"How is that possible?" JR Greer snapped.

"Not all of them," Grayson admitted. "But the man in the front. He was a Greer police officer. Named Archibald Thomson. He was on the force from 1947 until 1954, then that May, he vanished from the records. It has to be him."

TK wondered at the quick glance that the two older men shared. She had the sudden suspicion that their news wasn't a surprise.

The mayor spoke first. "Grayson, your collar's undone. I

do wish you'd wear a tie. Make sure that ink of yours isn't seen by any of that mob outside."

"I'm not ashamed of my beliefs." Despite his words, Grayson buttoned his collar.

"Nothing to do with shame or what you believe," his father snapped. "When you work here, you represent the entire town, not any one person. That's why we can't allow any of this nonsense about a Greer police officer being in that car to become public. Not until we have all the facts."

Grayson considered that and nodded. "Like the names of the other victims we found."

TK was still watching the grandfather. He had grown pale and now rested a palm against the mayor's desk, leaning his weight on its gleaming polished surface. She did a quick mental calculation: Philip Greer would have been in his early teens in 1954. Just a kid. But a kid who knew something, she was certain.

"Not just who they were," JR continued in a commanding tone. "How they came to be there. After all, just because this Archibald Thomson was once employed here doesn't mean he was still a police officer at the time of the incident. Maybe he was fired, went on some kind of rampage. Maybe he was mentally unbalanced. We can't tarnish the city's reputation or those of his victims until we have all the facts. Especially not with the current unpleasantness."

Sounded to TK as if the mayor had been working overtime on his white-washing campaign, painting Thomson as some deranged madman who happened to drive off a cliff with three bodies in his trunk. And there was nothing she could do about it: her job as a private consultant was to find what facts she could and report them. After that, she had no control over how those facts were presented to public.

The whole situation sucked eggs. Her first case as a lead investigator and stupid politicians were going to spin her findings into a twisted braid of lies. At least Lucy wasn't here to see it—although if Lucy was here, she'd be even more angry than TK. Lucy was used to exposing lies, not helping to create them. How would she handle this, given their non-disclosure agreement?

As TK pondered, a knock came at the open door. She couldn't help her smile when she saw David standing there, not at all cowed by his opulent surroundings.

"Mr. Mayor? David Ruiz from *The Crime Blotter.* I was hoping for a comment on why the DA decided to postpone the announcement of the Grand Jury's findings in the Jefferson case?

Also, if you'd like to comment on your feelings about the midnight vigil being held in the town square? Or the counter-protest the Klan is planning?"

# CHAPTER 21

TK SMILED AS the mayor bristled at David's interruption. Nice to know she wasn't the only one who pissed off His Honor.

"Out, now! Come back during regular office hours. Better yet, don't come back at all—talk with the public affairs officer; that's what she's there for."

David simply nodded and left, shutting the door behind him. He'd gotten what he'd come for: a response from the mayor that proved he'd done his due diligence in attempting to get all sides of his story.

"Guess I'll be going as well," TK said, her mood upbeat. After all, it looked like David was free for the night. Plus, she'd been on the case fewer than eight hours and had already ID'd one of her victims; not even Lucy could have done better.

The mayor jerked his chin in dismissal, obviously anxious to turn his interrogation onto his son. TK really didn't mind having Grayson spy on her, she just wished he'd be a man and admit that his father was using him.

She stepped outside and spotted David at the end of the hall, near the window overlooking the town square.

"I know something you don't," she teased him.

"If it's that the Grand Jury declined to indict, then I'm way ahead of you."

She pouted. Sometimes having a boyfriend who was an investigative reporter was no fun at all. "Everyone knew they would. It was a no-brainer, justified shooting."

"Not what I heard," David told her. "My sources say that Officer Jefferson was called to that address several times for domestic disturbances and that the last time, Eggers left the house unscathed but arrived at the county jail with multiple contusions."

"You think Jefferson beat him?"

"Might have thought he was giving Eggers a taste of his own medicine. But it could explain why Eggers ran."

She stared at him. "You're not suggesting that Eggers turned his gun on a police officer in self-defense?"

"Seeing as Eggers's dead, and the only witness is the man who shot him, guess we'll never know."

"No one will be satisfied by the verdict." Outside the window, the protestors were in a war of escalating chants, both sides' messages drowned out by the chaos. "But they knew that when they came here. What do they want?"

"Justice. Truth. I'm sure they'd start with being able to trust the men carrying lethal weapons who are charged with maintaining the peace."

"I think the cops would start with people not judging them before the facts are in," she retorted.

"People don't make decisions based on fact. They make them based on emotion. And once made, it's virtually impossible to sway them. In fact, studies have shown the more facts against their initial, instinctive position, the more they resist and create reasons to deny the facts."

Every time David talked like this, he made her want to go back to school. She'd joined the Marines straight out of high school—the chance for a guaranteed paycheck that would support her family was too tempting to deny—but always wondered where she might be today if she could have found a way to go to college.

As she watched the factions below, so clearly divided along racial lines, an image of an old photo flashed through her mind, a mob of angry white women viciously shrieking insults at little black girls trying to walk into a school, their teeth bared like wild animals.

How monstrous she'd thought those women—but maybe they were only mothers, not monsters? "So all those people during the civil rights marches, the bombings, the assassinations—"

"Exactly. Facts didn't matter. Nor did common sense or morality. People dug in, defended what they believed, even though it was obvious what had to be done for the nation, for humanity."

"So many lives lost, so much hatred sown. And nothing's changed. Nothing is ever going to change."

He frowned at that. "You're saying the laws, no matter how moral or ethical, can't make a difference? That's like saying it really is everyone for themselves. Let the mob rule."

"No. I'm just saying that freedom includes the right to hate." It was something she'd heard her grandfather say.

She remembered an old photo of grandpa with his VFW legion, all decked out in their uniforms and medals, standing so tall and proud. As they held a banner that said those very words. Protesting a gay rights parade. Those elderly men of valor, men who'd bled for this country, they smiled in that photo. Certain of how right they were, certain that they still served their country, protecting it from evil.

"Hate, yes. Kill, no."

"Obviously." She rubbed her eyes with the palms of her hands. She hadn't felt this drained since she was in the shit. Never during a mission or after, but before...before she'd always feel as if the desert wind had sucked her dry, devoured her whole. But then she'd lace on her boots, strap on her helmet and NVG, step onto the chopper, crowd in with her team, and they'd fill her up again. Not with vague ideas of glory or might makes right or even patriotism. Her team. Battle-worn men who trusted her with their lives as she trusted them.

Everything was so much clearer back then.

"It's just..." She paused, trying hard to get this right, even though she knew she was doomed to fail. Minds much smarter than hers hadn't risen to the challenge. "I feel like, where we are now, there's no right and wrong. For either side, for any side, for any one. We ask the cops to go out there, race into unknown circumstances, ready to sacrifice their lives to protect total strangers. And so many of them don't come home again. How's that right? Shouldn't their lives be worth something? Shouldn't they have the right to defend themselves? Shouldn't their families have the right to have them come home again after a hard day's work?"

He nodded, listening. She liked that about him. He did so love to talk—especially with her, since his disability usually didn't get in the way as much when he talked to her as it did with others. But as skilled as David was with words, he was an even better listener.

She continued. "And the people the cops are sworn to protect. They deserve to have some peace of mind. The ability to walk down their own streets without a gang of corner boys—"

"Not always gangs. Don't make them out to be violent thugs just because they have nowhere else to go," he cautioned her, a gentle reminder of his own childhood spent uprooted by his father's incarceration.

"Not gangs," she allowed. "Gaggle. A gaggle of corner boys, geese squawking and nipping at heels." She told him about her encounter with Franklin and his friends that morning. "But sometimes there are weapons. Sometimes they are thugs and they choose the corner not because there's nowhere to go but because that's where the innocent they prey on are."

He frowned but tilted his head in concession. "Sometimes. But not always. And what about the people of color killed by police officers who aren't armed? Where's the justice for them?"

"That's the problem, right? How's a cop, how's anyone supposed to tell the difference? Magical x-ray vision?" She bounced on her toes, warming up to the ideas spinning through her mind as if sparring with a dozen opponents. A gauntlet of contradictions and paradoxes.

She sighed, envisioning how she reacted this morning to Franklin and his crew. "I'm sorry. I have to side with the police. Everyone's a threat until proven otherwise. Maybe that makes me a racist bitch. I don't know. But thinking that way kept me and my squad alive—and we had a lot more going for us than a cop all alone with no backup."

"You're not racist." Despite his monotone his entire body radiated concern and warmth. "No more than any of us."

"I don't understand. I mean, I never had to really think about this. When I was part of a team, it didn't matter where we were from or what color our skin was, we were all focused on the mission. And most of the time, I was the only woman, so I never socialized with anyone—I was the one segregated during down times."

How she'd hated that. Even during their brief stints at larger bases like Camp Leatherneck, a base the size of a city, she and the other women quickly learned how dangerous boredom was in young, adrenaline-fueled men far from home.

They'd huddle in their cargo-container quarters, hating to admit to themselves or anyone exactly how stupid it was to go out alone, especially at night when the maze of temporary structures—the entire place was a mirage in the middle of an ancient desert, here tonight, gone tomorrow—became a stalking ground.

It was the first time she'd realized that being a Marine couldn't protect her from anyone. Not even her fellow Marines.

# CHAPTER 22

WINNIE GLARED AT the men making decisions about her life. She was so damned tired of stupid men thinking they could control her. Like her father. Like Mr. Greer—she knew the real reason why he was taking her dad's side in all this. He knew Philip liked her. Philip had once tried to kiss her, but she'd kneed him in the balls and ran.

Men. Boys. Same thing. All stupid. Except Henry. Most people called him retarded or dumb. Not Winnie. To her he was special. The only one willing to risk himself to protect her.

Of course she'd kissed him—that's what women in the movies did when the hero saved them. Especially if the hero was cute and nice and never, ever raised his voice much less a hand to her.

Who cared what color Henry's skin was? Winnie knew the color of his heart.

She marched past the doctor and his little girl, heading for the front door. Officer Thomson rushed after her, grabbing her arm to spin her around. Winnie yanked away and raised both fists to him.

"Winnie, where do you think you're going?"

"This is all my fault. I'm going to tell them the truth. I don't care what my dad does—won't be anything he hasn't done before."

"You don't understand." Officer Thomson glanced back at the doctor, his face suddenly grown sad. "This has gone beyond that. You need to let me and Dr. Mann handle this. Your job is to take care of his little girl, get her to safety. Can you do that?"

"What about Henry? I'm not leaving him."

Another look exchanged between the two men. She hated that, the silent language adults used when they thought they knew better than her.

The doctor whispered something to his little girl, stopping her tears, and set her on the ground. He held her hand and together they walked over to Winnie.

"Will you take care of Maybelle?" the doctor asked, crouching down so his eyes met Winnie's. "I'm trusting you. Can you do that?"

She looked from him to Officer Thomson. Saw that they weren't angry. They were afraid. This was bad. So much worse than she'd imagined. Nothing in the movies ever went this wrong. But this wasn't the movies, was it? It took all her courage and a little more for her to meet Dr. Mann's gaze and nod. "Yes, sir."

"Thank you," he said, solemnly transferring Maybelle's hand from his to hers. The little girl seemed stunned, her gaze as blank as Winnie's mind. What to do? Where to run?

Officer Thomson had the answers. He pulled his heavy key ring from his belt and selected a key. "The basement storage area is connected to the courthouse's basement next door. This time of day, courthouse is empty, you can get out through there." He handed her the key.

"Henry? Is he coming with us?"

"We'll take care of Henry," he said as he led her and Maybelle to the door to the basement. "No matter what you hear or see, stay quiet. If everything's okay, I'll meet you at Henry's house. Tell his folks they need to pack up and leave tonight. Can you do that?"

Winnie nodded and wiped her nose with the back of her hand holding the key.

Officer Thomson gripped her shoulders so tight it hurt— but in a good way. Like he was letting her know she was strong enough to bear it. He opened the door.

Maybelle made a sniffling noise. Her father came up behind her and gave her one last hug and kiss.

"Be a good girl now," he told her. "We'll get you back to Mommy as soon as we can, but until then you listen to Winnie, okay?"

The little girl nodded. She opened her mouth to say something but it was swallowed by her sobs.

"I love you," her father whispered as he kissed the top of her head. "Never forget that."

A gunshot sounded from the front of the building followed by the sound of fists pounding on glass.

"Go. Now." Officer Thomson said, shoving them onto the landing at the top of the steps and shutting the door behind them.

Then it was just Maybelle and Winnie. Alone in the dark.

# Chapter 23

TK WATCHED THE crowd below the courthouse window. The summer sun sat low on the horizon, and already the numbers of those protesting against the police were thinning as they realized there would be no answers here today. Those who remained behind lit candles and stood quietly, heads bowed.

Were they truly mourning the memory of the man Officer Jefferson had shot? Someone who had beat a woman? Hard to believe a man like that could touch so many lives. More from beyond the grave than when he was alive, she was certain.

More biased thinking. Maybe she had inherited more of her grandfather's racism than she cared to admit. David wrapped one arm around her shoulder, sensing her turmoil. Instead of bristling at the misguided gesture of gallantry, she rested her hand on his and gave it a squeeze.

Whatever had happened in that alley wasn't her business; finding the truth of the people who had been left to rot in that quarry were. Now that she had a name for one of her victims, she was certain she could find the rest.

"I need to check on Dr. Madsen and see what she's found," she told David, glad of a reason to change the topic. "How about if we pick up some pizza, bring it to her and her students?"

"Lead the way," he said.

She led him down to the rear entrance that faced onto the narrow alley that ran between the courthouse and police department on one side and the rear of the old Woolworth's building and municipal warehouse.

As they walked, she filled him in on her case—strictly off the record. He groaned at that, sensing a tasty story behind the few facts that she offered, but offered encouragement that brightened her mood immensely.

They emerged on the far side of the town square and turned down the next block where she'd seen a few restaurants including a sandwich shop and pizza place.

Half an hour later, they emerged carrying a variety of aromatic pies, including her favorite, a meat lovers with extra bacon. As they turned up the street she spotted a familiar group blocking their way. Franklin and his boys.

TK almost laughed as Franklin turned and sauntered toward them, his pack following close behind. Nothing was going to spoil her mood. Not with David here and her case progressing. Especially not a teen-thug wannabe.

"Isn't it past your bedtime?" she called to the boys in a jovial voice.

"Are these the guys?" David asked, taking the pizzas TK carried and adding them to his own stack. God, how she loved a man with tactical awareness. She had the weapons, she was the one trained in combat, of course she needed her hands free. "The ones from earlier?"

They were maybe a dozen feet from the corner boys. "David, meet Franklin and friends."

"You won't give us the time of day," Franklin said, hands open wide, palms up. But his smile most definitely did not make it all the way to his eyes. "In fact, you're downright rude when we pay you a compliment. First you run off with that Nazi creep and now you're hanging with this amigo? Girl, you need to get your eyes checked, see what you missing." He gestured to his crotch. "Don't you know, black is beautiful?"

"What I'm missing," TK matched his tone and expression of mock moral outrage, "is any idea where you misplaced your common sense. The cops are just down the street, in case you missed the men dressed in riot gear."

"That's where we're heading. Figure if they're stalling on the verdict announcement must mean black men ain't got no justice. As always. How about we walk with you and you can buy us dinner?" He jerked his chin and one of his guys—one of the two built like a linebacker, TK couldn't tell them apart in the twilight—helped himself to the top box of pizza from the stack David carried.

David didn't protest—no surprise, he'd seen TK in action and trusted her to handle herself. But what did surprise her was his scowl. Not aimed at Franklin or his cohorts, but at her. Warning her not to push things too far. She almost rolled her eyes. They were only kids, looking for trouble.

Maybe that was his point. Just because Franklin was looking for trouble didn't mean she had to give it to him.

"You can have the pizza," she said, strolling past them as if she'd planned to give them the pie all along. The top one was David's vegetarian delight, so no great loss. "Least I can do after embarrassing you this morning."

"Please. You embarrassed yourself. Going along with that Nazi thug. Did he show you his tatts? Came back with them from skinhead summer camp when he was a kid, so proud of them. Tried to parade them down our block, him and his jackboot friends. We showed them. His daddy wasn't so proud of his little Hitler then, not when our guys sent them back stripped naked, hogtied, superglued and feathered."

"Our guys?" she asked. "Grayson is what, five, six years older than you? When exactly did this happen?" Sounded more like urban legend than anything that might have actually happened.

"I was still old enough to watch and cheer," Franklin retorted. "Ain't anyone ever gonna forget that skinny white ass."

The boys around him jeered in agreement, their menace diminished by the pizza filling their mouths.

"No way in hell will he ever be mayor. Not after that. Folks around here got too long a memory. And if they really do let that cop get away with murder..." His eyes glinted as the street lights came on, their bright glow a counterpoint to the velvet-purple sky. "Well, now, maybe it'll be time for us to get some justice our way."

With that, he grabbed his own slice and knocked the box

with the remaining pizza away from the boy who held it, hurling it into the gutter. "C'mon, let's get this party started."

As one, they turned and left, heading toward the town square.

TK started to follow them, but David lagged behind. She waited. When he caught up with her, his expression was worried, despite the fact that Franklin and his crew had vanished into the night.

"What?" she asked, still a bit jazzed by the encounter. Just like this morning, she'd felt a familiar frisson of anticipation. Being in control but not in control...walking a knife edge...she didn't have words for it, but whatever it was, it was an adrenaline rush.

"I think that we're all racist," David started. The pizza boxes wobbled as he balanced them, obviously frustrated with his inability to adequately communicate without using his hands to gesture for emphasis. "But it has nothing, necessarily, to do with skin color. It's about fear. Not fear of someone having a different skin color. Not fear of them at all. Fear of the unknown."

He stopped and turned to her. "Like those boys. You met them this morning when you were alone. Outnumbered, five to one. Were you afraid?"

"No. I was angry, irritated, wondering what the hell right they had to do that, just because I'm a woman. But I wasn't afraid." They slowly continued down the street.

"Why not? Most women would be. Isn't that why men—whether it's construction workers or kids with nothing better to do—isn't that really why they catcall and jeer at women? Asserting their dominance over any woman who comes into their circle of influence—they control your attention, hell, the very pavement you put your feet on."

This she had an answer for—it was something she'd been dealing with all her life, especially after she joined the Corps. "Men like that, they want women to fear what might lie behind those so-called harmless words and whistles. They're bullies. Like cybertrolls—they aren't merely annoying, they're also instilling fear when they publish your intimate details, where you live and work, how to reach you when you're most vulnerable, and threaten real-life harm."

"Right. Because they've turned words, their right to free speech, into a weapon. Which, for a journalist who has the first amendment tattooed onto his soul, is a very, very difficult thing to say."

"Terroristic threats—that's the police term for it," TK told him.

"But it's not the actual words or threat that terrifies, is it? It's the randomness. The uncertainty. Will they follow through? When? Where? Terrorism is an act of dominance, taking over mental territory, more than physical. Doesn't matter if it's via intimate partner violence or large-scale ideology instilling fear in the masses. Once you control fear, you can wreak havoc over an entire nation, create chaos."

"What's that got to do with corner boys and racism?"

"You weren't afraid of Franklin or his gang. It didn't matter that they were black or white or purple, you would have had the same reaction."

"Because I had a plan. I knew what I could do, would do, to get out of there."

"Would you have shot them?" He was well aware that she always carried a gun—something that he despised but put up with.

"No. They never laid hands on me, it was only words. And I had other options."

"Because of your training."

"Right. And practice and experience." Where was he

going with this?

"See. I saw something different. I *was* frightened. When I read their body language, I didn't see a boy and his friends acting out. I saw a situation that could have changed in an instant. I felt choked by the possibilities. How volatile things were, how any one of those boys—or you or I for that matter—could have sent things spiraling out of control."

It was a long speech for him. Long enough that she swallowed her reflex reaction of dismissing his concern, that she had it all under control, and really considered his words. Because of his disability, David was an expert at reading body language, practically a human lie detector.

Could she have been wrong? Both this morning and now? "Which of us was right? Were they dangerous or not?"

"I'm not sure. That's my point. I mean, think about it. What if you're a police officer in a city where most of the crime in the area you patrol is black on black? Where the times when you are forced to react, when you fear for the lives of the public or yourself, when things happen so fast that however you react, right or wrong, becomes the practiced experience..."

"Okay, I see what you're saying. It's not necessarily prejudice. It's not consciously discriminating or making the assumption that every black man you see is someone capable of violence, but rather it's been ingrained through repeated exposure to violence." Train how you fight, fight how you train.

"Even if it's not actual violence, any pattern of behavior that occurs during a flight or fight adrenaline response is going to be programmed into the brain like a reflex—so the next time an encounter triggers those same feelings, you won't think of your training or of options or diplomacy."

"You'll be reacting, reflexively."

"Basic physiology."

She'd seen guys operate like that in battle, had felt it herself. Which is why soldiers spent so many hours trying to turn training into reflex, muscle memory. But the real goal was emotional memory—the short-cut that bypassed the brain's higher thinking areas and saved time when immediate action was needed.

Cops only received a small fraction of combat training and even less time to use it in the real world to reinforce it. A good thing—no one wanted the streets of Pittsburgh or Greer to turn into Fallujah.

But understanding the physiology of the problem did nothing to change the real-world consequences. "What's the solution? How do you fight subconscious reflexes? The problem goes too deep."

"Never said it was easy. But it is possible. There's new training that the DOJ is trying in places like Gary, Indiana and Stockton, California that shows real promise in mitigating innate bias. Keeping police safe as well as increasing their effectiveness in the community."

An experiment in a few cities seemed like an inadequate solution, but at least it was a start. Although it missed the bigger problem.

"Even if bias explains some of the blue on black violence, what about everything else going on?" She stood still, waving her hand toward the people milling behind the police barricades, now bathed in the harsh glow of streetlights. "Some of those people—no matter the color of their skin, on both sides—they don't care about peaceful solutions or better training or even justice or the truth. They want blood."

He leaned close, pressing his arm against hers, the pizza boxes still balanced between his hands, as if sensing the agitation that buzzed through her like an unexploded IED. She hated that sometimes she felt the same as that angry mob—out of control, wanting to use her fists, wanting to hit, to burn, to destroy.

Anything to purge this awful, uncontrollable rage that had the power to overwhelm her.

"I hate this." She lowered her head to his shoulder. "Feeling like this. Angry all the time."

"Where does anger come from?" He whispered the words as if they were a poem. "Fear. You're afraid of losing control. That crowd, they're afraid of never getting it back. Of being powerless, terrorized, their lives stolen by fear instilled by others."

"Of being enslaved." It was a bitter word—especially coming from her, a white woman, but it felt honest and true. It resonated through her, and she understood something deeper than words, she understood that same primal terror. She'd felt it herself—had been made to feel it. What was the other word he'd used earlier when he was talking about heckling? Dominance.

Yes. She remembered the power that had sparked in a man's eyes as she lay at his mercy, powerless to fight, no control over what happened to her—what he did to her.

It didn't last centuries, wasn't a wholesale subjugation of generations, ingrained into their memories, their traditions, their very souls. She'd only felt it for the better part of an hour, but it had been long enough to sear her psyche, to change who she was, right down to her DNA.

The memories hit her so hard she sagged against him. Immediately felt ashamed, relying on his strength instead of her own. But, for once, not afraid to let someone else get close enough to help her. To trust that a man would not betray.

That he saw her as human. Equal. Cherished.

Wasn't that what everyone, man, woman, child, deserved? Not as a right granted to them, but merely by the fact that they were born?

And if that basic, inalienable right was threatened, who wouldn't fight with everything they had to reclaim it?

David set the now-cold pizza down on the pavement and ignored it to take her into his arms. TK let him hold her. Tight. So tight she barely felt the ground beneath her feet. She had no idea what the answer was—maybe she never would. But she understood the problem.

More than a problem. A threat. One that could undermine more than neighborhoods or cities… It was at once both overwhelming in its universal, primal nature and still felt uniquely personal, private.

She had no idea how to explain it to David. Did the words even exist to describe this feeling? More than fear, less than fury…a sickening twist of her guts as if her belly had been ripped open and flooded with ice water.

But she understood. And with understanding came the realization that the people beyond those barricades were as vulnerable as they were powerful.

# CHAPTER 24

As THEY SKIRTED the town square on their way to the coroner's office, TK took over pizza duty to free David's hands so he could take photos of the protesters for the story he was writing. The police had cleared an eight-foot-wide alley, roughly down the center of the town square, lined with barricades to separate the two factions. They patrolled their narrow DMZ in full riot gear along with two K-9s.

It was an efficient use of their limited manpower, but TK couldn't help but wonder exactly how long the flimsy wooden barricades—nothing more than prettily painted sawhorses— would hold if either side of the crowd grew violent. The officers would be caught in the middle with no place to shelter, forced to fight their way through. Seemed like a recipe for disaster.

Earlier in the day, the anti-police protesters had been the loudest, most angry. But now they had their backs turned on the opposition as a minister led them in prayer.

On the other side of the barricades, the white supremacists—TK hated to think of them as the pro-police side; she doubted the police actually wanted their support—had grown in numbers and were chanting militaristic slogans in an attempt to disrupt the prayers opposite them. Boot stomps and raised fists slashed through the night, promising no peace for anyone.

David's photos and videos captured the contrasts and contradictions implicit in the scene: bulky police silhouettes with their weapons and dogs morphed into the elongated shadows of monsters surrounded by ghostly candlelight with outstretched, empty, questing arms on one side and a blur of angry motion threatening them from the other.

As she glanced over his shoulder to the screen, she realized he wasn't favoring one side or the other—or the third, if you counted the law enforcement presence—but rather offering insights into the paradox of democratic protest where everyone had the right to express their opinion but that did not mean that anyone was actually in the right.

*Freedom is the right to hate,* her grandfather's words sounded in her head as David became engulfed by the crowd, swallowed whole when a group of young skinheads surged toward the police barricades. For a moment she panicked until she saw him talking to a trio of middle-aged women on the edge of the fray: two white, one black, holding a Blue Lives Matter banner.

Leave it to David to calmly stroll past a bunch of hopped-up racists and find an island of sanity in the middle of this chaos, she thought as she joined him, still holding the pizzas. She offered some to the women, letting David do his work.

"I remember you from when you were on TV," one of the women gushed. "Before—"

"The IED," David finished for her. "You're all wives of police officers?"

"Terri and me, our husbands are on the force in Philly," one of the women gestured to herself and the woman beside her, "but Marianne, her husband was killed. Last year."

"I'm so sorry," David told the woman, his body language doing all the work of expressing his emotions. "What happened?"

"It was a lot like the case here. Foot chase, ended when

there was nowhere left to run, and the kid—he was only fifteen—he shot my Tyrone. Tyrone had his weapon drawn, but never got a shot off. I think maybe he was hoping, I mean the kid was just a kid, all he'd done was stole a car, I'm not even sure Tyrone knew he had a gun until it was too late." Her voice trailed off. David nodded his sympathy and waited, giving her space to collect her thoughts.

She jerked her head toward the raucous Neo-Nazis. "I want people to know that we're not racist just because we want our husbands to come home safe at night. There's big problems in this country and the answer isn't to lock up the police for doing their jobs, just like it's no good to have cops targeting black men unfairly. It starts with the kids. We need every child to have a fair chance from the beginning."

"It all starts with the schools," one of her friends put in. "You can't fund them with real estate taxes—that's true inherent bias, giving the rich kids an advantage and leaving everyone else trailing behind."

The first woman took over. "Not to mention getting the kids off the street and the guns out of their hands. We're a Second Amendment family, but there's no reason for all those kids to be running around with guns."

After they'd finished, David thanked them and they continued through the crowd. To TK's surprise, the white supremacists paid her more attention than they did David, despite his obvious Hispanic heritage. The power of video? Or maybe they didn't see him as either a threat or a challenge? He did radiate a calm certainty that made people drop their guard, want to tell him their side of things. TK watched, wishing she could learn how to do that herself.

As they wove through the crowd, David stopped to ask people from both sides of the barricades their reasons for being there. Their answers ranged as widely as their demographics. If someone had simply filmed the protesters from a distance, they would have seen only the obvious racial and political divides; David took the time to uncover the truth beneath the costumes and banners.

By the time they'd reached the other side of the town square, TK's ears echoed from the sounds of the crowd with their dueling bullhorns. It was a relief to finally move into the alley where the tall courthouse and solid police station muffled the noise.

"Looks like they're closed for the day," she said as they passed the police warehouse. "Otherwise, I'd show you the car—

it's a beauty."

"Mint condition 1949 Wayfarer," he said in reverence. "I can only imagine. Amazing that it was preserved so well."

"Dr. Madsen said it was a combination of the lack of oxygen and the constant cold temperatures at that depth. According to her, the bodies are also better preserved than she'd hoped for, given how long they were down there."

"Thought you said they were just skeletons?"

"They are. But she said many times not even skeletons will remain because the bone will be dissolved over time by the water." TK had listened closely as the professor answered her students' questions. It felt good to have the answers for once. "She thinks we might even be able to still extract DNA."

"After all this time?"

"She has a case where they were successful in finding DNA in a skeleton over two thousand years old that had been preserved in similar conditions." The door to the city offices was locked, but there was a buzzer labeled: CORONER AFTER HOURS. She pressed it and was rewarded with a click.

David held the door for her as she carried the pizza inside. The only lights came from the coroner's office. The building felt empty, their footsteps echoing with a hollow thud.

She nodded to the office door, and David pushed it open for her. They stepped into the area that had once been the former lunch counter. All of the lights were on, but the stools and microscopes had been abandoned except for one at the end manned by Madsen herself. She looked up as the door clicked behind them.

"We brought dinner," TK announced. "Where is everyone?"

"Sent them home. The mayor was just here, asked that everyone leave since they can't spare any officers to provide security until the state police arrive in the morning." She shrugged. "As if anyone would target the morgue. It's the cops pulling duty out there in the square that I feel sorry for."

"We just walked past and things were fairly quiet." TK set the pizza, now cold, on a clean section of the counter. "Dr. Marcia Madsen, this is my friend, David Ruiz. He's a reporter. I thought he could help if we need to go public with our story."

Madsen was no dummy; she knew that with TK and the Beacon Group bound by their non-disclosure agreement, she was the only public official who could break the story. After all, the coroner's office was a county position, not bound by any agreements with the town's mayor. She eyed David with suspicion.

"You can trust David," TK assured her.

"No photos of any remains," Madsen said. "It's disrespectful. Everything you see and hear here is off the record until I give you permission to use it. I get to fact-check any story before publication."

David considered her offer and nodded, extending his hand. "Deal." They shook on it. He perched on a stool and took a slice of pizza, not even grimacing at the meat slathered on top, a sign of how interested he was. "Tell me about what you're doing here."

Madsen led him through their work for the day, explaining first about the examination of the car at the quarry and then giving him the facts of what they'd found so far. She didn't downplay the gruesome details, but neither did she sensationalize them.

"There are many possibilities," she concluded. "All I can comment on now are the facts. What the true story behind them is has yet to be determined."

"That's an anthropologist's view," David challenged her. "But you're also coroner, charged with determining manner of death as well as cause. Can you give me any insights there?"

Madsen hesitated, obviously uncomfortable with making a decision without all the facts. But there was no way to get any more facts until they learned their victims' identities. Only then could TK retrace their steps, try to find out what exactly happened to them and why.

"Based on preliminary findings, I think we can rule out suicide as manner of death," Madsen told David.

"What about accidental? Hard to believe any of this, a police officer handcuffed away from the wheel of the car, three bodies with evidence of violent injuries in the trunk, could be accidental."

"The disposal of the bodies was not accidental. Nor was Officer Thomson's death. I need to finish my examination of the other bodies in order to better establish the cause of their injuries. But," she added before David could interject, "I am leaning toward homicide as the manner of death."

TK jumped into the fray. "You said, 'Officer Thomson.' Does that mean you've definitively established his identity? Did you find family? It's much too quick to compare DNA."

"Your partner Wash couldn't find any living relatives, so we don't have any DNA to compare. But, the computer facial recognition software finished its analysis right before you got here. Want to see?"

"Yes, please." They followed her into a small office area constructed between the lunch counter and the old kitchen. Probably an old storage pantry, TK thought. There, a large computer monitor showed one of the photos TK and Grayson had found of Officer Thomson. Beside it was a computerized version of a man's face—even without the fine detail of a real-life photograph, it appeared virtually identical to Thomson's image.

"This computer recreation comes directly from the skull we found. Watch what happens when I overlap it with Thomson's photo, using fixed physiologic reference points." Madsen leaned over the keyboard and the two images merged, matching perfectly. Then she dissolved the computer re-creation so that it was the actual skull on the screen, still matching with Thomson's photo.

"It is him," TK breathed.

"Without dental records or DNA, it's the closest I can come to a definitive identification."

"How did he die?" David asked.

"My current working hypothesis is that he was still alive when placed into the car and secured."

"He was alive? When the car went off the cliff and into

the water?" TK closed her eyes for a moment, unable to block her imagination as she visualized Thomson's death.

"Unfortunately, all my findings indicate that. I was hoping for his sake to be proven wrong."

"And the others?" TK asked. "Do you still think they might have been victims of a lynching?"

"I never used that term," Madsen corrected in a prim tone. "There have been only two documented cases of extrajudicial mob violence in Pennsylvania history. The last was in 1911 in Coatesville."

David snorted at her academic recitation. "Excuse me, doctor, but I'm from Texas. Hate to say it, but lynch mobs have been alive and well throughout American history. I don't think it's safe to assume Pennsylvania is above the rest of the nation."

"What happened in 1911?" TK asked, surprised that there had been a lynching north of the Mason-Dixon line so recently.

Madsen's mouth twisted in distaste. "An intoxicated black man was in a brawl that an off-duty policeman attempted to disrupt. He shot the policeman during the scuffle. A mob of some three thousand people, including many who were led by their ministers directly from church services, gathered to drag him through the streets and burn him alive. They turned the scene into a spectacle, men, women, and children watching, waiting for his remains to cool enough for them to take fragments of bones as souvenirs."

They were all silent for a moment. TK's mind went to the scenes of religious violence she'd witnessed in Iraq and Afghanistan. She'd felt so superior, so civilized, as if being American protected her from that kind of mob mentality—how wrong she was. Could the people in the Dodge have been victims of similar mindless violence?

"But to conceal a crime like this for over sixty years?" she argued. "How could they keep it quiet for so long? If it was a mob who killed them, wouldn't someone have talked?"

"Maybe their conscience weighed on them," Madsen answered, for once speaking in human terms rather than scientific facts. "Especially with a police officer, someone charged with protecting the town, involved?" She shrugged. "We may never know."

TK couldn't accept that. "No. We'll know. Give me time. I'm not going to let those people be erased from history. The truth is coming out whether the town of Greer likes it or not."

Madsen appeared doubtful, while David flashed TK a smile. Then he turned back to the doctor. "Can I see the car and take photos of it? Not to be released until you decide to go public, of course."

She considered that. "Wait here while I cover the remains in the back room. Then I'll take you through to the car."

Madsen left and TK turned to David. "Knew you two would hit it off."

"I like her, but she's a bit naive, thinking there are no lynchings happening anymore."

"I thought reporters are supposed to be objective."

"Objective doesn't mean blind." He gestured to himself. "Hispanic male growing up in Texas, the things I've—"

The building shuddered as the roar of an explosion threw them both to the ground, devouring his words.

# CHAPTER 25

MORE EXPLOSIONS FOLLOWED, booms and bangs and strange cracks splitting the air—and the walls. Projectiles splintered through the glass and plaster, dust and smoke filling the room.

Missiles? RPGs? TK's mind tried to catalogue the strange sounds and shapes even as she did the only thing she could: throw herself on top of David and roll them both beneath the desk, the only cover available.

The lights flickered and died, leaving them in darkness. She took solace in David's hand finding hers, squeezing tight as they cowered under the onslaught of the barrage.

Projectiles shrieked through the air above them, piercing walls, streaming smoke and in some cases strangely colored sparks. Her vision ghosted with scenes from the war, but this was nothing like that. There, she'd always felt some semblance of control, a sense that she had the power to take action, protect herself and her team. Here, she felt helpless.

TK had never taken fire from ordnance like this. The initial blast quieted, but now multiple explosions sounded all around—some large thunderclaps of sound, others whizzes and cracks. It was only after one spun through the partially demolished wall and hurled itself onto the floor, spinning like a top with a violent splash of color that she realized: they weren't under attack. It was the damn fireworks. Somehow they'd caught fire and exploded.

Bad news, because fireworks were just as deadly as any ordnance but also extremely unpredictable.

She dared to inch out from beyond the desk's shelter, David trying to pull her back to safety. Shaking free of his grasp, she crouched, straining to see if there was any sign of Madsen. The wall that separated the autopsy area where the doctor had gone and the office where she and David sheltered was mostly gone, a pile of sheetrock and splintered wood all that remained.

"Wait here," she shouted at David even though only inches separated them. She wasn't sure if he could hear—her own words didn't make it past the roaring that filled her ears.

The barrage had slowed, but she didn't count on it stopping. Probably merely a short respite while the fire burned through the wood of the next crate. Should she try to get David out? It would mean abandoning Madsen.

Small blazes dotted the otherwise dark space of the morgue. No signs of movement, no sounds of life.

A thick lab manual had fallen to the ground, its pages rippling with flames but the binding was still intact. TK carefully grabbed the makeshift torch and tossed it over the remnants of the wall to illuminate the space beyond. "Madsen!"

Coughing and squinting through the smoke, she made out stark, splintered remains of bone mixed with steel. Burnt building materials, a puddle of chemicals that blazed with a blue flame, and a woman's body, twisted, one leg splayed out at an impossible angle, her back to TK.

"Madsen," she shouted again, but there was no response, not even when the flammable liquid licked at the coroner's sleeve, giving her white lab coat a ghostly sheen.

TK braced the unstable debris, ready to climb over it when the flames illuminated a woman's face. Impaled by a length of rebar from the outer wall that had taken the brunt of the blast, and nowhere near the rest of Madsen's body.

TK choked on tears and smoke, letting herself slide back down the debris to the floor. As she crawled back to David, the world splintered with another barrage of explosions, collapsing part of the ceiling.

David grabbed her, rolling her back under the desk. She cursed him for leaving shelter to come after her, but then he cried out in pain, collapsing short of the cover the metal desk provided. Fighting through the sheetrock and ceiling tiles, she lunged for him. His leg had taken a direct hit from a piece of shelving falling through the ceiling.

She fought at the splintered wood that covered his leg until she was finally able to push it off him. There was no blood, but his leg was twisted to an unnatural angle.

Thankfully she couldn't hear his cries of agony as she dragged him back under the desk. He collapsed in her arms, and they huddled together, TK protecting him with her body as hell rained down on top of them.

# Chapter 26

IT WAS ALMOST eight by the time Lucy and Valencia reached Beacon Falls. She'd planned to simply drop Valencia off but then decided it wouldn't hurt to update herself on TK's case before she headed to Greer in the morning.

As she and Valencia climbed the steps to the second floor where Lucy's team had their workspace, she was surprised to see the lights on in the conference room.

"Why are you working so late?" she asked Wash, their technical analyst.

He was at his usual place in front of his computers, but he wasn't tapping keys or swiping touchpads. Instead, he sat extraordinarily still—at least extraordinary for Wash, usually a study in perpetual motion—his wheelchair frozen in place as he listened through his headphones.

Something was wrong, Lucy could feel it. She rushed to look over his shoulder, expecting to find him on a video call with TK. Instead, his screens were blank except for one lonely tab opened to a website that hosted live police scanners.

"What happened?" Valencia asked, joining them. She had her phone out. "I can't reach TK."

Wash finally acknowledged their presence, his face stricken. "There was an explosion. And fire."

"Where?"

"Greer. At the garage where the car they found was housed."

"Doesn't mean TK was there," Lucy said. "Did you try her hotel?" She grabbed her own phone and dialed David Ruiz. There was a good chance he was with TK. No answer—it didn't even ring through to voicemail.

"She's not at the hotel, she's not anywhere that I can find her. The explosion—there were fireworks in the building. The protesters at the courthouse, they panicked, ran. They're saying at least three people were trampled, dozens more injured."

"Try the detective she was working with," Lucy told Valencia who'd made the initial contact with their clients in

Greer. "Or the mayor; he should know what's going on."

"I'm trying. No one's answering." Valencia pulled a seat out from the antique dining table that served as the team's workspace. The house at Beacon Falls, Valencia's ancestral home, was filled with delicate, beautiful furniture like it. Too bad, because right now Lucy felt ready to break something.

"It was a body in an old car. Hell, you guys should have had leads on his ID narrowed down before TK ever even got to town," she muttered as she paced.

"Wasn't that easy. We couldn't find any leads on a missing man from that era before TK got there. But she still ID'd them. Well, the man, at least."

Lucy spun to him. "What do you mean at least?"

"Things kinda got a bit complicated," he said sheepishly. "Don't worry. TK had it all under control."

"Wash—"

"Complicated how?" Valencia asked, her voice encouraging instead of the "tell me before I wring your neck" tone Lucy was about to snap at him.

Wash turned to his keyboards, seemed relieved by the familiar routine. He was the youngest of Lucy's team, but in many ways, he was their guiding star, keeping them on course through investigations that often grew into tangled labyrinths. "First, they got the car out of the quarry. Then I noticed in the video they were taking before they opened it up that the guy was sitting in the passenger seat, not the driver's, and he was handcuffed to the seat."

"Handcuffed?" Lucy started but Valencia silenced her with a raised eyebrow. Handcuffed? What the hell had TK found in that quarry? Greer was nowhere near any organized crime hotspots—but maybe that made it ideal as a body dump?

"Yep," Wash continued. "And then things got weird. TK opened the trunk and found three more bodies crammed in there."

As he spoke, photos filled the large screen TV across the table from them. Gruesome images of skeletal remains coated with adipocere, a common part of the decomposition process when a body was immersed in water. Lucy glanced at Valencia, but the older woman was taking the images in stride.

"TK identified the guy in the passenger seat as a Greer police officer, Archibald Thomson. No record of his disappearance. Best we could narrow it down, he collected his paycheck in April, 1954 but not in May." Photos of a man in uniform appeared. First, as a soldier in the Second World War, then as a police officer. He looked straight at the camera, his face creaseless, someone more excited than fearful of the future.

Then Wash put up photos of a skull and superimposed it over Thomson's images. "This is what Dr. Madsen, the county coroner, was working on when I lost touch with her. We were running computer facial reconstruction algorithms on the victims' skulls. Thomson was an easy match because we had photos we could use."

"What about the victims from the trunk?" Lucy asked.

Why hadn't TK called for help when she'd realized she was in over her head? No need to answer. If she knew TK, the former Marine hadn't believed she was in trouble or needed help. Guess Lucy couldn't fault her too much. After all, the case was sixty-some years old, no urgency.

No urgency. Yet here she was, edging toward the door, her gut clenched with a need to be there, *now*. Silly impulse. There was no help she could offer during a mass casualty response; she'd be more likely to get in the way of first responders. Still...she couldn't deny her sense of urgency.

Wash distracted her by sending photos of three skulls to the screen. "It takes longer when the computer has no photos to compare with, has to start from scratch. Basically it loads tissue thickness just like a forensic sculptor would, building a face from the bone out."

As he spoke, the faces slowly began to take shape. An African-American man, woman, and boy stared out at Lucy and Valencia. "That's as far as we can go for now. Dr. Madsen is going to examine the bones, try to find more distinguishing details."

"A family?" Lucy was surprised. "And the car came from DC? So, if the police officer was from Greer, maybe the family was visiting someone there as well?"

Wash shook his head. "No missing persons reported match their description from either DC or the entire state of Pennsylvania. Not for the three people in the trunk or Officer Thomson. At least nothing that made it into the databases or the records TK could find in Greer." He shrugged. "Small towns, even big cities, sixty years ago..."

"No computers, you're talking hand-written police blotters and paper reports," Lucy said.

"*If* they were even reported missing," Valencia put in. Both Wash and Lucy stared at her. "You're both too young to remember how things were back then—I was just a girl myself, but if you were black and in trouble, you could vanish without anyone reporting it."

"An entire family? I mean, we're not talking criminals on the run here," Lucy protested.

Valencia shrugged. "If you got the wrong people after you and yours, it was easier to disappear, start over fresh. But also easier—"

"For someone else to kill you, and your loved ones would be too intimidated to report it to the authorities," Lucy finished for her. She frowned at the photos on the screen, unable to abandon her previous argument. "But an entire family? Why would anyone want to kill an entire family?"

"Not to mention a police officer," Wash added. "How'd they get away with that?"

Lucy had had enough of speculation. "Only one place to find the answers. I'm headed to Greer. Call me right away if you hear anything from TK."

# Chapter 27

TIME LOST ALL meaning as the fireworks continued their bombardment. TK's hearing became useless, and every time she closed her eyes, flashes of bright color stabbed at her vision. Smoke choked her, sulfur and black powder, burning like hellfire.

All she could rely on was her sense of touch, gripping David tight. Then the rain began. Lashing, driving rain coming from all directions. Until finally a man's arms pulled her away from David, and she realized it wasn't rain at all, it was pressurized water from a fire hose.

Everything became a blur. At first she fought, until she was certain they weren't abandoning David. Then she was out of the building, random fireworks still whizzing and blaring across the night sky.

The firemen carried her to the town square. The barricades had fallen, splintered on the ground. People from both sides of the protest, some crying, some with blood on their faces, staggered through the space in front of the courthouse where the night was crisscrossed by the lights of police and fire trucks. Others huddled on the grass of the town square, once so pristine and manicured, now torn up as if it had suffered a stampede.

From the shocked looks and the ambulances streaming back and forth, people being helped into the back of any vehicle available, taken away, she realized that the crowd must have run for their lives when the explosions began.

As her hearing slowly returned, she heard someone say that people were dead. A part of her wondered where they would put the bodies now that the morgue was destroyed—that was the part of her that couldn't decide between hysterical laughter or uncontrollable tears.

Then they carried David out on a stretcher. She pushed away from the medic trying to force oxygen on her, losing most of the bandages he'd applied to her assorted burns and lacerations. They were nothing compared to the anguish that cast David's face into a mask of pain.

She ran to him, grabbing his hand and refusing to let go until she was with him in the ambulance. One leg was twisted, shorter than the other, and he howled as they attached a splint and ratcheted it like a medieval torture device. She almost hauled off and hit one of the paramedics, but then David's morphine kicked in and he fell back, blissfully unconscious.

The rest of the night was a blur. The hospital over the mountain in Altoona went into disaster mode as the casualties swarmed their ER.

TK blocked out everything except David, allowing herself to be separated from him only when the orthopedic surgeon took him away to operate on.

She sat stunned until a kind nurse took pity on her, cleaned and dressed her wounds, got her cleared by a doctor, and put her in David's room to wait. She even let TK keep her weapons, although it was against hospital policy, once TK explained who she was and showed her carry permit. Good thing her wallet and phone had been in her pockets. She'd lost her computer in the carnage along with everything in her messenger bag.

Finally, they wheeled David back in, now on a large bed,

one leg swathed and placed on a machine that kept it elevated. He was asleep, his body wired with monitors and IV tubing. The nurse assured her he was fine, so TK had scraped her chair close enough to take his hand in hers and did what any good soldier did after the battle was done and there was nothing left to do except prepare for the next one. She slept.

When she woke the next morning, it was to the irritating beep of a monitor, the invigorating scent of coffee, and the intriguing sound of Wash's voice. "I know, you gotta love amateur enthusiasts, right? They come through every time."

TK pried her eyes open. David sat upright in bed, his laptop—the source of Wash's voice—open on a table. Before she could say anything, or find her voice through the scratchy, smoke-scented, sleep-thickened cotton that filled her mouth, Lucy walked through the door, carrying two cups of coffee in a cardboard carryout box along with a white bag stained with grease.

"Morning," she said, setting the bag onto the windowsill and handing TK a cup of coffee. "You doing okay?"

TK took a sip of coffee. "I am now. David, are you all right?"

"Yep," he said absently, peering at his computer screen.

He held up a small button attached to a wire. "They let me regulate my own pain meds. All I have to do is push."

His tone was much too mellow—didn't he realize how close they'd come to dying?

She blamed it on the hit of caffeine as she bounced out of her chair, the events of the night pummeling her. "You're not pushing yourself too hard, are you? Why are you talking with Wash? You just had surgery—Wash, he just had surgery!"

All eyes pivoted to TK—including Wash's through the webcam. She clapped a hand over her mouth. "Oh, my God, I think I'm channeling my granny's ghost."

"Even your West Virginia hillbilly twang got worse. Did you hear it? You called me 'Warsh.' I was waiting for you to say something like holler or ain't." Wash laughed.

"Yeah, you all," she purposefully clipped it into two distinct words, "can just forget that ever happened."

"Right, like that's gonna happen," Wash answered. "Don't worry about David—he's already had a free consultation with Tommy."

"Not that he was acting like a child," Tommy put in from off screen. As the Beacon Group's resident MD, the former ER pediatrician was their go-to for all things medical. "Valencia is here, too."

"Good morning." Valencia's face tilted in above Wash's shoulder. "Tell her the good news, Wash."

"Right. Well, thanks to the fact that Washington DC totally changed their license plate design in 1953, and a search of Mopar along with several classic car databases that narrowed the original car dealer to one in Alexandria, Virginia who happened to specialize in selling cars to African-Americans—a niche customer base back then—"

Wash paused for breath and David took over. "And my suggesting he reach out to vintage car aficionados as well as searching the personal columns of the DC black dailies from May, 1954...we think we've found your victims."

"I still need to confirm them," Wash put in. "Hopefully the facial reconstruction software will give us enough to make a positive ID, but it's a solid lead."

TK was barely listening; she was too busy searching David's face. He was lit with excitement, no pain that she could see, despite his leg and the multiple smaller lacerations and superficial burns that matched her own.

She shifted her weight, releasing a new wave of aches and pains and wished she also had access to a magic button that whisked pain away. But really, most of what she felt was sheer relief. They'd been lucky...so very lucky.

For a moment, the image of Madsen's decapitated head filled her vision, but it was quickly replaced as Wash filled the computer screen with the breadcrumbs he and David had followed. "And here they are...the Mann family. Last seen leaving Cleveland on May 17, 1954, headed back home to Washington DC. Father was a surgeon, mother a schoolteacher. Neither was ever seen again. Or their four-year-old little girl, Maybelle."

That caught her attention. "Dr. Madsen said it was a boy in the trunk with the two adults. She thought from the size of his skeleton he was at least ten to thirteen years old."

Wash's face reappeared. "Sorry, I couldn't find anything about a boy. Maybe he was a hitchhiker they picked up?"

"But then where is Maybelle Mann?" Lucy asked. She'd been so quiet, TK had almost forgotten she was there. "She'd be in her late sixties now, if she's still alive."

"Wait," TK said, her mind still cloudy. She took another gulp of coffee. "Are you saying we might actually have a witness?"

"We won't know what we have until we find her." Lucy's

tone was somber, but it did little to erase the grin from Wash's face.

"Don't worry, boss. I'm on it."

"Me, too," David added. "Seeing as I'm kind of worthless for much of anything else."

TK bent down to kiss his forehead. "Not to me you aren't," she whispered. "I kinda like you tied to a bed."

His blush was her reward. Before she could say anything more to totally embarrass him, her phone rang. She was amazed it still worked after the beating it had taken last night, gave credit to the waterproof, supposedly unbreakable case she'd invested in.

"TK, are you all right?" Grayson's voice was hushed, almost reverential. As if he'd expected her to be dead or something. "What were you doing there? That building was supposed to be empty."

"I'm fine, Grayson. Good morning to you."

"Hey, so, my grandfather asked me to call."

"The judge?"

"Yeah. He wants to see you. Says it's about the case. That he remembered something from around the time the car would have gone into the quarry."

Interesting that the old man hadn't said anything yesterday when they'd met in the mayor's office. But even then, she'd had the feeling that Philip Greer had known more than he'd let on in front of his son and grandson. "What's his address?"

"Oh, I'm happy to drive—"

"No problems, just text me his info. I can make it there in half an hour." She wrinkled her nose as she realized that the stench of smoke and sulfur that she couldn't shake came from her own scorched and stained clothing. "Well, maybe—"

Lucy grabbed TK's rucksack from the floor and held it before her. She must have retrieved it from the hotel in Greer. TK nodded her gratitude, the thought of a hot shower too tempting to ignore. "No, strike that. We'll be there in forty-five minutes. Thanks, Grayson."

# CHAPTER 28

LUCY DROVE—Lucy always drove, but TK was okay with that; she liked being free to scan her environment.

They took the interstate from Altoona to Bald Eagle and then hit the back roads that wound around the mountains to Greer. TK navigated them to the address Grayson had supplied. Turned out it was on the river, between the quarry and the college, an elegant white colonial with enough square footage to definitely qualify as a mansion.

"Imagine growing up here," TK said as they exited the vehicle.

The front yard stretched out wide as a football field. The house stood at the fifty-yard line with a view of the river sweeping through the forests and down past the town.

"The first Greer had his iron forge and trading post on a river landing decades before the American Revolution," Lucy told her as they hiked up the front walk. "I wonder if that was near here. House looks at least a hundred years old."

"One hundred and fifty, give or take," a man's voice called to them from the front door. Judge Philip Greer stood waiting for them, dressed in a nicely fitted suit complete with vest and tie. His only concession to his retirement seemed to be his shoes, a pair of comfortable crepe-soled lace-ups suitable for the office or a quick hike on a trail.

As they joined him on the front porch that had more square footage than TK's entire apartment, he gestured to a tree-lined path leading to the river. "We've kept the original log cabin and forge as intact as possible. Teachers bring school children on field trips to see it."

He smiled at them each in turn, then led the way inside. The foyer was adorned with paintings of Greers, some of them life-sized. They crossed through a formal living room decorated with antiques and then reached the doors to what was obviously the judge's private study. Here the furniture was more comfortable and showed actual use. The decor consisted of hunting trophies including an elk, moose, bear, and a twelve-point buck.

"My first kill," he said proudly. "I was eight." There was a gun case in the corner and over the fireplace were photos of generations of Greer men hunting as well as pictures of the judge and the mayor in military uniforms, carrying sniper rifles. "Greer family tradition," he said, noticing TK's interest in the photos of her fellow Marines. "Too bad Grayson never served. First male Greer not to see combat since the Civil War."

He gestured to them to sit. TK chose an overstuffed chair while Lucy remained standing, slightly to one side and behind the judge. Handing the conversational baton off to TK.

"Thank you for coming," the judge said in a formal tone. "Ms. O'Connor, I understand you were caught in the blast. Are you all right?"

"I'm fine. Just a few bumps and bruises. Dr. Madsen wasn't so lucky."

He nodded sorrowfully. "I know. JR told me her students are already planning a memorial." He paced away from them, his steps heavy on the plush carpet. "This is very difficult for me. Maybe I should have said something sooner, but I'm not sure that it would have been helpful anyway."

"What is it, Judge Greer?"

He pivoted and leaned against the window, the morning sun highlighting every line of his face and glinting against the white in his hair. "The policeman, Officer Thomson. Do you know...was he gut shot?"

TK exchanged a look with Lucy. "I'm not sure. Dr. Madsen hadn't yet found any evidence of injury other than his broken arm, where he was handcuffed to the car."

"Handcuffed?" He blinked at that, his posture slumping. For a moment she thought he was going to collapse.

TK stood, stepped forward and reached for his arm. "Maybe you should sit down, sir?"

He let her guide him to the nearest chair. "Thank you. I'm fine now. Thank you."

"What makes you think Officer Thomson might have been gut shot?" Lucy asked, her tone crisp and official.

"I think my father might have seen it happen." He licked his lips.

TK spotted a decanter of water on a side table along with some glasses. As she poured, she realized that they were made of crystal and probably cost more than she made in a year. He drank eagerly, then handed her back the glass. She perched on the corner of the chair nearest to him while Lucy remained standing in the background. Lucy was playing bad cop to her own good cop, but it seemed so unnecessary. It was obvious the judge wanted to help them.

"I was just a kid," he started. "Don't know anything about what exactly happened. But I still remember that time. How awful it was—people marching and shouting. There was a labor dispute at the paper mill. The Negroes wanted the same pay as the white men. But they didn't do the same work, so Daddy—my father—wouldn't give it to them."

"A labor dispute left four people dead?" Lucy asked.

The judge shuddered at her words. "I don't know. I remember there was a riot—I wasn't there, but I heard my mother talking, worried. She said a police officer had been shot by a Negro and that fighting had broken out. Then after my father returned home late that night, I crept out of my room to see that he was all right...he wasn't."

His voice trembled. "I'd never seen him like that. Frightened. Blood covered his shirt and pants, but it wasn't his. I couldn't hear everything. But I heard him say Archie was gut shot. I knew Archie was Officer Thomson. Then he said something about the pain being so bad they had to restrain him while they were trying to get him to a doctor." He glanced up.

"Perhaps that was your handcuffs?"

"Maybe," Lucy conceded. "But why would they transport him in a civilian vehicle instead of a police car? And how did that car end up in the quarry?"

"I'm sorry. I don't know. I remember that night and the next day being filled with worry. School was canceled, kids locked up in their homes with their mothers, shotguns brought out of closets. My father said the Negroes were rioting, that he and the other men had to stop them before they destroyed the town and killed anyone else. He changed clothes and left again that same night, didn't return for two days. My mom cried the entire time, she was so scared he'd never come home."

"And he never said more about what happened?" TK asked.

"No. Refused to talk about it. None of my friends' fathers would talk about it either. I remember the minister's sermon— don't remember what he said, but I remember church that next Sunday, and about all the women and half the men were in tears. Back on the town square there were places where you could tell there'd been fires set and windows were busted on the police station, but other than that, everything looked normal. But it wasn't normal, nowhere near normal—even a kid could see that.

People walked around town, their lips tight, nodding to each other but not talking, not like usual. And the blacks—a lot of them moved away, never to be seen again."

He shook his head. "It was the worst time of my life. When you see your parents decimated to empty husks, filled with fear, it changes a child. Changes them forever. My father, he was never the same after that."

"Did Officer Thomson have any family? Do you remember if there was maybe an obituary in the newspaper? Anything that might give us more information?"

"Newspaper back then was the *Greer Gazette*, came out once a week. Not even sure if the *Gazette* went to press that week—my father probably had all his men out helping the police with the riots. That's how it was done back then. You took care of your town, didn't call in outsiders like the way they handle things today."

He leaned back, his gaze searching the photos on the mantle. "I remember Officer Thomson. He was a nice guy. When it snowed he limped—said it was from getting shot somewhere in Italy during the war. Didn't have any family, no wife or kids. The single women used to swarm all over him at church socials, act like a man couldn't be relied upon to feed himself, living alone like that." He smiled. "I remember thinking—I was only thirteen, fourteen at the time, just starting to wonder about girls—and I remember thinking how nice it'd be if some of those ladies treated me as nice."

He glanced up. "Sorry. I think that's all I remember. It wasn't anything we ever spoke about, you understand?"

"Maybe your father kept records? A journal?" Lucy asked. "With all his business interests, he probably lost money during the riots or had to pay overtime for his men to provide extra security?"

"He probably did keep records—he was a much better businessman than I ever was. But they're all gone. Back in 1972, Hurricane Agnes flooded the whole town. Anyone who kept anything down in a basement or cellar, sometimes even the first floor for houses near the river like this one, it would have been destroyed. All I know is when I went through his papers after he died there wasn't anything from back then. Sorry." He spread his hands wide. "I wish I could be more help."

TK stood and joined Lucy. The judge made a feeble attempt to rise, bracing his hands against the arms of his chair but then fell back again.

"I can't believe this nightmare has returned to haunt us

after so long," he said. "This town needs time to heal, now more than ever. Rather than having memories of a long-ago scandal dragging us into the limelight."

For the first time, TK detected a note of insincerity. Was this all an act? Designed to convince them that there were no more leads to follow, maybe even get them to give up on the case? Without any physical evidence remaining, his story made for an easy explanation. All they had to do was accept it and walk away.

Lucy caught TK's gaze and gave a small nod. TK turned back to the judge. "Oh, I almost forgot. Have you ever heard of a family named Mann? A doctor and his wife and their little girl? They were from Washington, DC but may have been visiting here."

"Mann? No, I never met a doctor or anyone with that name. Why?"

"Because the doctor and his wife were two of the other victims in the car, along with Officer Thomson. We're off to talk with their daughter, now. Apparently, she saw everything that happened."

The last was a bold-faced lie, of course, but well worth it to see the way all the blood drained from the old man's face.

# Chapter 29

THE DANK MOLD of the courthouse basement made Winnie want to sneeze. Even though she knew there was no way the men outside could hear her through the brick walls, it felt much too dangerous. Maybelle clung to her hand, muffled tears her only sound.

"It's gonna be all right," Winnie whispered as they navigated through the shelves stuffed with papers, the single bare light bulb casting more shadows than it dispersed. "You'll see. Everyone's gonna be just fine."

Her words were more to comfort herself than the little girl she was suddenly responsible for. None of this would have happened if not for Winnie. She had to find a way to make everything right.

They reached the stairs leading up to the courthouse. Crept up them slowly, wincing with every creak and sigh the wood made. Until finally they reached the door at the top. Winnie pressed her ear against it and listened. All she could hear was Maybelle's anxious panting and her own heart pounding. Good enough. She slid the key into the lock and turned it. Then, biting her lower lip without even being aware that she did it until she drew fresh blood from the cut left by her father's slap, she opened the door.

The lights were out, but the courthouse's large windows were more than enough to illuminate the corridor, the late afternoon sunshine reflecting from the tan marble floor.

"Let me see if it's clear." Winnie tried to pull her hand free of Maybelle's, but the little girl held on tight as they walked together to the window at the end of the hall, hugging the shadows on the one side of the corridor. The windowsill was deep, and a bench stood before it. This was the front side of the courthouse, the side that faced the town square.

She lifted the girl up onto the bench then climbed up herself. The windows soared high overhead, but the sun was setting, leaving a shadow cast on this side of the building, hiding them from sight. At least she hoped the shadows were enough.

Just to be sure, she moved Maybelle down to the far corner where the fancy woodwork along the window frame created a recess.

The men weren't gone. In fact, now that day shift at the mill had ended, there were even more of them—seemed like everyone her father had ever met was standing, hollering at the police station. Including Philip's father, Mr. Greer, who was the mayor and owned the quarry and the paper mill and most everything else worth owning around here. He didn't stand at the front with the rest, she noted. Instead, he sat inside his fancy car behind his driver, window rolled down so he could watch and whisper instructions to a man in a suit at the rear of the crowd.

The man nodded and moved quickly through the crowd, other men pausing in their shouts to listen and bow their heads. After he finished whispering to them, they'd raise their faces once more with new gleams in their eyes. Then the first rock came. Followed quickly by others.

Mr. Greer didn't smile, but he seemed mighty pleased as the rocks shattered the plate glass at the front of the police station. The men with him were the same ones she'd seen in the alley, taking Maybelle's mother. But she couldn't see the doctor's wife anywhere—maybe she was in the car? No, Mr. Greer would never let a colored woman in his fancy car. Maybe they'd taken her somewhere else?

Winnie had heard talk of the immigrants and Negroes trying to form some kind of union—stealing money and food from the mouths of the white workers who'd been here first, her dad complained. She had a feeling that maybe this mob with their angry fists and rocks had to do with something much, much larger than a colored boy helping a white girl escape a beating from her father.

She clung to the idea, hoping it would ease the stab of guilt, but of course it didn't. All she could think of was Henry's busted face. The faces of the men below were almost as devastated, red not with blood but with rage that twisted them until they were almost unrecognizable as human.

"Give us the boy," her father, emboldened by the mob behind him shouted. She'd never before seen him stand so proud and tall. As if he was a different man. A stranger she'd never met.

"We'll come in after him!"

"Teach him a lesson."

"Him and all the Negroes. Need to learn their place!"

The shouts, accompanied by insults and slurs she'd rarely heard before in private much less ever in public, grew with a vengeance. More rocks flew, more glass shattered, sparkling ruby red in the bloody sunset, until suddenly the crowd hushed and took a step back.

Winnie craned her neck to search the area in front of the police station. Officer Thomson stepped out to the edge of the stoop that adjoined the courthouse stairs. He carried a shotgun, holding it with casual knowledge of a soldier accustomed to violence. For a moment, her heart steadied, and she was able to draw a breath unfettered by fear. Officer Thomson was in charge, not the mob. He'd take care of things, make sure no one else got hurt.

"Time for you all to go home to your dinners, don't you think?" he asked as he stared down the crowd, seemingly searching out and meeting each of their gazes. "Law's the law, and we've got this under control."

His voice was calm, not rushed. As if chatting with the men who liked to stand around outside the barbershop on Saturday mornings. Most of those men, including her father, were among the crowd. "Send Mrs. Mann back inside with me, and we'll all call it a night."

But then she saw something that Officer Thomson was blind to, given that her window was much higher than where he stood. Mr. Greer leaned his head out of his car window and beckoned to the man in the suit, who went over to where a truck had just pulled up behind the car. He and two men in overalls took something from the truck bed and then divided up.

She lost the other two in the gathering dusk that had darkened the square to the purple of a fresh bruise. But the man in the suit she could see as he leapt up to the base of the gazebo. Sidling behind one of the supports so that all she could make out was the barrel of a rifle. Aimed at Officer Thomson.

She was too far to shout a warning—and too late, as the shot cracked like man-made thunder, followed by two more. Then more from the crowd, although the few pistols and rifles she spied were aimed up to the sky.

The crowd surged forward, cheering and jeering, not seeming to notice as Office Thomson stumbled back, one hand trying to raise his shotgun, the other flailing for support. It wasn't until he suddenly sat down, legs collapsing beneath him, that she spotted the dark stain on his uniform shirt. Gut shot.

Maybelle gasped as her father ran out of the police station, kneeling to tend to Officer Thomson. "Daddy!"

Then the mob was on him, a mass of arms and bodies lunging and grasping and tearing him away.

Another shot sounded, then another, muffled by the crowd—not coming from the man in the suit, she noted with a quick flick of her gaze. He'd vanished. So had Mr. Greer. Driven away to his big house with his fancy china and gourmet dinner.

Then the men—bent over so they no longer appeared as men, but rather hungry beasts surging to tear at their prey before the other wild animals could steal it away—rushed into the police station and emerged, dragging Henry with them.

Within a blink, the mob had devoured him like they had Maybelle's father. She could see movement as the crowd dragged their prey into the town square, but she couldn't see Henry or Dr. Mann at all as the other men's bodies surged over them.

Only Officer Thomson remained behind on the police station's stoop. One hand pressed against his belly, blood staining his fingers. And all he could do was watch, helpless.

Winnie tugged Maybelle off the bench and pulled the girl face first, tight against her, wrapping her arms around her as they huddled out of sight of the nightmare horror beyond the window. She held her hands over Maybelle's ears, trying to shelter the girl from the screams, but there was no way she could protect herself.

"Don't worry," she crooned, as much for herself as for the stunned little girl who whimpered with terror. "I'll keep you safe. I promise. Nothing's gonna happen to you. I promise."

A shout of triumph rattled the window as flames blossomed below the courthouse steps.

# CHAPTER 30

"THINK I WAS TOO OBVIOUS?" TK asked Lucy as they walked back to the Subaru.

"I think he was too worried to suspect anything. Sure as hell spooked him with Maybelle's name."

"That or the idea that she saw everything."

Lucy opened her door. "Yeah, that might have been pushing it a bit too far. Especially given that we have no idea where Maybelle is. Or if she was even there. Wash still needs to confirm her parents' IDs."

TK got into the passenger seat, wincing a bit as her weight dropped.

"Sure you're okay?" Lucy asked. "You got pretty banged up last night."

"I'm fine. But speaking of last night, I want to call David, make sure he's not pushing himself too hard."

"He put on a good show for you this morning, but I guarantee he'll be napping most of the day. That is, when the nurses and doctors and x-ray techs and lunch ladies aren't waking him up."

"Right. I forgot, you went through the same thing with your leg."

Lucy grimaced. Almost losing her leg after a dog mauled it and then struggling with infection, muscle loss, and now permanent nerve damage wasn't quite the same as a simple break repaired by a few plates, but TK didn't know that. "He'll be fine. A few weeks on crutches then a few of rehab and he'll be good as new. I can give you the names of good people in Pittsburgh if he wants to move up from Baltimore, let you take care of him."

To her surprise, TK actually gave her offer some consideration. "I'd be fine with that. And he can do his job from almost anywhere as long as there's WiFi. But how can we convince him?"

We? Suddenly TK's love life was dependent on Lucy? Exactly what she'd been hoping to avoid. "Best person I know, can talk anyone into anything? Valencia. Put her on his case and he won't know what hit him."

TK smiled. "You're right. That's a perfect plan." She slid her phone out, but before she could place a call, Lucy's phone rang through on the car speaker.

"Guardino."

"It's Wash. Guess who I found?" His voice was jumping with excitement. "Or rather who found us."

"You found Maybelle Mann?" Lucy said. "So soon?"

"Well, to be honest, like I said, she found us. Remember I told you about all those vintage car enthusiasts? And my posting photos of the Wayfarer on their sites asking for more info? Turns out Maybelle is a regular visitor to several of them—has alerts set up for any mention of a 1949 Dodge Wayfarer. She's spent most of her adult life searching for her dad's car, it's one of the few clear memories she had left of her family."

"Really? So where is she? When can we talk with her?" TK asked, leaning forward and practically shouting into the speaker.

"She's here. Well, not, here, here, like in Beacon Falls. More like there—not far from you guys. She's a professor at Penn State and head of their campus ministry. She's a religious studies scholar—has published several books under the name she goes by now, Henrietta Mann Rawling. But it's her, everything checks out, she's Maybelle Henrietta Mann."

Lucy pulled into a left-hand turn lane, preparing to make a U-turn. State College was only forty minutes away. "We're on our way."

"Hang on. You need to drop TK off first. Guess the mayor's son has been trying to reach you?"

"I've been ignoring him," TK said. "Why, what's up? Is he pissed we talked to his grandfather without him?"

"I'm not sure if he's pissed, but Mayor Greer sure is. He called here, said he needs to see you in his office right away."

"Thanks, Wash," Lucy answered before TK could let out the expletive she knew was building inside the younger woman. "Text me Maybelle's info and let her know I'll be there in an hour. Don't give her too many details, I'll handle that."

"Will do. Bye." He hung up.

TK twisted in her seat, her knees knocking against the dash. "You need to take me with you—if I go to the mayor's office, he's as likely to fire us as he is to do anything. The man cannot abide a whiff of scandal, not with his congressional campaign, and with Madsen dead and all our evidence destroyed, he has no reason to allow us to continue the investigation."

She paused to take a breath, and Lucy glimpsed her opening but TK started talking again before she could take it. "We have nothing: no concrete evidence, just suppositions based on computer analysis of photos that we're missing the originals of and we're missing the bones that analysis is based on—hell, we don't even have the car anymore. Please, I know this case looks hopeless, but we can't give up. Not when we're so close to maybe finding out what really happened."

"*If* Maybelle Mann actually was present at the time of the killings, and *if* she actually saw anything, and *if* she still remembers it. She was, what, four at the time?"

"So, you're giving up. My first case as lead and it's ruined." TK slumped back in her seat, reminding Lucy of Megan, her fourteen-year-old daughter.

Although Megan hadn't been almost blown up, seen her boyfriend injured and a colleague killed, so Lucy could excuse TK's whining. A bit. "I didn't say that. And this has nothing to do with you being lead. It's about finding the truth and some measure of justice for that family—don't forget Officer Thomson and that unknown boy, as well. Of course we can't give up. But we also have a contract to fulfill and a client to keep happy. Which means I'm dropping you off at the courthouse."

TK opened her mouth to protest, but this time Lucy didn't give her a chance. "And you'll entertain the mayor and his staff, jump through their hoops, see what they want and most importantly why they want it. If they want us to keep working the case but they want to control when the public learns our findings, that's one thing. If they want us to bury what we know, that's entirely different. But we need to buy some time. Can you do that, TK?"

"Ma'am, yes, ma'am," TK answered, snapping to attention until her seatbelt ratcheted her back. "Happy to play patsy and take one for the team. As long as you let me in on the final down."

"Absolutely. After all, you are lead investigator. It's your case."

# CHAPTER 31

TK NAVIGATED FOR Lucy once they reached Greer. The streets were blocked off around the town square, but past the barricades, she could see the blackened remnants of the warehouse and government center.

The old Woolworth's building had collapsed in on one side—the side closest to the warehouse where the explosions and fire had originated. Piles of brick, blackened wood, and twisted metal clawed through the space where the coroner's office had been. Puffs of smoke and ash filled the air as fire crews doused any hot spots and worked to clear the debris. The entire town smothered beneath the stench of smoke.

At the outer perimeter, they were stopped by a state trooper who had them wait in the car while he called to clear

TK's entry into the courthouse.

While they waited, a familiar figure came jogging past the barricades, waving to them. Grayson. Great, her favorite shadow puppet.

"TK, wait," he shouted.

She was tempted to tell Lucy to drive off but instead rolled down her window as he arrived at her side of the car.

"Hey there, you must be Lucy Guardino. It's so very nice to finally meet you." He thrust his hand into the car, past TK, so Lucy had no choice but to shake it. "Guess I'm coming with you then, while TK updates my father."

"Coming with me?"

"Sure. The judge called, said you had a lead on a witness? My dad wants me to go with you, record the interview, document all the pertinent details, that kind of thing."

"I can handle it, thanks." Lucy clearly thought that was the end of the discussion, but then again, she hadn't met Grayson. TK hid her smile. Rock meet immoveable object.

He opened the car door for TK, then hopped into her seat as soon as she vacated it. "No problem at all. The press conference is postponed until one, but we'll be back by then, right?"

TK grinned at Lucy, happy to share the unique burden that was Grayson. "Don't forget to show Lucy your tatts, Grayson. And tell her your ideas for urban development. Give you two something to chat about on your way there."

The state trooper waved her through the barricade. TK in turn waved to Lucy and Grayson as they drove away.

She started across the town square—it had turned into a sea of mud from the firefighters' water, so she changed directions and took the long way around using the sidewalks. Debris filled the gutters, some from the burnt buildings, most from the crowd that had abandoned everything when they fled the square.

Blood-red Nazi flags mixed with peace signs. Water-stained banners floated in puddles, their words turned into dripping swirls of color, messages of hate and freedom combined into an incoherent rainbow.

Both groups caught in the violence, entrenched in their beliefs. A spark of sunlight struck a smashed bottle, its glass stained with blood.

Her grandfather may have been right: freedom was the right to hate. But what he hadn't seen, what the men and women caught in the melee last night hadn't seen, was that hatred was also freedom denied. It locked people into a prison of their own making.

How many wonderful people had changed her life, people who, if she'd isolated herself behind a wall of prejudice like her grandfather, she'd never have met? Valencia, Wash, fellow Marines who'd saved her life and she theirs, David... How empty her life would have been without them.

She loved her grandfather. But maybe in this he was wrong—no one person had the right to dictate how others lived. Maybe she'd been raised to believe that hatred trumped others' freedom, but she didn't have to choose that way of life for herself.

The sound of people singing rode across the wind. She stopped, searching for the source. A small group, black and white; men, women, and even little children, stood on the other side of the police barricade, holding hands and singing. Not a song of rebellion or protest. A song of peace and hope: *My Country, Tis of Thee.*

She blamed her sudden tears on the morning sun glinting in her eyes and continued forward.

When she arrived at the courthouse, she stood looking up the imposing set of stone steps. Then she glanced at the modest and less intimidating police department beside it.

Lucy said to buy time; she didn't say how. TK turned her back on the courthouse and instead entered the police department.

A few minutes later, she was escorted up to the second floor where the department's two full-time detectives had a small office—well, there was no door or walls, but it was definitely a separate space from the file cabinets and desks that cluttered the main area—in the rear corner.

Karlan stood, two mugs of coffee in his hands, waiting for her. She stopped beside the two desks that had been positioned so they faced each other, caught by the view from his window. From there you could see across the alley, down into the disemboweled remnants of the coroner's office.

"One thing about the crime scene being just across the alley, makes it easy to keep an eye on it." The joke fell flat as they both thought of the body found in that crime scene.

He extended her a cup of coffee as a peace offering. She accepted, grateful for anything that could keep the pounding in her head at bay. Karlan wore the same uniform as yesterday, and she assumed it was not his first cup of coffee of the morning.

"So, what can I do for you?" he asked.

"Give me a place to hide out? The mayor summoned me to his office, and I'm not sure if it's to get a statement about last night, a summary of what we found about the bodies in the car, or to fire me now that all of our evidence has gone up in smoke."

"Probably all three."

"That's one weird family. His father, the judge, called us to his house this morning, told us about a night of riots back in 1954 and a cop that was shot during them."

"Let me guess: Archibald Thomson?"

"Exactly. Said the riots were from a labor dispute and he didn't know anything else."

"Like how three bodies, including a juvenile and a female, ended up in the trunk of the car Thomson was in."

"Wait. You heard we identified two of the bodies, right?" Her mind was fuzzy—no, it'd just happened this morning, she hadn't had a chance to call Karlan, so he couldn't have known. "Well, potentially identified. We're waiting for confirmation."

"No. When did that happen? *How* did that happen with Marcia Madsen dead and the skeletons destroyed?"

"Our tech guy. He was helping Dr. Madsen run a computer facial reconstruction program while he was also running down leads on the car. Found the owner. A doctor named Samuel Mann from Washington, DC. He was reported missing in May, 1954 along with his wife and four-year-old daughter."

Karlan arched an eyebrow. "So if it was Samuel Mann and his wife in the trunk, how'd they get there? Victims of a carjacking or something during this so-called labor dispute that somehow never made it into the history books? And who was the kid with them? Not to mention, where's the little girl?"

"No idea, no idea, no idea, and State College teaching religious studies."

That got a reaction as he choked on his coffee. "Excuse me?"

"The girl—woman now—was also looking for the car. She found us. My boss is on her way to interview her now. Guess who invited himself along for the ride? After his grandfather the judge said he'd never heard of the Manns?"

"Grayson. That kid. He's either a stone-cold sociopath or just so desperate for his daddy's love and attention that he's been brainwashed. Probably both, given those two. The judge, he isn't exactly known for his religious or racial tolerance either. And while the mayor talks like he's Mr. Working Class Man's Best Friend, rumor has it most of his friends come from Philly and have Italian last names."

"The mayor has ties to organized crime?" That would explain how a small-town nowhere mayor could be mounting a bid for Congress. Maybe the mob had been using Greer as a dumping ground for unwanted bodies? Perhaps even for generations?

"No proof, but word is both he and his father owe their success to the Philly mob."

A judge and congressman both in the control of organized crime? No wonder the mayor was so desperate to quash their investigation along with any suspicion that might fall on their family. And it explained why he came to the Beacon Group instead of turning the investigation over to the State Police or FBI.

"Do you think they started the fire last night? No evidence means no case, means no negative publicity. Or maybe they got their mob friends to start the fire?"

"Greer would never give anyone something as big as that to hold over him. He'd keep it in the family. He's holding a press conference at one. Word is, he's planning to blame the protestors for the fire."

"Do you have any actual evidence?"

He made a sour face. "Evidence? Hell, we haven't even been allowed access to the crime scene yet." He jerked his chin to the window where the firemen were still at work on the smoldering remains of the building. "Greer doesn't care about evidence. Or the truth. All he cares about is shutting up the opposition and getting the reporters out of town—hopefully to write about how well he's handled this crisis. What a leader he's been in this time of need."

"And as soon as the press conference is over—"

"Your case will be erased forever and mine will be marked closed. Marcia deserved more." He leaned back in his chair. "I feel like I've failed her."

"We still have a few hours left."

"Yeah, but where to start? Security footage was stored on drives in the government building, so it's destroyed. Did you or your friend see anything? You're the closest things to witnesses I have."

"No. We were in the other room." She thought about it. "Weren't there officers on duty at the warehouse? That's where you have your evidence lockup, right?"

"One officer from seven to seven. Patrols both the warehouse and the government center. The desk sergeant stopped him when he was clocking in, reassigned him to protest duty. On orders of the mayor."

"Madsen said the mayor came by, sent everyone home."

His eyes creased. "You realize this is absolute, wild conjecture and speculation. We have no facts, we have no witnesses, we have no evidence."

"You mean that a politically corrupt official took it upon himself to destroy all the evidence that could cost him his next election? Right. Could never happen..."

He finished his coffee but made a face as if it had suddenly turned bitter. "If he was involved." She noticed he wasn't using Greer's name anymore much less his title. "Purely hypothetically. He'd have to create some kind of delayed timer for the fireworks to go off after he cleared the building. Or at least thought he'd cleared it."

"Not so hard. Anyone who knew the truck with the fireworks would be there would have ample time to jury-rig a delayed ignition device. Hell, even a smoldering matchbook might have been enough. I'm guessing with all the black powder and other flammable chemicals in the fireworks, it wouldn't take a huge flame to get things started."

"Which means we're looking for someone who knew the

bones would be at the morgue…"

"You, me, my people." She ticked off possibilities. "Madsen and her people, the tow truck driver, officer at the quarry, evidence officer on day shift, and pretty much the entire Greer family, all three generations."

"And who also knew about the fireworks arriving yesterday."

"Pretty much anyone who walked through that warehouse entrance—the truck was parked right in the front, along the wall beside the coroner's office."

"So we have plenty of folks with means and opportunity. Guess that leaves us with motive."

They were both silent for a long moment, the only sound the back-up beeping of one of the fire trucks outside the window. "Everyone involved in our cold case is probably dead by now."

"Except the judge."

"Except the judge," she allowed. "But he was just a kid back then. No way he killed four people and got away with it clean."

"Maybe he was protecting someone else?"

"Like who? Some ninety-year-old guy rotting away in a

nursing home?" She sat up. "Unless…don't tell me the judge's father is still alive? He did say he had blood on his clothing when he came home after this labor dispute."

"No, he died a long time ago. Back when I was a kid myself. They had a funeral parade and big memorial service. Got us out of school for the day."

"I didn't realize you grew up here."

"My folks moved here in the 1960s. Well after this mysterious labor dispute I've never heard of. Town lost a lot of jobs when the paper mill was closed, but after JFK took office, they got some big government contract to build radio parts for the space program. Paid decent money, so my folks moved here. Then after the Apollo missions ended, plant shut down, no more money." He waved his hand out the window. "Town's been dying ever since."

"And so's our case—both of them. We need evidence, not just speculation."

"I'm all for evidence. But unless the arson investigator finds something on whatever ignited the fireworks, I've got nothing."

# CHAPTER 32

LUCY WAS ONLY twenty minutes into their ride when she was ready to reach across Grayson, open his car door, and hurl him over one of the steep mountain cliffs as she sped away. How the hell had he survived a full day with TK without TK killing him? The kid never shut up, and most of what he said was pure racist drivel.

"I think what you're proposing is called apartheid," she interrupted. "Pretty much already failed. Big time."

"Apartheid was a legally sanctioned form of racial and class discrimination. What I'm talking about is different. People choose where they live and who they live with. They choose their government and what laws—local laws, at least—they want to enact. It's actually self-determination. Democracy at its finest."

As much as she wanted this conversation over, she could not let that stand unchallenged. "Doesn't sound like democracy to me. Sounds like discrimination."

"Discrimination is about depriving people of their rights. I'm talking about giving people back their right to choose." However wrong-minded the kid was, he was passionate, she'd give him that. "Take Greer, for example. We're just a small town in the middle of nowhere. We used to be a quaint, pleasant small town, the kind you'd see in the movies. But we're not anymore. So my father used eminent domain to take over some of the neighborhoods that were literally falling apart, riddled with crime and drug use, unsafe for anyone to live, much less raise a family. He sold the land to developers who will demolish them and then build the college expansion. Win/win for everyone."

"Except the people whose homes you just stole."

"They were paid. Now they can find new homes, better homes, safe homes. If they choose to. Like in Detroit. They're trying to give houses away—all folks have to do is promise to maintain them. Basically just say, I choose not to live like a rat in cage, I want my own home, I promise to mow the lawn and paint the walls and not turn it into a crack house. And yet, they're having a hard time finding anyone." He leaned across the center console. "Why do you think they're having such a hard time giving houses away?"

"Because who wants to live in Detroit?"

"Exactly. But...what if instead of calling it Detroit, you divided the land into communities, gave each one autonomy? Then people aren't just getting a home, they're getting self-determination, they get to decide where their tax dollars go, how their kids are educated. I'm not talking slums or housing projects. I'm talking real homes here. Wouldn't that be better for everyone?"

An idealistic racist...wow, where to start? Maybe by labeling the problem? "You do know how racist that sounds, right?"

"I'm a separatist, not a racist. And how is it any different than a bunch of rich white folks getting together to build a private gated community or taking over a suburb? I'm just saying, why not give everyone an equal chance to raise their family the way they really want? Those people my father displaced when he took over their buildings for the town, do you think they wanted to keep living like that? In buildings that should have been condemned years ago, gangs roaming the hallways, drugs and guns everywhere? Think that's how they'd choose to raise their families? I'm saying, give them a choice. That's all."

"Like the people shoved into the trunk of that car had a choice?" she snapped.

He flinched, his expression turning contrite. He was silent for a long moment—the most he'd gone without talking since he'd gotten into her car. "Do you really think she watched her own parents die?"

"I'm not sure. Even if she didn't, she was a little girl whose family was ripped away from her."

He sank into his seat, his mood somber. "I can't even imagine. I lost my mom when I was about that age, but I always had my dad and my grandfather. I always had someone."

From the looks of him, he'd not only had family to help him through the trauma of losing a parent, he'd also had wealth to comfort him.

"She didn't just lose her family," Lucy reminded Grayson, "she lost her identity. She would have lived in fear that the men who killed her parents might someday come after her."

"Maybe they weren't killed because they were black. Maybe there was some other reason. They were from DC, right?

Maybe they made enemies, were involved in some kind of political corruption."

"A doctor and a schoolteacher? I doubt it." Thankfully they arrived at the address Henrietta Mann Rawling had sent before he could continue arguing. A black woman with long hair artfully arranged in a complex weave of braids stood waiting at the entrance to a townhouse.

Lucy turned to Grayson. "You will move to the back seat. You will remain quiet. You will be respectful."

He opened his mouth, ready to protest. She snipped any mention of his first amendment rights with a wag of her finger. "No. This is not some theoretical debate. Not for this woman. Her family was murdered, thrown in the trunk of a car, disposed of like garbage. She did not deserve that. They did not deserve that. Do you understand?"

To her surprise, he suddenly couldn't meet her gaze. Instead, his face fell, a little boy who realized Santa Claus wasn't real. His shoulders hunched, he nodded. And then he reached for his collar, making sure it was buttoned tight.

Lucy pulled the car up to the curb and rolled down the passenger window. "Ms. Rawling? I'm Lucy Guardino."

The woman nodded and smiled. Grayson nodded and

hopped out, holding the door for Rawling before climbing into the rear seat.

"Ms. Rawling, I want to thank you for taking the time to speak with us," Lucy said after she'd made introductions.

"Actually, it's Dr. Rawling. Most folks call me Henrietta, but I think maybe y'all should just call me Maybelle, seeing as that's who you came all this way to talk about."

Her accent was Deep South, warm and soothing. Lucy could well understand how she came to be a minister—her cadence and rich voice made you want to pay attention and reflect upon each word.

"Your Mr. Gamble," Maybelle continued, "he told me why you were looking for me." Lucy smiled. Wash was the youngest of their team; no one ever called him Mr. Gamble. "Amazing the power of the Internet, how it can foster and build human connections. I tried, a few years ago, to trace back my parents—my real parents—through some of those genealogy sites, but," her sigh whispered past them, "there was nothing there. The car forums were a lark, but I figured if anything brought my daddy back to me, it'd be that car. Lord, how he loved that car."

"Where would you like to go to talk? Is there a convenient restaurant nearby?"

"Let's talk on the way. I want to go to where you found my parents' bodies. I want to go to Greer."

Grayson made a small noise at that, but Lucy silenced him with a glare in the rearview mirror. She reached past Maybelle to the glove box and took out an old-fashioned micro-cassette recorder. "With your permission, I'd like to record our conversation. But if you say anything you regret, you can take the tape."

"Thank you for your consideration. But I don't believe that will be a problem. My pappy—Mr. Rawling—he was a lay preacher. I think, even though we weren't blood relations, he shared his gift of words with me. Fitting, since he lost his son."

"His son?"

"Henry. You don't know about Henry? He's how all this started."

"What happened in Greer?" Lucy asked as she pulled away from the curb. "It was started by a Henry Rawling?"

"No. Not started *by*," she corrected Lucy in a firm tone. "Started *because*. You see, Henry Rawling was raised to help people. He was a little slow, didn't do so well in school, but he was kind and gentle. I never even met the boy, except when my daddy cut him open to save his life, but it was his folks and aunt who saved me, and they told me all about Henry. He was only thirteen when they killed him."

Lucy sensed Grayson's tension as he fidgeted in the backseat. He wanted to know if Henry Rawling could be their third body in the trunk. So did she, but this had to unfold at Maybelle's pace, no one else's. "Why did they kill him, Maybelle?"

Maybelle's eyes drifted half shut as she dabbed them with a tissue from her purse. "He didn't do anything except try to help a little girl. Her daddy was beating her and Henry helped her get away."

"Was it you he helped? Were you running away from home, is that how you ended up in Greer?" But how did a four-year-old make it all the way from DC to a small town in rural Pennsylvania? Especially back in the 1950s?

"You really don't know anything, do you?" Maybelle's tone turned stern. "Greer." She sighed the name. "I've been searching for that blood-soaked town most of my adult life— never knew the name until you folks came calling."

"What do you remember?"

Maybelle settled into her seat and continued, "I was only four. My momma, she was a beautiful woman, she was a schoolteacher. And my daddy, he was a doctor. Not just any doctor, he was a surgeon. Saved lives in two wars, as a medic in World War Two and a battalion aide surgeon in Korea. I don't remember any of that, just remember the pictures of him in his uniform, how proud and handsome he looked."

She chuckled. "Or maybe I'm just getting him mixed up with Denzel Washington, and all I remember is how I want him to look—the mind plays tricks like that, you know. Especially when you're trying so hard to hang onto any wisp of memory you have."

She turned to Grayson in the back seat. "Remember that, son. You have to appreciate what you have here and now. Just never know when the good Lord has a change of plans in store for you."

"Yes, ma'am," Grayson mumbled.

"We drove to Ohio for a funeral. I don't remember who died—someone in my mother's family—or where the funeral was. I only remember a bunch of church ladies mussing my hair and pinching my cheeks and talking to me like I was a baby. And pie. Lots of pie—my daddy and I would sneak a piece and go sit on their back stoop where it was quiet. And then we were coming home. I was asleep most of the time."

She stopped as Lucy turned onto the narrow two-lane highway that would twist them over the mountains. "Still can't believe I was so close all these years. I looked it up when Mr. Gamble said where you were. Less than forty miles, and I never found it. That's why I took the job at Penn State, you know. Spent all my life down south. The Rawlings, they had family in Alabama, near Selma. By the time the civil rights movement was going strong, I was right there with them—lied about my age more than once. Met John Lewis and Dr. King. Wasn't much impressed at first—I started out more of a Malcolm X kind of activist. But then I came around to Dr. King's way of thinking. But I wanted to do more than preach to a few familiar faces week in, week out, so I went back to school, got my doctorate. Taught and preached at schools like Emory and Clemson, then North Carolina, then Penn State...as if the Lord was leading me back here to where everything started. And everything ended. My alpha and omega. In a tiny town called Greer."

# CHAPTER 33

TK AND KARLAN were brainstorming possible avenues of investigation when Karlan suddenly straightened in his chair, glancing past TK to the space behind her. She turned to see the mayor approaching, weaving his way through the desks without actually touching them. All of the officers on duty were out of the building, leaving TK and Karlan as his only targets.

"Mr. Mayor," Karlan said, not exactly jumping to his feet, but at least making a gesture as if inviting the mayor to join them.

"Detective Karlan, Ms. O'Connor." The mayor favored them with a hit and skip smile that barely grazed his lips before settling himself against the filing cabinet, forcing both of them to crane their necks to make eye contact. "Forgive the intrusion. I realized that as hectic as this day and these investigations must be, I should not expect you to come to me with progress reports but rather reach out to you myself." He spread both hands wide as if to say, "here I am."

"We were, ah, just going over TK's statement," Karlan said.

"Right. I understand you and a friend were there last night with Dr. Madsen. And your friend, he's in the hospital? Is he all right?"

"Broken leg, a bit banged up, but he'll be fine, thank you."

"I'm sure he will." The mayor nodded as if he had access to some arcane orthopedic crystal ball. "Perhaps, after you give your statement, you should join him? I know when my wife was ill, I hated leaving her in the hospital alone. So draining on the psyche, all that medical hustle-bustle."

TK actually wanted nothing more than to be with David, make sure the nurses knew how to read his body language since they'd never know if he was in pain or had reached the point of exhaustion simply from his voice alone. But some contrarian impulse forced her to smile at the mayor and say, "No worries, Mr. Mayor. I'm here for the duration. I'd only drive David crazy if I stayed at the hospital, hovering over him."

The mayor—he was about the same age as Karlan, in his

mid-fifties—made a face that clearly questioned the commitment level of modern-day relationships, but then shrugged. "Very well. Please, don't let me interrupt. I'd love to hear your statement about the tragic events of last night."

Karlan hesitated, but the mayor slid a chair over, crowding in at the desk, giving them no room to maneuver.

"All right, then," he said as he opened his notepad. "You left the courthouse at what time?"

"Around six," TK answered. "I met David and we talked a bit, then went to get pizza for Dr. Madsen and her students."

"And then you proceeded to the coroner's office? Did you see anyone on the way?"

She hesitated. Mayor Greer leaned forward as if he already knew what she was going to say. "Yes. Franklin and his friends."

Karlan glanced up at that. "The ones from yesterday morning?"

"Yes. We gave them one of the pizzas and had a...chat."

"And you can positively identify them?" the mayor asked, earning a frown from Karlan for his encroachment.

"Yes, I'd met them earlier yesterday. Franklin and four other boys, I don't know their names."

"Did you see where they went?" Karlan asked before the mayor could butt in again.

"They walked toward the town square. I lost sight of them when they went past the police barricades."

"So they were headed toward the government center?" the mayor asked.

"Mr. Mayor, please—"

TK wasn't about to allow her testimony railroad anyone. "No, sir. I saw them walking north. I saw them reach the police barricade. I have no idea where they went after that."

Karlan nodded but the mayor didn't appear satisfied. "What time did you encounter these hoodlums?"

"We reached the coroner's office around seven-twenty, so about fifteen minutes before then. Maybe twenty—we stopped so David could take photos of the protesters and interview them."

"Which would give them plenty of time to set the fire and leave again before you arrived," the mayor concluded triumphantly. He turned to Karlan. "I want these boys located and brought in for questioning as soon as possible, Detective."

"Of course. We'll be pursuing every angle—"

"This takes priority. I want to be able to announce at the

press conference this afternoon that we have suspects in custody. The people need to know that they're safe on their own streets." The mayor stood, hands braced against the desk, leaning over both TK and Karlan. "I expect results, Detective."

Karlan stood, meeting the politician head on. "Yes, sir."

The mayor swung his attention to TK. She remained sitting, at ease, refusing to kowtow to his authority. "My son texted me that this new potential witness he and Ms. Guardino are meeting might have pertinent information. I'd like to meet with her as soon as they return."

As if Grayson wouldn't make sure that happened no matter what TK said. TK simply nodded, waiting to see what Greer's true agenda was.

"It would be interesting to see how her memory of events sixty-plus years ago correlates with my father's. After all, the girl was only, what, four at the time? Not old enough to be a credible witness. We can't have her story getting out until we vet every detail."

Ahh...so he planned to discredit Maybelle before he even met her. Which would leave the judge's account as the only one available.

Now she stood, aligning her body with Karlan's. "Yes sir.

That's our job. We'll dig out every ounce of the truth, don't you worry."

His frown suggested he detected the rebellion in her tone, but he nodded without saying anything and left.

Karlan followed his progress out, and once the door had shut behind Greer, said, "Did you just declare war on the mayor?"

TK grinned and bounced on her toes, that feeling of anticipation that she'd first felt when she arrived in Greer returning. "Yep. Want to help me nail that smug sonofabitch?"

"I want the truth," he admonished her, reminding her once again that he was old enough to be her father. "I want Marcia Madsen's killer. I want justice for the people we found in that car."

"So do I," she assured him. "But if it means pissing off Greer, I'm happy to take that as a bonus for a job well done."

"Okay, then. Just so we're clear. Guess we should go find Franklin, see what he has to say for himself."

# CHAPTER 34

AS LUCY DROVE them over the mountains, Maybelle told her version of the events leading up to her parents' deaths.

"We were at the courthouse window, watching the mob. Officer Thomson came out to stop them and they shot him. Then my father tried to help, but... Winnie tried to hide it from me, but I still saw, saw what they did..." Her voice trailed off.

"Winnie." The name was a sigh. "She was my hero. All my life I wanted to be as strong as she was that day. Somehow I can hang on to her memory as a real person more than my parents, not sure why. They were heroes as well, just like Officer Thomson and Henry Rawling. Makes you wonder when so many good people can die for no good reason. Makes you doubt. Question God's plan."

Lucy tried to steer Maybelle back to her story. "How did you escape?"

"Winnie got me out, knew all the back ways through yards and gardens and fields to get us to the Rawlings' house. Said we had to warn them, get them out of town before the men came for them. When we got there, it was just Henry's mom and aunt, so we packed up anything they could carry and waited for his father to get home with the truck. Never been so scared or have time move so slow—and yet it all went so fast, like my parents were being rushed away from me before I could even finish crying."

"You must have been terrified, all these strangers taking you away from your parents."

Maybelle nodded, her gaze caught in distant memories. "I guess I was in shock. I remember thinking that maybe I hadn't really woken up in the car, that I was still asleep and this was just a dream brought on by sneaking too much pie. I kept waiting to wake up, but things just kept getting worse and worse, and there was nothing I could do except pray. That's my first memory from when I was just a baby, my momma and me praying for Daddy to come home from the war safe and sound. So that's what I did."

"And you escaped with the Rawlings?"

"Wasn't quite so easy. Henry's father was the only black preacher, and their house and little church were beside the black graveyard. New Canaan, that was how they always called it—for the longest time I thought that was the name of the town, could never figure out why they said it with such reverence after everything that happened there. But it wasn't the real name of the town, it was their name for the congregation."

"The Rawlings never told you about Greer?"

She shook her head. "When I was little, there were only so many secrets I could safely carry, like my new name. And it was too painful for them to talk about. By the time I got older, they were gone. They were always worried that the white men from Pennsylvania would find them, hunt them down, kill them in their sleep. But it was nothing like that. Just a rainy road on a dark night, driving the church bus, went off a bridge. Six people died, the rest of them—my friends, the entire youth choir— ended up in the hospital. I should've been with them, but I was being a bratty, sulky teenager and when I didn't get picked for the solo, I had a hissy fit and stayed home. One rainy night, and everyone who could have given me any answers was gone."

They drove in silence until Lucy began to maneuver

down the switchbacks leading off the mountain. As they came to a small cleared plateau with a modern-day glass and timber log cabin perched at the top, taking advantage of the view over the valley and river below, Maybelle gasped. "Is that it? That little place hugging the river?"

"That's Greer," Lucy confirmed. "The college takes up most of that green space between the river and the mountains. The quarry where we found the car is on the other side of town—"

"There, I see the sun hitting water. That must be it, right?" She sat forward, sounding like a little girl despite the solemn nature of their journey. "Everything looks so different from how I remember it. Not that I saw very much, and it was a long time ago."

They rounded a bend, giving them a different view of the town. "That dome, is that the courthouse?" This time her voice was laced with anxiety.

"Yes." Lucy eased off the gas. "You don't have to do this. If you'd rather—"

"No." Her voice was firm. "I've waited all my life to see this place. But I think we should find Winnie first."

"Find Winnie? You mean she's still alive, here in Greer,

after all these years?"

Maybelle shook her head. "No. I mean find her grave. I saw her get killed. Saw where he buried her body."

"What happened? Was it her father, did he finally catch up with her?" Lucy was surprised by how invested she'd become in the fate of the brave little girl who'd saved Maybelle. To learn that after everything, Winnie had died as well that night...it felt as visceral as if she'd known her in person.

"Not her father. A boy. He came to Henry's house. Winnie said he was there for her, made us run out the back while she stalled him. We hid in the woods, covered in mud and leaves, huddled behind a log, nowhere else to go until Henry's father came with the truck."

She stared out the window at the brilliant July morning, shook her head as if shrugging away the years and pain. "We could hear them yelling. The boy must have hit her or something, because she came running around the side of the house, heading away from us, through the graveyard. He came running after, caught up with her. She had a knife—guess she took it from the kitchen—and cut him across the arm."

She held up her right forearm and gestured. "But he picked up a rock, hit her on the head, and down she went. That didn't stop him. He kept swearing and yelling at her, saying she was a tease and a whore and all sorts of names, all the time he kept bashing her with that rock, over and over. Until he just kind of collapsed. Sat right down on the ground, cradling her bloody body and cried."

Another pause. "But then he stopped crying. Stood up, fast, like he'd heard something that scared him—maybe it was me, I was sobbing but Henry's aunt had her fist in my mouth. I bit her so hard I drew blood, but she never let me go. Never made a sound, either, not her or Henry's mother. There was an open grave nearby, freshly dug, ready to go. The boy, he just kicked Winnie's body, rolling it into that hole in the ground, tossed the knife and rock in after her. Then he shoved some dirt on top of her and he walked away. Like nothing happened."

"You think you can find that grave?"

"I know I can," she said with certainty. "I saw the marker on the grave right beside her. I've been reading since I was three—my momma taught me—and it was an easy name to remember. Abe Brown. I remember because of President Lincoln. And Brown was the name my parents were talking about before we stopped. In the car, there was a news report. My father told me that because of this Brown, I could grow up to be anything I wanted."

"1954," Lucy mused. *"Brown versus the Board of Education?"*

Maybelle nodded. "May 17th, the day that changed everything."

"This boy who attacked Winnie, did she ever say his name?"

"Yes. She called him Philip. Said his father was mayor. Said he was the one who beat up Henry and started the whole thing."

Grayson lurched forward so fast that Lucy almost hit the brakes, thinking he'd seen a deer in the road or something equally dangerous.

"No," he said. "That's wrong. It couldn't be him."

"What is it, Grayson?"

"My grandfather. His name is Philip, and his father was mayor back then. But, I'm sure you're mistaken. It couldn't have been my grandfather who did that to your friend. I mean, he was a judge. He spent his whole life upholding the law."

"Winnie said Philip. The mayor's son." Maybelle was firm, refusing to compromise.

"I'll take you by his place, you can meet him for yourself. See that it wasn't him."

"Grayson," Lucy said, "it was sixty years ago. Maybelle was four years old. How can she possibly recognize him in the man he is now?"

"I'd know him," Maybelle insisted, not flustered at all by Grayson's protests. "If I saw a picture of him from back then. That face. It haunts my dreams every night."

Grayson frowned, unwilling to concede. In the rearview mirror, Lucy could see him swiping through his phone, undoubtedly searching for photos that would help his case.

"You're wrong," he said, sounding more than a little petulant in his defense of his family name. Not that she totally blamed him—after all, Maybelle had just accused his grandfather of murder. "We'll find a picture. You can see what the judge looked like back then, see for yourself it wasn't him." He leaned toward Lucy. "Take us to my grandfather's house."

"No," Maybelle said. "I'd like to go to the quarry where my parents were left, and then I want to visit Winnie's grave. Pray over them both. After that, I'll go anywhere you want, tell my story to anyone you want. No more hiding the truth."

# CHAPTER 35

WHILE KARLAN DROVE them to Franklin's home, once again using the dilapidated patrol car he'd had yesterday, TK called Lucy to update her. Her call went straight to voice mail, which she hoped meant Lucy was too busy gaining valuable insights from their new witness to answer her phone. She left a message letting Lucy know what the mayor was up to as well as a warning that Grayson was feeding his father information.

Next, she tried David. He sounded a bit groggy but insisted that he hadn't been sleeping and that he wasn't in pain. "Can't sleep. I forgot how some of these pain meds make me itch all over, and scratching only makes it worse."

"Tell the doctors. Ask them to change to something different."

"Haven't seen them. Besides, it's better if I tough it out, get off the meds as soon as possible."

Typical. He'd complain to her but wouldn't take the necessary steps to solve the problem if it made him lose face. As if a total stranger cared how high his pain threshold was. Was there anything more stubborn than male pride?

"David. You've just been blown up. Literally. For the second time in your life. Take the damn meds and give your body time to heal."

"I'm fine," he insisted. "How's the case going?"

She quickly filled him in on her and Karlan's frustrating side of the investigation and what little she knew about Lucy's progress. "We're on our way to interview Franklin, see if he or his buddies saw anyone near the warehouse."

"We were all headed in that direction, so I guess it's possible." His tone didn't sound very hopeful. "But with all those people in and around the square uploading photos and videos, why don't you crowdsource your search?"

"Ask for random tips? I don't think the mayor would approve," which, honestly made the idea more appealing, "and we don't want to set off any vigilantes like what happened with the Boston bombing."

"Right. What if Wash and I combed through the videos posted online? We know where we're looking and when, should be able to narrow things down. I'll bet he could even create some kind of algorithm."

"Actually, that would be helpful." And it would keep David's mind off the pain and the itching and most of all, the boredom that came from lying in a hospital bed. "I'd really appreciate it."

"Good. Because if we find anything, I'll absolutely be expecting a reward."

"Like what? An exclusive story?"

"No, I was thinking more along the lines of a naughty-nurse costume…"

She hung up. Karlan slanted her a look, and she knew her blush gave her away. "I take it the boyfriend is feeling better?"

"It's the pain meds, makes him goofy. But he did have a good idea." She told him about David and Wash searching the online media for leads.

"Why the hell not?" he said as he pulled the cruiser to the curb. Up ahead, a block away from where she'd first encountered Franklin yesterday morning, there he was, sitting on a stoop with two of his friends. One of the linebackers and

Skinny Kid.

As she and Karlan left the car and walked toward them, the boys glanced up and fell silent. They all seemed strangely subdued compared to her encounters with them yesterday. That's when she noticed that the linebacker had his arm in a sling and Skinny Kid's scalp bristled with staples.

"You guys okay?" Karlan asked as they drew near.

"What do you care?" Franklin asked in a bitter tone, as always speaking for all of them. His eye was bruised and swollen and his lip had a crusty scab where it had been split.

"What happened?" TK nodded to their assortment of injuries.

"What do you think? Got caught in that stampede when the fireworks blew. Not that the police cared. More concerned with herding us than protecting us. Like we were cattle, animals."

Karlan frowned. "Are you saying a cop did this to you? Assaulted you?"

At first TK thought Franklin was going to say yes—he straightened, his chin held high in defiance. But then his shoulders slumped. "Nah. But they pushed us all back from the fire and that sent us right into the path of a bunch of Nazi thugs."

"Anyone you'd recognize? Want me to file a report?"

Franklin stared at Karlan as if he was from Mars. "Our business, we'll deal with it. Don't need you to get involved."

"And I don't need you headed back to prison for taking the law into your own hands," Karlan said in a stern tone. Stern, but caring, almost fatherly. "This time it won't be juvie, you know that."

Franklin glanced at the other two boys. They stood, gave him a nod, and sauntered off, skirting past TK and Karlan as if they weren't even there.

"Can't tell you who did it because we couldn't see past their boots and fists. It was crazy mad out there, folks running away from the fire, toward the fire, pounding on each other, running over each other. Never seen anything like it—and I never want to again. We were animals. All of us. Never mind color, we were all just scared and seeing blood."

Karlan considered that. "You and your friends, always out on the street, nothing better to do. You know they're going to need people to help put the town square back together. You guys could sign up, make a few bucks, show folks that this town never quits fighting no matter how bad things get."

"No one will hire me, not with my record."

"Let me take care of that. Come see me after the Fourth, bring your crew."

Franklin nodded as if sealing a solemn vow. Then he tilted his head to TK. "You look a little banged up yourself—were you caught in the riot?"

"No. I was inside the government center when the fireworks blew."

His eyes widened as he pursed his lips in appreciation. "You were right there, eye of the storm? Damn girl, you're made of steel, some kind of Wonder Woman."

"I got lucky, had some good cover to hide under. My friend is in the hospital and Dr. Madsen was killed."

"Yeah, I heard they was still pulling body parts out."

"That's why we're here," Karlan said. "We were wondering if you or your friends saw anyone near the government center or warehouse before the explosion?"

"You think we did it?" He didn't seem upset by the implied accusation, rather seemed a bit proud. "Like we built us an IED, timed it to blow up the fireworks?"

"Not you, but someone. Probably close to the same time you and your friends were walking that way."

He frowned. "We walked around the barricades, scoping the crowd, you know? Passed the alley behind the police station but didn't go down it."

"So you didn't see anyone?"

"Just the mayor. Strutting around like he's king of China—damn fool didn't even seem to care about the people yelling and screaming for justice, other side of the courthouse. Like that Italian dude, fiddling while Rome burned."

Karlan leaned back as if this information wasn't anything important. "Don't suppose you noticed what time it was that you saw Mayor Greer?"

Franklin slid his phone out, thumbed through the screens. "Was gonna post a GIF, show folks just how stupid he is, so I snapped a few pix." He held the phone up to Karlan and TK. "Time stamp is right there."

So it was. 7:07. The mayor was leaving the warehouse, brushing his hands together, a grin sparking his teeth against the light of the streetlamp. The next photo caught him mid-stride, making it seem as if he was capering. And that's when TK noticed his hands—he wore gloves.

"Who wears leather gloves in July?" TK muttered to Karlan.

He nodded, thumbing through the photos, his smile quickly masked. "It's a start."

She barely heard Karlan's negotiations with Franklin over the phone with its evidence. All she could think of was David, his face twisted in pain, and Marcia Madsen's torn and battered body.

She expected politicians to be liars, thieves, and crooks—part of the job description, even if they weren't connected to the mob. But murder? Just to cover up evidence of a scandal from six decades ago?

Or had Mayor Greer done it to protect his family name? That made more sense to her; not an excuse, but she could somehow wrap her mind around the idea of saving your family even if it meant extreme measures. Still boiled down to stubborn pride taking precedent over actual people and lives.

No matter why he'd done it, if JR Greer was behind Madsen's death, she was going to nail him. Dig a hole and bury him and his political aspirations so deep they'd never be seen again.

# CHAPTER 36

LUCY DROVE TO the quarry, following Grayson's directions. There was no one at the gate, so he hopped out and opened it for them. She parked the Subaru on a cleared area of packed earth and stone and walked with Maybelle to the edge.

The sparkling granite walls, interspersed with startling patches of green where wild plants had found soil to thrive in and birds had nested, reflected from the vibrant, unearthly turquoise of the water far below. It was a desolate spot, carved out of an otherwise verdant plateau with the river to the south and the mountain ridge to the east. But also filled with its own unique beauty.

A hawk soared overhead, a silent witness to their pilgrimage. Lucy stood in silence alongside Maybelle, not wanting to intrude upon the older woman's private thoughts but also not wanting her to feel abandoned, alone in her re-awakened grief.

A few minutes later, Grayson joined them, standing at a respectable distance, his gaze focused on the dark depths of the quarry.

"Do you think any of them are still alive?" Maybelle asked in a *sotto* voice. "The men who did this? Do you think any of them have ever stood here, thinking about who those poor murdered souls were, who they left behind?"

Once upon a time, Lucy had been an optimist. Back then, she would have said yes as an affirmation of hope in the human race. But too many years and too much blood shed by uncaring, unfeeling men had come between her and optimism, so the only way she could answer was, "I don't think so. Because if they did, they would have found a way to make things right. Or they would have admitted to themselves the cowardice that polluted their hearts and jumped."

It came out harsher than she'd intended—Nick was always telling her she needed to work on her boundaries—but Maybelle simply nodded. "Guess the best any of us can do is to pray for all of them. The ones who still have a soul and the ones who forever lost theirs that day."

Lucy noticed that the minister said nothing about forgiveness or God's will or any of the other platitudes that to her often smacked of surrendering human responsibility to the universe at large. She decided that she preferred Maybelle's interpretation: take care of what you can here on earth and let God take care of what you can't.

The hawk seemed to agree, letting loose a piercing screech as it dove down into the water, its flight causing endless ripples across the placid surface as it emerged with a fish grasped in its talons. Maybelle's gaze followed its path until it was lost in the afternoon sun.

"Take me to Winnie, please."

They returned to the Subaru. Grayson had no idea where the old church and graveyard were located, suggesting that they go to the courthouse first and check the county property records, but Wash, as always, came through with what Lucy needed. The GPS coordinates he gave her were less than three miles away from the Greer town square.

At first the narrow two-lane county road wound past fields of corn and soy, but then it quickly gave way to forest. When their last glimpse of a building was over a mile back, Lucy started to doubt Wash, when a tiny, whitewashed chapel appeared as they rounded a bend in the road. Good thing, because she'd lost cell reception and couldn't call him if she wanted.

"That's it," Maybelle said, leaning forward. "The house is gone, but that's Henry's father's church. I'm sure."

It looked like any of the dozens rural churches that punctuated the Pennsylvania farmland, but it matched Wash's coordinates. Lucy pulled off the road into a small dirt parking area beside the chapel. The sign out front read: NEW CANAAN. It didn't list a denomination, instead simply said, "All welcome."

They got out of the car. The forest was thick, their sudden arrival silencing the wildlife, creating an eerie auditory vacuum. On the far side of the church was a clearing overgrown with wild roses and honeysuckle. Lucy strolled over and was able to make the faint outline of a foundation and fallen chimney, its bricks stained and scorched with soot. Below the brambles lay the remnants of burnt timbers.

"Henry's house," Maybelle said as she and Grayson approached. Grayson seemed nervous, looking around, jumping at every cracked twig or random noise.

"We hid in the woods back there." She pointed to the rear

of the foundation. Then she pivoted about forty degrees, aiming for an area at the rear diagonal from the church's back corner. "The cemetery was there."

The others started across the overgrown grass and weeds. Lucy stopped, her attention caught by sunlight glinting off metal in the opposite direction.

She took a few steps back toward the road. Farther down from the chapel there was a SUV pulled off the road, parked in a clump of daylilies. Hiker? Maybe, but given the absence of any traffic or other human presence, she couldn't help but feel on guard. She listened but didn't sense any movement other than Maybelle and Grayson behind her.

She was armed, of course, a nine-millimeter semi-automatic holstered at her waist, but she wondered about detouring back to the car to grab the Remington pump-action she kept in her trunk.

The others passed out of her sight as she headed toward the Subaru. That's when the first shot shuddered through the air.

# CHAPTER 37

WHILE KARLAN FINISHED negotiating with Franklin for possession of his phone—sounded like it was going to cost Karlan a brand new phone, probably out of his own pocket—TK called the mayor's office to see if he was available for an update. She thought he'd be there prepping for his press conference since it was meant to start in fifteen minutes.

"No, I'm sorry," his assistant told her in a flustered and worried tone. "He canceled the press conference and left, said he had family business to take care of. Now I have to call all these TV stations and reporters, and I have no idea what to tell them."

TK hung up, leaving the poor woman to fend for herself.

"Greer is gone," she told Karlan, gesturing him back to the car. He deposited Franklin's phone in an evidence bag and secured it in the cruiser's trunk, then hopped in. "Any ideas where he could be?"

"If he's willing to kill to protect his family's reputation over what happened six decades ago, do you think he'd let the witness your boss is bringing here to walk around, free to talk to anyone? My bet is, wherever she is, he is."

"Yeah, that's what I was thinking but Lucy isn't answering her phone. Neither is Grayson."

He hit the gas, the cruiser sparking against the curb as it lurched away. "I don't like the sound of that."

TK didn't answer. Instead she called Wash. "Can you give me the coordinates of Lucy's phone?" Their phones had a location app installed, but it could only be accessed with Valencia's permission. "I can't reach her, and I'm worried she might have some unexpected and unwelcome company headed her way."

"From Mayor Greer?" he asked.

"Yeah, how'd you know?"

"David found footage of him entering the warehouse last night. He's in the background, but I enhanced it and saw he's carrying a small bag."

"We just found photos of him leaving, and he's not carrying anything but is wearing gloves. What do you want to bet that bag contained a delayed fuse or ignition device?"

"No bet. I just texted you with the coordinates of where I sent Lucy. Must be no cell coverage there, I can't locate a tower that she's pinged outside of the one in Greer, but GPS says her phone is there."

"Then that's where we're headed."

"If there's no cell coverage, how will I know if you need back-up?"

TK thought about that. "Anyone you could send would be too far away. Let me work with the locals."

"You need to know what Lucy learned." He quickly explained about Maybelle Mann and the girl she'd seen murdered. "We can't trust the locals. If you don't call back in twenty minutes, I'm calling the State Police."

She didn't bother telling him that she was with a local right now. Instead she hung up and pulled up the map on her phone, showed it to Karlan. "This look like a likely spot? It's the last place we can trace my boss's phone."

He considered. "No cell reception out there. It's an old church—still has a small congregation even though they lost their minister. African-American, I forget which denomination."

"Maybelle Mann is a minister. Maybe she wanted to pay last respects to her family or something?"

He steered them onto the highway headed toward the quarry. "It's not far from the Greer estate. Mainly forest. Good hunting area."

She remembered the judge's room filled with trophies. "Let's hope they're not the ones being hunted. Got any friends you trust for backup?"

"Yeah, but no one who will make it there before us. And we probably shouldn't use the radio, too public."

They turned off the highway and onto a rural route that quickly left any trace of civilization behind. He drove with one hand as he worked his phone with his other, quick, pointed conversations that were over quickly. Then he hung up. "Lost reception, you have any on your phone?"

"Nope."

"Okay then. Just you and me until the cavalry arrives."

"What have we got as far as armaments?"

"What you see," he gestured to his duty belt and ballistic vest, "plus I've got a backup piece at my ankle and the shotgun." He nodded to the Remington secured at her knees. "You?"

"A Beretta nine millimeter and two knives."

He frowned at her. "You been riding around with me for two days strapped?"

"If you'd've asked, I would've told you. I've got a concealed carry permit."

"Teach me to trust a civilian." He slowed the car, easing it off the road and killing the engine. "Church is ahead, around that bend."

They both exited the vehicle, neither shutting their doors, moving silently into the trees edging the berm.

"We're going to look pretty silly if this is all for nothing," he said with a nervous laugh that told her it had been awhile since he'd been in the field. Small town like Greer, he might have never seen any real action.

"We're going to look alive," she reminded him. "That's all that counts." She took the lead, her Beretta at the ready, and he didn't protest.

A shot rang out, sending birds screeching toward the sky. Then a sudden hush fell over the woods.

TK jogged over the uneven terrain, something on Karlan's duty belt clacking as he followed. She pulled up as the trees gave way to a clearing.

There was the church, a pretty, whitewashed building

with a steeple. Lucy's Subaru waited beside it. She couldn't see anyone near, but there was motion behind the church. She squinted, wished she had her monocular, but it was in her messenger bag, which had been destroyed last night.

She spotted a patch of white—Grayson's shirt. He was huddled on the other side of a split-rail fence at the far corner of the clearing behind the church. Beside him was an older woman, Maybelle Mann, she guessed. She didn't see Lucy—was she down?

"The shot came from there," she pointed to a spot between nine and ten o'clock. "I'm going to circle around to the shooter. You go protect the civilians." She directed Karlan's attention to where Grayson and Maybelle were hiding at his two o'clock.

"Take this." He handed her the shotgun and drew his pistol. She nodded and turned back into the trees, leaving him behind.

A second shot cracked through the air. This one came from a slightly different direction than the first. Both sounded like rifles, not shotguns or pistols. Was she dealing with one shooter on the move or two?

And where the hell was Lucy?

# Chapter 38

THE FIRST SHOT came when Lucy was totally exposed, the church between her and the others as well as her and the Subaru. Thankfully, the shot wasn't aimed at her; it came from the trees to her left and was aimed behind the church in the direction of the graveyard.

She wasn't the target. It had to be Maybelle. Which meant she had to decide: circle the long way around to get the shotgun from the Subaru and lose time, leaving two civilians unprotected. Or, get there as fast as possible, even if it meant exposing herself to fire.

Her feet were already moving before her mind finished its trail of logic: she had her pistol; adding a shotgun wasn't going to appreciably increase her odds against a sniper using a long gun; and someone needed to provide cover and get Grayson and Maybelle back to the car so they could escape.

Ignoring the pains of protest radiating from her bad ankle as she moved in a zigzag formation, taking advantage of the low-lying overgrowth of bushes as cover, she ran as fast as possible to the back side of the church. Hugging its shadows until she ran out of building, she scanned the cemetery, searching for Grayson and Maybelle.

Two more shots had sounded—one from the same position as the first, one from a second position farther north. Had to be two shooters. No way could one man have moved through the forest and found a second vantage point that quickly, not even if he knew the terrain.

If they were smart, one would keep shooting to keep them pinned down while the other moved to engage them.

Finally, she saw Grayson and Maybelle. They were on the other side of the split rail fence, using the foliage as concealment. Unfortunately, she didn't see any gravestones or statues tall enough to use as cover—as soon as either of them moved, they'd be visible to anyone within range. And it was open ground between her and them. If she tried to get to them, she'd be totally exposed herself.

She wasn't far from the Subaru. Changing direction, she sprinted for the car and lunged into the driver's seat. Then she steered it across the uneven terrain, hoping she wouldn't take out the axle on one of the many boulders and fallen branches that littered the ground.

A bullet hit the rear window, starring the safety glass as the car lurched toward the fence where Maybelle and Grayson waited. The tires spun on a thick patch of leaves, but she shifted down and regained traction. Another shot pinged off the hood. She bashed into the fence, mowing it down so they wouldn't have to climb over it.

"Get in!" she shouted.

As Grayson scrambled to his feet, she noticed movement on the far side of the cemetery. An armed man coming through the woods.

Grayson and Maybelle were hopelessly exposed with their backs to the man. Lucy crawled across the front seat and out the door. She opened the rear door to use as cover and aimed at the man. "Drop it!"

"I'm Detective Karlan," he called back. "TK sent me."

She kept her weapon trained on him as he approached. Grayson was helping Maybelle past the shattered remains of the

fence but was taking his sweet time about it. The boy seemed to
have absolutely no situational awareness, leaving Maybelle fully
out in the open as he moved a length of wood out of her way.

Suddenly Karlan's chin jerked up and he leapt in front of
Grayson just as another shot split the air. Maybelle made a small
noise of terror, but Lucy was already there, hauling her past the
fence. Another shot, then two more, splintered the wooden
railings. Lucy pushed Maybelle into the Subaru, then turned to
where Karlan and Grayson had fallen.

Karlan had tackled Grayson, probably saving the boy's
life, but he'd taken a bullet in the chest. Lucy knelt beside him.

"Help me get him in the car," she ordered Grayson when
the boy didn't move. "Now."

"He saved my life," Grayson breathed. "Why'd he do that?
He saved my life." Then he looked up at the trees where the
shots were coming from. "They shouldn't be aiming at me."

Lucy ignored his adrenaline-fueled prattling, instead
working to lift Karlan's bulk. He had a vest on, good. Was
gasping for breath, but that meant he was still breathing, also
good. Didn't mean they were out of the woods, not by a long
shot.

"Grayson." Her voice was as good as a slap in the face,

finally breaking his trance. "Pick up his other arm and help me."

They both crouched to lift Karlan. As they did, a man wearing a business suit emerged from the trees at the far side of the cemetery, nothing standing between them and the rifle he aimed at them.

"Stop right there."

# CHAPTER 39

TK CROUCHED, MOVING stealthily through the woods. It reminded her more of hunting with her father and grandfather back in West Virginia than it did combat patrols in the war. Same principles applied, though: watch where you step, always check your six, and don't forget to look up.

Several more shots sounded, all from the same location, the first she'd clocked. At least two shooters: one on the move, one stationary. Karlan had said there was good hunting back in these woods, so she began scanning for tree stands and hides. Another shot sounded, and she was able to pinpoint its origin within a few trees. It was a good sign that he was still shooting; meant that his partner hadn't zeroed in on their target yet. All she could hope was that Lucy was busy turning the tables on the partner and protecting the civilians. And that Karlan reached them in time.

She focused on her mission: neutralizing the sniper. Leaning into a tree, a thick hemlock, willing her body to blend with its trunk, she scanned the leaves above her, searching for the sniper's perch. A hint of motion, the faint sound of brass being ejected: he was reloading.

Pinpointing the sound to a nearby oak, she made out the silhouette of a man concealed by camouflage netting draped over top of a deer hide's metal framework. Not exactly a full-fledged Ghillie suit, but good enough to fool a deer. Scanning down the tree, she spotted the wooden slats nailed to the trunk, forming a ladder. Too slow and noisy to climb it, besides she really didn't want to give him the chance to finish reloading and continue shooting at her friends. Instead, she dropped on one knee to get a better angle, steadied her aim, and fired three shots in rapid succession.

It was a gamble—she'd revealed her presence and her location to both shooters. But she was rewarded by a muffled curse as the man lurched upright, then tried to swing his weapon around toward her, got caught in the net, and tumbled the sixteen or twenty feet down to the ground. He landed with a whoosh and a loud grunt, his rifle hopelessly tangled in the netting.

She didn't let down her guard as she approached. It was the judge, snarling up at her, still trying to get his rifle aimed properly. Hard to do with one arm obviously broken. She sidestepped the rifle's barrel and reached over his head to yank it from his hand, taking the netting with it.

"You broke my damn hip," he moaned. "And my arm. What the hell? You're going to pay for this."

"Like Officer Thomson and the Mann family did?" she asked as she searched him for more weapons, removing a fixed-blade hunting knife and a pistol. "Or how about Winnie Neal? That's the name of the girl you killed with your own hands, isn't it, Judge?"

"Bitch," he snarled. She wasn't sure if he meant her or Winnie. "Deserved what she got. I'm not going to let her ruin things now, after all this time."

He was stalling. Wanted to keep her away from the second shooter—his son, the mayor, she suspected.

The judge wasn't going anywhere, not the way his one leg was noticeably shorter than the other, and he didn't seem in any immediate danger, so she left him there, taking his weapons with her as she circled around to the graveyard where she'd sent Karlan.

TK quickened her pace, wondering where Grayson was in all this. Did Lucy have a traitor in her midst?

She reached the graveyard's outer perimeter just in time to see the mayor raise his rifle at Lucy and Karlan. They were in front of Lucy's Subaru, half driven into the fence. Grayson stood on Karlan's other side, helping to support the police officer. Pretty obvious Karlan had been shot, but she couldn't tell how badly he was injured.

The car blocked her line of fire, so she kept moving, trying to find a clear bead on the mayor. Before she could get a shot, an older black woman wearing a navy blue dress climbed out of the Subaru, her hands up in surrender.

"Please. Don't hurt them," she said. Had to be Maybelle Mann.

TK kept moving, skimming through the brush as quietly as possible, crouched low now that the trees had thinned out. She needed to move another ten yards or so before she'd have a clear shot. All she could do was pray that Maybelle could stall the mayor long enough.

"It's me you want. I'm Maybelle Mann."

"Grayson, take Karlan's gun and hers as well," the mayor ordered, gesturing with his rifle. He didn't seem as comfortable with the long gun as his father—or maybe it was his fancy suit and shoes that weren't made for walking in the woods. "Bring them here."

Grayson hesitated. TK strained to get a clear line of sight on both him and his father. What if he turned Karlan's weapon on Lucy?

Maybelle stepped in front of Grayson as if protecting him.

Of course, she had no idea it was his father with the rifle. She was willing to sacrifice herself to save total strangers.

"Go on," she told Grayson and Lucy. "Get him out of here. Leave me. It's okay. Go on now."

"Grayson, do as I say," the mayor snapped, his patience clearly at an end.

Grayson grabbed Karlan's service weapon, shoving the larger man's weight onto Lucy so that she staggered beneath it. TK quickened her pace, just a few more feet.

But then Grayson raised Karlan's Glock at Maybelle.

TK debated breaking cover, making herself a target—but there was no guarantee she could draw both Grayson and his father's fire.

Grayson's aim wavered. "Is it true? What she said? What the judge did?" His voice broke with anguish. "How could he?"

Lucy was making a show of helping Karlan to the ground, but TK could see that she was really maneuvering to draw her own weapon out of sight of the mayor. He was still the real threat, more so than Grayson. She hoped.

"It's the past," the mayor answered his son. "Now it's our job to protect our future. To protect our family." Leave it to the mayor to turn a hostage negotiation into a political speech.

Grayson shook his head. TK kept moving, getting into position to take out the mayor. She trusted that Lucy would deal with Grayson if need be. Right now, the kid was serving as a damn fine distraction.

"So you knew? Did he kill the others, the ones in the car?"

"No. That was his father. Doing what's best for the town. We're Greers. That's who we are. Now shoot her. Show me you're worthy of the Greer name." JR's tone snapped across the graves, crackling with command.

For a tense moment, TK thought Grayson was actually going to do it. He held the heavy Glock with both hands, aiming at Maybelle. She stood, facing him, her face filled not with fear but compassion.

"It's all right," she told Grayson, ignoring the mayor. "Just let them go first. This man needs a doctor. Let them go."

TK was screaming at Lucy in her head. Why didn't she take the shot, kill Grayson? She was so close, she could do it easily.

As she moved into position, she answered her own question. If Lucy shot Grayson, then there was nothing standing between the mayor and Maybelle. And if Lucy tackled Maybelle, Karlan would be hopelessly exposed, in the line of fire.

No way could one person move fast enough to save both Maybelle and Karlan.

Good thing there were two of them. TK was about to break cover, when Grayson surprised her, whirling to aim at his father. "Did you start the fire last night? Did you kill all those people?"

"Those people died as a result of their own stupidity."

"Why?"

"It's not your place to ask why. It's your place to do. Stand aside, I'll take care of the bitch myself."

Grayson raised his arm and fired. At his father.

The shot went hopelessly wild. The mayor didn't flinch, merely frowned as if not very surprised at his son's betrayal. His aim at Maybelle never wavered. No way would he miss her, not as close as he was.

TK leapt out from cover, almost tripping on a half-buried gravestone. She held the shotgun up with her left hand as if surrendering. "Mr. Mayor. I have your father. Let's talk this over before anyone else gets hurt."

As a diversion, it was potential suicide. The mayor's aim jumped toward TK.

Lucy pushed Maybelle down and fired at the mayor. Grayson threw his body over Maybelle's as his father whirled and fired at her.

Gunfire thundered through the air. Three more shots from Lucy and one from TK's shotgun.

The mayor staggered back then sagged to the ground.

TK went to cover him as Lucy checked on Karlan and the civilians. Grayson cautiously rolled off of Maybelle. Guess the kid had finally made a decision for himself, chosen a side instead of following lockstep in Daddy's path.

There was no doubt the mayor was dead. She kicked his weapon away and felt for a pulse, more for Grayson's sake than anything. Only question was whose round had killed him. He'd taken three to the chest, one to the face—all from Lucy—while her shotgun round had pretty much blasted away most of one arm and part of his abdominal cavity.

She turned and shook her head at Lucy. Grayson looked up, his face streaked with mud and dead leaves, tears seeping down his cheeks. "My dad?"

"Sorry. Nothing anyone can do. But your grandfather should be fine—a few broken bones, is all." She joined them, crouching beside Karlan.

"Is Maybelle okay?" the detective gasped.

"I'm fine," Maybelle assured him, moving to where he could see her. "Thanks to all of you."

"I think I was shot." Karlan's face was red, sweat pooling around the collar of his uniform shirt. "I've never been shot before."

"You haven't yet," Lucy said. "Hit the vest."

"Still counts," TK argued as together she and Lucy ripped at the Velcro straps holding the vest in place, giving Karlan room to breathe. "Bullet impacted his body even if it didn't penetrate."

Lucy rolled her eyes at TK. "I can tell you've never been married or had to make that particular phone call to a loved one."

Grayson got to his feet, stumbled toward his father's body before TK could stop him, then lurched and vomited. Maybelle wrapped her arm around his shoulders and guided him away from the gruesome sight.

Then suddenly, they stopped. Grayson straightened. Maybelle let go of him and crouched down, her fingers tracing a grave marker that had fallen over.

"Abe Brown." She circled around until she was patting the ground above the grave beside the marker. "This is it. This is where we'll find Winnie."

# Epilogue

*JULY 4TH*

MAYBELLE STOOD BEHIND the podium on the courthouse steps as if she was the president ready to give his State of the Union address. Straight, tall, a touch defiant.

"What are you going to say?" TK asked her as she adjusted the microphone. Lucy, David, and Karlan stood behind them at the top of the steps, along with, at Maybelle's personal invitation, Grayson Greer. TK was still pretty pissed off at Grayson—at his entire family—so she was stalling, avoiding joining him and the others for as long as possible.

Maybelle flattened her lips together in a grimace. "I don't intend to say much of anything. Other than to finally confess the truth."

TK wasn't sure what that meant. In the past few days, it felt as if hidden truths had emerged from all around her. Or maybe it was that they'd boiled to the surface from inside her.

The conversation she'd had with David about fear and facing the truth of who you were still resonated. Especially now as she looked out on the faces of the people crowded into the town square: black, white, brown; some angry, waiting for Maybelle to give them an excuse to act on that anger, some curious, some hopeful, most weary.

Maybelle touched the cross that had been her mother's— one of the few items from the Wayfarer that had survived the fire at the coroner's office. One of Madsen's students had brought it to Maybelle along with the news that they had found Winnie's body exactly where Maybelle said they would. Along with the knife and rock, which would hopefully be enough to put Philip Greer behind bars for the rest of his life.

"Ready?" TK asked.

Maybelle nodded, and TK turned the microphone on then moved back to stand beside David. He leaned against his crutches, said it was easier to stand than try to sit down and get up again. Despite the crutches, he managed to free a hand to interlace with hers.

Then Grayson sidled behind the others, moving from where he'd stood on the far side of Karlan to stand beside TK. She scowled at him, but as usual, he didn't take the hint.

At first Maybelle stood in silence, the gravitas of her countenance enough to draw attention and quiet the crowd nearest the steps. Then she began to speak, not in a loud or strident voice, rather in a quiet voice that had everyone leaning forward, paying attention.

"My father died at the bottom of these steps," she began. "And when I say 'died,' I of course mean he was murdered. Killed in a war we're still fighting today, sixty years later.

"Despite your cheers and chants and cries for justice, this is not a war between white and black, not a righteous battle of good and evil. This is a war of anger and fear. A war of lies and fists. A war driven by shame and shouting that threaten to drown the truth. A war that has been fought for two hundred years in this land of freedom and justice for all.  A war that will continue to be fought until we—each of us, every one of us—embrace those freedoms and turn our energy to fight for justice and truth.

"My father used to say that all blood is red—he'd fought in two wars, killed men in combat and then as a surgeon fought to save them, his arms plunged up to the elbows in their blood. All blood is red. No matter the color of the skin that holds it inside. It's not the person's color or blood that makes them different or dangerous. It's their fear.

"Fear is our enemy. Fear makes us rage at the change in the world and search for an enemy to unleash our fury upon. Fear gives us false hope that our might makes right even as we know the truth we refuse to give voice to: that violence comes from cowardice, not courage.

"I was only a little girl when my parents were murdered. Some would say that excuses my silence. But my father didn't sacrifice himself solely to save an innocent boy from a lynch mob, he did it to save me. And he wasn't the only one courageous enough to stand for the truth. A white man stood beside my father. Police officer Archibald Thomson. A white lawman, charged with bringing justice to this town and keeping the peace, he had the courage to break the peace, to refuse the mob the false justice they sought, and he died."

She pointed to the base of the steps. A few people in the front row stepped back.

"Right there. Right where you stood with your rocks and bottles and signs and tear gas and guns and riot batons. Right there three black people—my mother and my father and an innocent boy—and one white law man stained the earth forever with their blood sacrifice."

Maybelle continued, "It shouldn't have happened. Not here, not anywhere. And I'm ashamed to my very soul that it did. That I watched. That I hid. That I ran. That my life was paid for with my parents' blood and the blood of two innocent children and the blood of a white police officer. To this day, over six decades later, I still dream of their blood. All that blood. It haunts me. My father was right: all blood is red. And you can't tell it apart.

"All courage comes from love, my mother used to say. My mother. White men killed her just for showing her black face to them when they were angry and afraid. They killed her without knowing her name or who she was. They would have killed me as well. But I lived. I'm here today, and it's taking all my courage to stand here and tell you the truth, but I'm here now and here's the truth you need to know: I'm ashamed. Ashamed of myself. Ashamed of that mob of angry white men who thought that killing innocents would salve their fear.

"Ashamed of all of us here today. Because when we treat each other like beasts without brains or hearts or voices or souls, we are all cowards. Our fear knows no bounds and its cry silences any hope for truth, justice, or a future.

"So, I'm begging you. Lay down your weapons. Stop the bloodshed. Look, listen, think, and talk. Sit down and listen and talk.

"We live in a country where speech is free—but not cheap, never, ever cheap. That free speech was paid for in blood—including the blood of my parents. Your parents and grandparents and great-grandparents as well. Respect their sacrifice. Sit down."

She raised her hands, palms down, and patted the air like a kindergarten teacher summoning her students to sit down for story time.

To TK's surprise, it worked. Several of the onlookers in the front of the crowd lowered their signs and sat down on the pavement. Then more people behind them, until like a wave, it spread out through the crowd, with the law enforcement officers standing guard backing away and lowering their weapons as well.

Finally, only a scattering of men—why was it always the men who were the last to surrender their anger, TK wondered—both black and white, stood like islands in a sea of quiet, glaring at each other, fists at their sides.

Grayson edged closer to TK, brushing her arm.

"Still think we're better off separate?" she whispered to him. Lucy said she should take it easy on the kid—after all, in the end, he'd made the right decision, even if it had meant betraying his family. But TK knew all too well that decisions made in the crucible of battle didn't always mean a permanent change of heart.

"Then what's the answer?" he asked, for the first time sounding unsure of himself.

"All courage comes from love," Maybelle repeated. "Have the courage to learn the truth—all of it. Not just the bits and pieces that ease your fear. Face the truth, and you never need be ashamed again.

"Because in our hearts, we know the truth," Maybelle's voice rose but was not strident as it echoed across the square. She waited a beat and then lowered it to an intimate whisper. "We know the truth. Don't we?"

Many in the crowd nodded, entranced. A few shouted, "Yes!" or "Amen!"

Maybelle continued to weave her spell. "We know what needs to change in this country, and we know how to change it.

One of the last things I remember from the day my family was killed was how happy they were about a man named Brown who that very day had won the right for all children to receive equal education no matter what color their skin. All they had to be was American.

"My parents, they were so proud that day to be American. So happy because they knew I could be anyone I wanted. I could grow up to be a doctor, a surgeon, saving lives like my father. I could grow up to be a teacher, saving minds and molding futures like my mother. My parents gave their lives, and so did a white policeman. Why would they do that to help a stranger, a boy they'd never met?

"Because they had a dream of what this country was and how decent people should behave and stand up for each other. Because that was how Americans acted here in the land of the free and home of the brave.

"And when they took me away," Maybelle continued, her voice now threaded through with the hint of the girl she'd once been, "and I had nightmares about that day and could barely remember my parents' faces and people told me to forget all about it, it was only a dream, a bad, bad, dream, and everything would be okay once I woke up and forgot it... Do you know where we ended up? Where the Lord in His infinite wisdom sent me to try to forget my little girl dreams? He sent me to the one place where a decade later I could witness first-hand the power of a dream.

"You know where He sent me? To a factious town called Selma, Alabama. And soon I was a teenager, too smart for my own britches, those little girl dreams of who my parents were and why they died and what they wanted from life long gone and forgotten.

"But then I woke up. And I realized that way back in Boston, those men two hundred years ago had a dream, and Dr. King he had a dream, and my mommy and daddy, long dead and forgotten except in my nightmares, they had a dream. A dream that starts with: *We the people...in order to form a more perfect union, establish justice, insure domestic tranquility, and secure the blessings of liberty...*

"Over two hundred years and all that killing and rioting and shooting and burning and hate and fear and lack of justice, tranquility, or liberty, and we're still dreaming. But it's time to wake up."

Maybelle's voice grew louder once more, her Southern accent sharper, no longer soothing or intimate, but rather a call to arms.

"We the people need to wake up to the fact that killing each other is not the answer. Wake up to the fact that we are *all* the people and ain't none of us going anywhere, so we'd best step up into this marriage, this perfect union of domestic tranquility. Like any sacred union, ours is based on love, honesty, respect, and caring for each other more than we care for our own lives.

"The blessings of liberty. That was my father's dream. That was my mother's dream. That was Officer Thomson's dream. That was the Rawlings' dream for their son, Henry. That was Winifred Neal's dream before Philip Greer murdered her before my very eyes. A dream they died for, them and so many others.

"But you and I, we aren't dreaming. We the people, we're awake now. We see that violence hasn't worked, no matter how many bodies you try to hide.

"We know we need to stop the killing and the fear and the hate. We're awake to the fact that the only way out of this nightmare is by holding on tight to each other—and you can't tell the color of anyone's skin in the dark, can you? We have to lead each other by the hand out of this chaos, this screaming, bloody mad hate and fear.

"There will be people trapped in the nightmare, too afraid to join our more perfect union. We can't ignore them. We must gently, oh, so gently, nudge them awake, offer a hand, help them to see the light of day. Because we're awake now. And we know it's going to take all of us, listening, helping, learning, to find that courage to make things right.

"Because if all courage comes from love, then all that anger and hate comes from fear. The stuff of nightmares.

"But we're not dreaming those dreams of hate anymore; we're not running scared in those night terrors like I had when I was a little girl, seeing my daddy's blood run out on the steps of this very courthouse, beneath the flag he fought for in two wars. I'm not dreaming anymore about that brave white police officer who put his own body between an innocent boy and an angry mob. Instead, I remember him. Every day. And I honor his courage and sacrifice.

"We no longer have the luxury of dreams. Not anymore. Because we're awake now. And things are going to change. They have to change. Starting today. Starting with me. Starting with you." She pointed to the crowd. "Yes, you. Put away the hate. Wake up. It's a new day. Time to wake up, America."

As the crowd roared and applauded, TK turned to Grayson. "There's your answer. Building a community together instead of apart. Wouldn't that be a better legacy for your family than the hate they've left behind?"

He blinked, his expression grave, but finally nodded. Then he swallowed hard, the motion revealing a glimpse of the eagle's wings tattooed on his chest and neck. "I'm not sure I know how. What if I'm just like them, like my grandfather and great-grandfather and father?"

She shrugged. "We can't choose our families. But we can choose how we live our lives."

Together they stood side by side, looking out at the crowd. Maybelle leaned against the podium, exhausted, tears glistening in her eyes. David's hand squeezed TK's—he'd heard what she'd told Grayson, understood that she was speaking for herself as much as to the boy beside her.

Grayson drew in a deep breath, swiped his eyes with a knuckle. "Do you think she'd help? Dr. Rawlings? If I asked her? After everything that's happened, everything we've done?"

As if in answer, Maybelle turned away from the podium and gave him a soft smile filled with hope. More than hope. A promise for tomorrow.

# LETTER TO READERS

Even though many of the events of OPEN GRAVE reflect current events, I've been busy researching this story for years.

Most recently, by participating in the same "shoot-don't-shoot" firearm training simulations that federal agents, SWAT officers, and other police officers train with. But long before I knew I wanted to use an officer-involved-shooting scenario (which, because of recent real-life events actually became a subplot rather than the central plot of the story) in a book, I'd had this idea nagging at me, this conundrum of a paradox that I couldn't wrap my mind around.

What did I do? Same thing I always do when I need to make sense of the chaos that is our world. I wrote about it in a story. This story.

You see, that photo of TK's grandfather? It's real. I have no idea who the veterans were who appeared in it, but I first saw the photo almost three decades ago in an old magazine. Veterans dressed in uniform, with their ribbons and medals, men who had shed blood to protect our country and keep all of us safe, holding a sign at a protest (I can't even remember what they were protesting—it was a black and white photo, so maybe abortion, maybe gay rights, maybe something else).

And the sign read: FREEDOM IS THE RIGHT TO HATE.

What do we do with that? Of course I defend any American's right to free speech—it's the foundation of our democracy.

But speech that preaches hate? That turns neighbor against neighbor, brother against brother, that threatens to divide rather than unite? Speech that by its definition allows for no chance at rebuttal much less debate or civil discourse?

How do we reconcile these two diametrically opposing facts?

When I began OPEN GRAVE, I had no idea how timely these questions that had nagged at me for decades would become. I wish I had answers. But, just like democracy, answers to questions this complex do not come easy. They take work. Hard work. And thought.

My hope is that by exploring each of our stories we can find the answers. Because we're all in this together.

Thanks for reading!

CJ

PS: Lucy will be back later in 2017 in GONE DARK. She'll be on the hunt for a fugitive who leads her into the path of a raging wildfire. Catching her quarry becomes more than a question of serving justice, but a matter of survival.

# About CJ:

*New York Times* and *USA Today* bestselling author of twenty-nine novels, former pediatric ER doctor CJ Lyons has lived the life she writes about in her cutting edge Thrillers with Heart.

CJ has been called a "master within the genre" (Pittsburgh Magazine) and her work has been praised as "breathtakingly fast-paced" and "riveting" (Publishers Weekly) with "characters with beating hearts and three dimensions" (Newsday).

Her novels have won the International Thriller Writers' prestigious Thriller Award, the RT Reviewers' Choice Award, the Readers' Choice Award, the RT Seal of Excellence, and the Daphne du Maurier Award for Excellence in Mystery and Suspense.

Learn more about CJ's Thrillers with Heart at www.CJLyons.net

Lightning Source UK Ltd.
Milton Keynes UK
UKHW012141070520
362945UK00003B/1032

9 781939 038494